What You Do to Me

ALSO BY BARBARA LONGLEY

Love from the Heartland series, set in Perfect, Indiana

Far from Perfect
The Difference a Day Makes
A Change of Heart
The Twisted Road to You

The Novels of Loch Moigh

True to the Highlander
The Highlander's Bargain
The Highlander's Folly
The Highlander's Vow

What You Do to Me

BARBARA LONGLEY

Montlake
Romance

Published by Montlake Romance, Seattle

www.apub.com

Amazon, the Amazon logo, and Montlake Romance are trademarks of Amazon.com, Inc., or its affiliates.

ISBN-13: 9781503939233
ISBN-10: 1503939235

Cover design by Eileen Carey

Printed in the United States of America

This book is dedicated to Nanci Longley.
Thanks for the inspiration.

Chapter One

Brrr. Thermal coffee cup in hand, Sam walked out of his apartment building and crossed the parking lot. He huffed out a breath, and a cloud of steam formed in front of his face. Minnesota winters were frigid, and the frigid had started early this year. They'd already had a couple of near-freezing nights, and it was just the beginning of November.

If it weren't for hockey, snowmobiling and ice fishing, he'd consider moving south. But then he'd miss Grandpa Joe and Grandma Maggie, along with his younger brother and sister, cousins, uncles and aunts. His siblings might be willing to make the move with him, but his grandparents would never leave Saint Paul. All of their kids, grandkids and great-grandkids were here, which meant he was stuck.

Sam circled to the driver's side of his old Ford work van and climbed in. Turning the key in the ignition produced nothing but a reluctant *RrrrRrrrRrrr.* "Come on, buddy. I don't like the cold or Monday mornings either, but you don't see me staying in bed." He patted the dashboard, like that would somehow encourage the van to start. He tried again and got the same refusal. "I'll let you think about it for a minute or two, and then you have to crank. We have work to do." He waited a few moments and tried again. The engine turned over, earning another pat to the dashboard.

Content to sit while the engine warmed, Sam sipped his coffee and turned on the radio. He had plenty of time before he needed to show up for work, and his favorite morning talk show was about to begin. He tuned the radio to *Loaded Question* and adjusted the volume so he could hear the radio over the heater fan and grinned as the cheesy music announced the morning show was about to begin.

"Good morning, Twin Cities! You're listening to the wake-up crew, Dianna Barstow and Russell Lund, and it's time for . . . da, da daaaah, Loaded Question!" the male counterpart of the duo announced. *"What's our question for today, Dianna?"*

"Well, Russ, I think we have a real winner this morning. Today's question is: What's the sluttiest thing you've ever done?"

This ought to be good for a few laughs. Sam adjusted the vents so they blew only on the windshield. He could get out and scrape off the ice, but why bother? The glass would just frost up again by the time he was back inside. Better to let the van warm up and defrost on its own. Grandpa Joe always said there were two kinds of people in this world: smart lazy and dumb lazy. If you're smart lazy, you do things right the first time, so you don't have to do them over again. Smart lazy. That's how Sam saw himself.

"Whoa! Good one! What is the sluttiest thing you've ever done, Dianna?"

"Ahhh." She laughed. *"Spring break five years ago. No details."*

Their banter went on for another few minutes before the DJs announced their telephone number and turned it over to the listening audience. Since the talk show hosts often gave out some pretty sweet prizes—like hard-to-get concert tickets or cash—Sam had the number in his speed dial. He hadn't won anything yet, but he wasn't about to give up. For the next few minutes he listened to one outrageous story after another, choking on his coffee when laughter sent it down the wrong pipe.

A husky, feminine voice came over the air. *"Hi, my name is Yvonne."*

"Hello, Yvonne," Dianna and Russ said in unison. *"What's the sluttiest thing you've ever done?"*

"Well," she began, hesitating slightly.

Her voice sounded familiar, and her name . . . "Nah. Couldn't be."

"I'm recently divorced, and I kept the house," Yvonne finally blurted.

"Go on," Russ prodded.

"It had been a while since I'd . . . you know . . ."

"Had sex?" Dianna chortled. *"We're listening. We're all listening."*

"I had a few things that needed to be done around the house, and a couple of my girlfriends kept telling me I should hire this handyman named Sam. So I did."

Sam froze, and not from the cold. "Cripes!" It *was* her. He'd done some work for Yvonne two weeks ago. He thunked his head against the steering wheel and groaned. "Great. *I'm* the sluttiest thing she's ever done."

"OK, Sam the handyman," Russ teased. *"Tell me. Just how handy was he?"*

"My oh my. Let me tell you. He was plenty handy and incredibly hot. After he did the job, I did him." She sighed. *"He was wonderful."*

Yvonne's happy sigh over the air brought a smile to his face. He should get an award for leaving customers *completely* satisfied, something like those Employee-of-the-Month plaques you see on walls sometimes. He imagined what his award might look like hanging on the wall at Haney & Sons. Polished brass mounted on an oval piece of oak, and the engraving would read: Sluttiest Carpenter Award of Excellence—for going above and beyond the call of duty.

"You were plenty hot yourself, Yvonne." Maybe she'd have another job for him to do soon. He shook his head. Not a good idea. Women got ideas when he came around a second time—*relationship* ideas.

He shuddered at the thought. His life was exactly the way he wanted it. Who needed all the drama, all the demands and upheaval that came with the whole relationship package? Who needed the heartache? Not him. Strings-free, protected sex and the bachelor life suited him just fine. He had his buddies, his brother, sister, grandparents and a great extended family. He lived *la dolce vita*—the sweet life. *Why fix it if it ain't broke?*

Listeners were weighing in about Yvonne. About him.

"It would bother me knowing my partner had probably done it with half the women in the Twin Cities," the first listener commented.

"He's the slut," another caller said.

"Yvonne was just a lonely divorcée. Maybe he's a sex addict. For all we know, she was just one of a dozen he did that day," caller three remarked, sending Sam over the edge.

"Sex addict?" He scowled at the radio. "Wait just a doggone minute. I've done nothing wrong." Before he realized what he was doing, he'd grabbed his phone from the cup holder and hit speed dial. His outrage grew with each passing second. He was a good guy, honest and upfront. He never led anyone on. Plus, his moral compass worked just fine, thank you very much. His call was answered on the fifth ring.

"This is Russ, and you're on the air. What's the sluttiest thing you've ever done?"

"Yeah. This is Sam Haney. I'm Yvonne's handyman, and—"

"Whoa! No last names here, Sam Haney. We like to protect the innocent, Handyman Haney. Did you get that, ladies? Sam Haney, the handsiest handyman in the Twin Cities."

"Hands-On-Haney, the handyman!" Dianna chortled with glee, and the two of them laughed. *"Get his number for me, would you, Russ?"* Dianna chimed. *"As a matter of fact, Sam, why don't you share your number with all of us?"*

Aww, cripes. Idiot. Their jokes were stupid, and he didn't appreciate being the punch line. "Listen, you wouldn't believe how women throw themselves at me on the job. I can show up for work scruffy as all get-out, raggedy flannel shirt, faded torn jeans, unshaven and hair a mess, and they're still all over me. Women love me."

"I'm sure they do," Russ said, and both hosts sniggered lewdly.

The word *cliché* popped into his brain. He shoved it aside. There was nothing clichéd about him. He just needed to find a different morning talk show, that's all. "Look, I don't mess with married women, or women who are involved with someone, and it's not me who comes on to them. *They* come on to me. We're consenting adults, enjoying a little safe, recreational sex. That's all there is to it. No addiction. No taking advantage. Nobody is getting hurt. I'm unattached, clean, healthy and a decent guy. Can I help it if women want me?"

Trudy laughed out loud, delighted by the latest installment of *Loaded Question*. She turned the bacon frying in the skillet and headed to the fridge for eggs. She liked to send her husband off to work with a good, hot breakfast in his stomach. Returning to the kitchen counter, she set the eggs down and turned up the radio.

She gasped, hardly believing Yvonne's handyman had the audacity to come on the air. Pulling her iPhone out of her apron pocket, she called her sister's number. Nanci picked up right away.

"Is that you, Trudy?"

"Are you hearing this?" Trudy demanded. "Are you listening to *Loaded Question?*"

"I am. I already looked up Handyman Haney's place of business on the Internet. Haney & Sons Construction and Handyman Service. No job is too big or too small, according to their website. Might have him do a few jobs for me." They both giggled like teenagers.

Trudy sighed. "I know it's wrong, but I wish my Haley would have an encounter like Yvonne's. She needs something to shake her out of her slump and bolster her self-esteem since you-know-who did you-know-what to her."

"Still can't believe that twerp bolted like he did, and only two weeks before their wedding." Nanci huffed. "Who does that? Who just up and suddenly decides they *have* to live in Indonesia—without the high school sweetheart they've been engaged to for two whole years?"

"I think there may have been another woman involved." Trudy forked the bacon out of the pan and set it on a stack of paper towels to drain. Cradling the phone between her ear and shoulder, she moved the pan, replacing it with a smaller one for the eggs. "Don't you think so?"

"Not for one single minute," her sister snapped. "I think he had a *man* waiting for him over there. I can't imagine any heterosexual male walking away from my gorgeous niece for any other reason."

"Aww. That's sweet—in a warped kind of way." Trudy melted a little butter in the pan, pushed the bread down in the toaster, and cracked the eggs over the skillet. "Haley is really down in the dumps, and it's been months. She needs something other than remodeling projects to shake her out of her slump. Have you seen what a disaster she's made of her house?"

"I have, and it's frightening."

Frank Cooper, Trudy's own high school sweetheart, walked into the kitchen and kissed her cheek before helping himself to coffee and meandering into the dining room with his newspaper tucked under his arm. Trudy transferred her phone to her hand. "Can I call you back after breakfast?"

"Sure. Later."

Trudy put her phone back in her pocket and focused on flipping the eggs so they were over easy, just the way she and Frank liked them. The toast popped up, and while buttering the lightly toasted whole-grain bread, a plan began to coalesce in her mind. She loaded two plates, cut a banana in half, and carried their breakfast to the dining room. As usual, Frank had his nose buried in his newspaper.

She set his plate in front of him. "Frank, Haley's birthday is coming up."

He lowered the edge of his paper to send her an indulgent smile. "If I'm not mistaken, our daughter's birthday is in May. This is November." Setting aside the news, he put a napkin on his lap and reached for the salt.

"I know when her birthday is. *I'm* the one who carried her for nine months and went through seventy-two hours of labor bringing her into this world." She lifted her chin. "Excruciating labor, I might add."

"Seems to me the number of hours you were in labor grows with each telling." He raised an eyebrow and cut an egg with the edge of his fork.

Trudy's chin came up another notch. "Her birthday *is* coming up—"

"I can't argue with that, sweetheart. Birthdays do come around once a year. They're always *coming up*. Even for you, though to me you're still as beautiful as you were the day we met."

"Oh, Frank, and you're still the sweetest man in the world." She slid her palm over his arm, warmth for her husband of thirty years filling her with gratitude. He'd given her two amazing children and a very comfortable life. She wanted the same for her only daughter. "Well . . . I was thinking maybe we could give Haley an early birthday present this year." She squirmed in her seat a tiny bit. "She's had such a rough time of it, and I want to help her out. Don't you want to help her out, honey?"

"Mmm-mm," he agreed around a mouthful.

"Her house is a disaster area, what with all the home improvement projects she starts and never finishes. She has no idea what she's doing, and I'm afraid she's going to bring the place tumbling down around her ears or worse. It's going to go up in smoke."

Frank frowned and nodded.

"What if we pay a handyman to help her put things back together so that her house is livable again? I want my little girl to be safe. Don't you want our little girl to be safe, Frank?"

Her husband's eyes twinkled as he swallowed his mouthful. "Haley isn't a little girl anymore, Trudy. She's twenty-six, with a well-established career and a home of her own. Still, it's an excellent idea. Take care of it, would you, sweetheart? Hire somebody, but check for references on Angie's List first."

"Oh, I will." *No I won't.* She crossed her fingers in her lap against the small white lie, knowing exactly whom to hire. She rose from her chair. "More coffee?" Trudy could hardly wait to run the plan by her sister before making the call to Sam the Handyman. She hurried to the kitchen and grabbed the coffeepot to fill their mugs.

The more she thought about it, the more convinced she became that Haley needed a little fresh male interest to get her through her heartbreak. If a gorgeous hunk made a pass at her, she'd realize just how desirable she truly was, and she'd get past the Michael debacle. She'd be ready to get out there and date again, and then maybe, just maybe, Haley would marry and give her a few grandchildren before she got too old to enjoy them.

As her oldest, it was up to Haley to produce grandchildren first, especially since Frank Jr. hadn't even finished college yet. Another worry, since he'd been working on his undergrad degree for six years now. He kept changing his major. Ah, well. One problem at a time, and right now Haley Helen had to come first.

Trudy finished her breakfast, kissed her husband good-bye as he left for work, and then she headed for the family room. The dirty dishes could wait. Settling into her favorite chair, she put her feet up on the ottoman and called her sister. Nanci was always good for a brainstorming session, and this plan would require some finesse.

"Trudy?" Her sister picked up. "Is that you?"

"Of course it's me. You can see my name on your caller ID. Why do you always ask if it's me?"

"Because I enjoy having to make you tell me it's you."

Trudy rolled her eyes. "I have a plan."

"Uh-oh."

"Don't say that until you've heard what it is."

"I've known you your entire life. I don't need to hear your latest plan to know it's a mistake."

"It's not a mistake. Don't you *want* Haley to have a love life again?"

"Ha! This ought to be good. Let's hear it."

A little miffed, Trudy resisted the urge to bring up a few of her older sister's less-than-stellar ideas, like the doughnut-hole she'd married—and divorced. To be honest, the divorce turned out to be one of Nanci's better ideas. "Frank and I have decided to give Haley an early birthday present. We're going to hire a handyman to help her bring her house back up to code. Guess who the handyman is going to be?" she chirped, hardly able to contain her excitement.

"Sam Haney, the handsiest handyman in the Twin Cities?"

"Exactly. What do you think?"

"Are you serious? You *want* to set your own daughter up for a one-night stand with a man who has done practically every single woman in the Twin Cities? Who are you, and what have you done with my straitlaced little sister?"

Doubt cast a shadow over what she'd thought was a wonderful idea. Mothers didn't encourage their daughters to be promiscuous. Not good mothers, anyway. A spark of indignation ignited. She wasn't a bad mother. She was a concerned mother. Her daughter had lost her mojo, and Trudy wanted to see that she got it back. Besides, she knew her daughter.

"Not exactly. I want the man to make a pass at her, that's *all*. You know as well as I do Haley would never act on it, but having a gorgeous man want her might be all it takes to get her moving in the right direction again."

"That's fine, Trudy, but I can't see Haley making a pass at Hands-On-Haney, and like Sam said on the radio, it's the women who come on to him, not the other way around. There's no guarantee he'll do anything but the job if she's not the one to make the first move."

"Oh, crap." Her bubble of optimism burst. "I hadn't thought of that."

"Not only that, but . . . say you set this up, he *does* make a pass at her and she says no? What if he's the type of man who won't take no for an answer. You don't know anything about Sam Haney. You could be setting Haley up for a dangerous situation."

"I don't think so. You heard Yvonne on the radio. Her *friends* recommended the handyman to her. Surely the women he's been with would have sensed if he were a bully or the predator type. The divorcée spoke about him in glowing terms. She said he was wonderful."

"That's true but—"

"Besides, he divulged his full identity on the air for everybody to hear. Criminal and predator types wouldn't do that."

"That's also true." Her sister's voice held a thoughtful note. "You know what?"

Yay. Here comes another idea-squashing comment. "What?"

"Nobody can tell your voice apart from Haley's over the phone, right?"

"Yeah, so?"

Her sister sighed, and said nothing for a few seconds.

"What am I missing here?" Trudy asked, a tad curtly.

"Haley isn't going to proposition Sam the handyman. We know that, but what if you make the call pretending to be Haley when you set up the appointment? You could make the first move on her behalf. That way, by the time he gets to her house, he'll already be primed and raring to go. He'll make a pass at her thinking he's only responding to her come-hither request."

"You're saying I should come right out and tell him I want him to . . . as Haley, that is . . . that I want . . ." It came to her in a flash. She knew exactly what to say. After all, Sam must know lots of women had listened to this morning's radio show. She'd make it clear that she'd heard *Loaded Question* and hint that she wanted his *special touch*. "Oh, that's brilliant."

"Of course it's brilliant, but if it ends up being another one of your calamities, I know nothing. Nothing at all. We never had this conversation."

"Fine, and if it ends well, I get all the glory."

Chapter Two

"Caffeine . . . I need coffee." Haley yawned and picked up the empty mug from her desk. She stood up and stretched before heading for the law office's break room. This was going to be a busy Monday, and once again, she hadn't slept well the night before. Gee, it would be nice to get a good night's sleep. Maybe she'd try one of those over-the-counter sleep aids tonight.

The sound of laughter drifted out of the break room. How long had it been since she'd laughed? Too long. She walked into the kitchen area and headed for the coffeepot. "What's so funny?"

Their newest law intern, along with Haley's two best friends and fellow paralegals, Kathy and Felicia, sat at one of the round tables. Kathy gestured toward the radio on the counter. "It's over now, but we were laughing about KS96's *Loaded Question*. This morning's question was: What's the sluttiest thing you've ever done?" Kathy went on to give her a brief description of what had transpired with the divorcée and the handyman named Sam Haney.

"The woman actually said after Sam did the job, she did him!" Felicia giggled. "The handyman said women throw themselves at him on the job all the time. Can you imagine?"

"It's going viral. I'm seeing tweets and Facebook posts already, and the radio station's website is flooded with comments," Kathy added, scrolling down the screen of her tablet. "I can't believe the guy gave his real name—his entire name."

"Let me see that," Haley said, holding her hand out for Kathy's tablet. She read a few of the comments before handing the tablet back. People had plenty to say about the handyman, and none of it was good. The guy probably regretted making that call this morning.

"Identifying himself on the air the way he did is a lawsuit waiting to happen." The law intern's face lit up. "I'm going to call him and offer my services—pro-boner, of course."

Another round of giggles ensued. That joke was as old as the Egyptian pyramids. Haley returned to the counter to pour coffee into her mug. "Do you believe it really happened? I think shows like that are setups. They're staged."

"Oh," the law intern—what was her name again?—nodded. "I know it happens. I have a friend who brags all the time about how she's done it with the UPS guy and the guy who does her townhouse's lawn care. You'd be surprised."

"I guess I would be." Haley leaned back against the counter. "There's no way I'd crawl into bed with a complete stranger. Would any of you do that?"

"You mean to tell me you've *never* had a one-night stand?" Felicia asked, her coffee-brown eyes widening.

"Nope, I never have." Her heart wrenched. She'd gone from high school to college to being engaged to being dumped—all with the same man. Her one and only lover, the man who had broken her heart and left her. Practically at the altar.

"Haley, you need to get out more." Felicia waggled a finger at her. "We have to plan a girls' night out. You've been moping around here for months now. It's time to move on."

"Yes." Kathy thumped her empty mug on the table like a gavel. "Girls' night out. Count me in."

"Me too." Law Intern's face lit up. "I know where there's a male strip club. How about it, ladies? Get a stack of ones and let her rip?"

"All right." Felicia pushed the intern's shoulder. "You're OK, Melissa. I like you."

Oh, yeah. Melissa. That was her name. "Sounds like fun." *Not really.* "But I think I'll pass. I'm in the middle of remodeling my house and—"

"Girl, you're in the middle of *destroying* your house." Felicia shook her head. "Kathy and I have been there, remember?"

Heat crept up her neck to fill her cheeks. She and Michael had intended to remodel the place together, and she was bound and determined to do so despite his defection, or maybe because of it. She had to prove to herself that she could manage on her own. "Of course I remember. Thanks again for helping me with the wedding's-been-cancelled cards." She turned to the sink and grabbed a paper towel to wipe up any coffee drips she could find. "Anyway, a strip club isn't exactly my thing."

"All right, a nightclub crawl in Minneapolis then," Melissa offered. "Anywhere where there are single men, loud music and alcohol."

"Come on, Haley," Kathy cajoled. "It'll be fun. We haven't gone out for more than lunch in ages. Let's do this."

"All right." She sighed. "I'll be the designated driver." Felicia was right. She needed to stop moping. It *was* time she moved on, and going out with friends might just be the best thing for her.

"Uh, no." Felicia snorted. "We're all going to pitch in and pay my little brother to be our chauffeur for the evening. He's in college. That boy is always broke. We'll be doing him a favor." She pushed her chair back and rose from her place. "This coming Saturday good for everybody?"

"I'm free." Melissa got up as well. "Kathy?"

"It'll work for me, and I'll make sure Haley doesn't bail on us. Your brother can pick up both of us at her house . . . if it's still standing."

"Hey." Haley frowned. "Things are coming along just fine with my house," she lied. "If you're that concerned, I can come to your place to be picked up."

"Nu-uh. I'll be at your house at seven sharp. We'll go have dinner somewhere first. Be ready to party." Kathy rose from the table. "I have to get to work. I have depositions to process this morning."

"Me too." Felicia followed. "E-mail me your address, Melissa. We'll be by for you right after we pick up Kathy and Haley."

"OK." Melissa grinned. "This is going to be great. I don't know about you, but I could use some fun."

Haley caught the intern's infectious smile and returned one of her own. She'd never really done the club scene before. Sure, she'd gone to dinner and a movie with friends, and she'd gone dancing with Michael, but a club crawl? Not so much. Maybe it would be fun. She took her coffee from the counter and headed for the door. Once she settled herself at her desk, her cell phone chirped with her mom's ringtone. She fished it out of her purse. "Hey, Mom. What's up?"

"Hi, honey. Are you going to be home late Saturday afternoon?"

"Sure. What do you need?"

"It's not what I need, Haley," her mom muttered. "It's what *you* need."

"Oh?" Haley blinked. "What do *I* need?"

"Help with your house, that's what. It's a disaster area, and your father and I are concerned."

Why today of all days was everyone ragging on her about her house? Her brow creased. "No, it's not. I'm just in the demolition phase. The tear-out is always messy. Wait until I start the new install part, and then you'll see. It's going to be great."

"Give it up, Haley Helen. You're in over your head." Her mom let go one of her famous long-suffering sighs. "Your father and I have decided to give you an early birthday present. We've hired a construction company slash handyman service to help you put things back together. We're paying, so you *cannot* argue with me about this. Any day now I expect to hear on the news about a poor woman whose house has collapsed on top of her, name not to be released pending notification of her relatives. That would be us, your family."

"Mom!" OK, so her mother wasn't far off the mark. How-to videos and do-it-yourself books weren't really working for her. She wasn't finding it difficult to tear things apart, but putting them back together eluded her, and that made her feel helpless and overwhelmed to the point where she became immobilized. She and Michael had purchased the post-WWII story-and-a-half bungalow together, and he'd signed over full ownership to her before he left. Her heart thumped painfully at the thought of him.

She forced her mind away from the hurt. "I guess it would be nice to have a functioning kitchen again . . . and a bathroom." She glanced at the clock. She had to wrap this call up and get to work. "The only time this construction company can send someone to do an estimate is on a Saturday afternoon? I'm leaving at seven sharp. Do you think they'll be done in enough time for me to get ready?"

"They're a busy company. Besides, Saturday was the only time I could make an appointment for you that didn't interfere with your job." Her mother paused. "Do you have a date Saturday night?"

The hopefulness in her mother's voice really sucked. Haley pinched the bridge of her nose. "No. I'm going out with Kathy, Felicia and a new law intern from the firm."

"Oh."

How could one two-letter word carry such a load of disappointment? She bit her lip again, this time to refrain from responding. Her mother was an expert at this game, and Haley didn't want to provide her with the next volley.

"I'm sure the estimator will be finished well before you need to leave."

"Thanks, Mom." She knew better than to fight this. Trudy Cooper was no quitter when it came to managing the lives of her children. "Maybe I can watch and learn while things are being fixed. I do appreciate the help. Tell Dad thank you for me."

"Tell him yourself. You *are* coming for Sunday dinner, right?"

Haley smiled. Sunday dinners with her family were a tradition, one that had definitely helped her get through these past few months. "Of course. I'll bring a vegetable dish. Will Junior make it this time?"

"He'd better. It's a requirement for his continued support while he flounders away our money on multiple undergrad majors." Trudy snorted. "Frank Junior is giving me gray hair."

"You've been completely silver since you turned forty, Mom." Haley laughed. "You keep trying to pin that on me and Frank, but we're not taking the blame."

"Just wait until you have children, Haley. Just wait."

Haley's eyes misted. What if she never did have children? What if she never found anyone to love her ever again? Why had her fiancé felt he had to move to the other side of the planet just to get away from her? Not knowing was the worst part. He'd refused to discuss his decision with her. He'd just . . . up and left.

"I've got to get back to work. Thanks, Mom. I really do appreciate the gift. I'll see you Sunday, and I'll bring the estimate for the work on my house with me."

"You do that, sweetheart. See you Sunday."

Sliding her phone back into her purse, Haley forced herself to focus on work. Some wounds were just too painful to prod, and her broken heart was one of them. She should be looking forward to her girls' night out, and she would, dammit. She would look forward—not backward.

◆ ◆ ◆

Sam's phone vibrated in its belt holster. He put his nail driver down and pulled it out, checking the caller ID before answering. "Hey, Gramps. What's up?"

"Are you going to make it into the office for lunch today?"

Sam glanced at the clock on his client's wall. Unless a job kept them from it, he, his siblings, uncles, a few cousins and Gramps always gathered at the office for lunch. If they were lucky, Grandma Maggie brought lunch to them. If not, they had enough stuff in the fridge to feed an army. Eating together gave them a chance to run things by each other and talk about business. "Yeah, I'll be there. Why?"

"Come back to my office when you get here." Grandpa Joe grunted. "We need to talk."

Uh-oh. "OK. See you then." Grandpa Joe had already hung up by the time he got the last word out—as usual. Gramps hated to talk on the phone.

Sam wiped his sweaty palms on his jean-clad thighs before picking up his nail driver again. Maybe Gramps hadn't heard about this morning's radio show, and he just wanted to discuss a job. A man could hope.

Two hours later, he pulled his van into a parking spot in the small lot of Haney & Sons. He still got a rush of pride at the addition of the *Handyman Service* part of their sign. That had been his brainchild.

When the housing market crashed, he'd suggested they offer repair and handyman services along with the remodeling and new construction that had always been their bread and butter. Folks were hunkering down, fixing up the houses they were in rather than trading up. Things were improving in the construction industry now, but the handyman service had kept them afloat during the rough patches, and they'd decided to keep it going.

He enjoyed the variety of jobs he did as a handyman, though his first love would always be carpentry. They were at a point where they could take on a few more apprentices. In fact, he'd bring that up today.

Sam stomped his feet, freeing his boots of construction debris, and walked through the side door and into the kitchen of the house they'd remodeled into their offices. He continued on down the hall to his grandfather's office. The door was open. His grandfather sat behind his desk with the phone pressed to his ear. He scowled at Sam before scribbling something on the yellow message pad in front of him.

They really needed to hire someone to answer the phones, file and do general office stuff, so Gramps could focus on other things. His cousin was there, dusting the shelves. "Hey, Jerry." He gave his cousin a high five. "How's it hanging?"

Jerry's slanted eyes and Down syndrome features lit with a radiant smile. "It's h-hanging." He waggled a finger at him. "You're in t-trouble, S-Sam."

Great. Sam nodded and took a seat just as his grandfather hung up the phone.

"Just what is it you think we're selling here, son?" Gramps gathered up a wad of yellow phone messages strewn over his desk and thrust them at him.

Sam took them. "You heard about—"

"Hell yes, I heard. Three-quarters of the Twin Cities' female population heard. The phone has been ringing off the hook ever since your asinine on-the-air debut. You'd better hope your grandmother doesn't know, because she's on her way over."

He gulped. "I don't suppose she's bringing lunch."

"Lunch?" Grandpa Joe slapped his palm against his desk. The phone began to ring. Gramps ignored it. His bushy gray eyebrows dipped so low they nearly hid his eyes. Nearly. "Again, just what is it you think we're selling here?"

Sam shrugged, feeling like an eight-year-old. He ran his hand over the lower half of his face and studied the pile of messages in his fist. "There are a lot of potential jobs here. I—"

"No," Gramps gestured toward the messages, shaking his head, "this is not the way to *get* new business."

"I'm only human." He crossed his arms in front of him. "Women throw themselves at me. It's not me who—"

"And what? You've eliminated the word *no* from your vocabulary? Don't think for a minute I don't know what goes on out there." Gramps leaned back in his chair and waved a hand to indicate *out there.* "You might not believe this, but I was young and studly once. Believe you me, I had plenty of *invitations* on the job back then."

"You turned them *all* down?" Sam arched a brow. "You *always* said no?"

"That's not the point." Gramps shifted the piles of clutter around on his desk. "Once I met your grandmother, that was it for me. I only had eyes for her. Still do. We Haney men can't help ourselves when it comes to *the one.* After I met your grandmother, even the thought of being unfaithful shriveled my—"

"I'm not looking for *the one.*" *I just wanna have fun, not lookin' for the one* . . . He put his thoughts to rock-and-roll music inside his head. He should try his hand at songwriting. Another award sprang to mind, best songwriter of the year, a blue-collar blues award . . .

Grandpa Joe cleared his throat and waved his hand in the air again. "Find a nice girl and settle down. In the meantime, keep it professional on the job."

"I *always* keep it professional on the job. You know that." Sam shifted in his chair. How many hot-blooded, young, single guys out there would refuse a gorgeous woman when she came on to him? Not a lot, he bet. Besides, there hadn't been *that* many women. It all started when the handyman service began. The phenomenon had taken him by surprise and had gone to his head. "I've never engaged in any *extracurricular* activities until the work is finished."

The aroma of Italian food wafted into the room, and his grandmother's familiar step echoed down the hall. Sam slunk down in his seat. Nobody could reduce him to a mass of guilt and remorse like his silver-haired dynamo of a grandmother. Was it too much to hope she hadn't heard?

"S-sam, we gonna coach h-hockey soon?" Jerry came to stand next to him.

"Of course we are, Jer." Sam grinned at his cousin. "I already sent in the registrations and fees. We're just waiting for the schedule." They'd been coaching for a couple of years, including hockey camp during the summers, but things were different now that they were in Saint Paul's Pee Wee League. They'd be competing in the upcoming tournament season, a new experience for them both.

"Samuel Joseph Haney." Gran stomped into the room with her hands fisted on her hips and storm clouds in her eyes. "I cannot believe what I heard this morning."

"Uh-oh," Jerry whispered. "You're in t-trouble again, S-sam."

Sam flashed his cousin a *don't I know it* look and shot up from his chair, intent on working his way around his grandmother and out of the building. He'd have lunch somewhere else today. "You can save your breath, Gram. Grandpa Joe already laid into me. I gotta go."

He hurried toward the door to the parking lot, regretfully passing up his grandmother's spaghetti with meatballs sitting on the kitchen counter. He opened the back door and ran straight into his uncle. "Hey, Uncle Dan."

"Not staying for lunch?" His uncle blocked his escape.

Sam edged past him. "Nope, not today."

Dan turned away from the door and walked beside him. "I heard the radio show this morning." He shook his head. "If your mom and dad were alive—"

"Well they aren't, are they?" They hadn't been since he'd been a teenager, not since his fifteenth birthday. And there it was—the shortness of breath, racing heart and sweating palms he always got whenever he thought about his mom and dad's accident. If his parents hadn't been flying their single-engine plane over Lake Superior to be home for him, they'd still be alive.

He hadn't let anybody new into his circle since that day, and he didn't plan to anytime soon. Yep. He'd closed himself off after losing the two people who mattered most. He wasn't an idiot. He realized his thinking was messed up, but it was what it was, and it worked for him. The friends he had today were the same friends he'd had since grade school—the few girls he'd dated included. The females in his circle were all married now, thank goodness.

Uncle Dan placed his hand on Sam's shoulder and gave it a squeeze. "Your birthday was just a few days ago, and I know this is a rough time of year for you. But Sam, I also know my brother would expect better of you. As your uncle, it's my duty to say *something* about your behavior. Just think about it. You're a good kid." He patted him on the back. "Keep it in your pants, OK?"

"Uncle Dan," Sam rolled his eyes, "I'm not a kid."

Dan nodded, his gray eyes solemn. "Then don't act like one."

"I gotta go. Got a job to do." There was nothing *wrong* with his behavior. He didn't have a mean bone in his body. No one was getting hurt. He wasn't taking advantage of anyone. If anything, it was the other way around. Women were taking advantage of him, and he had no problem with that.

Haley stood in front of the full-length mirror behind her closet door, armed with a hair dryer. Already past five o'clock, she wondered if the estimator for the company her parents had hired would still make the appointment. At any rate, she'd be ready for her Saturday night out with friends. It *would* be nice when she could dry her hair in her bathroom again.

Her hair dried and twisted up into a loose knot, she applied her makeup and contemplated what she'd wear. Black leggings, high-heeled boots and a jersey tunic or a slinky black dress? She glanced toward her window. Clouds obscured the little daylight left, and was that a snowflake or two? *Brrr. Leggings it is.*

A loud knock on her front door sent her blood rushing. This was it. A professional was going to look at the mess she'd made of her house. Whoever it was, he or she had better not judge.

Still wearing her jeans and a long-sleeve Henley, she hurried to open the door. Her breath caught. Before her stood a man who could easily be featured in one of those "Stud of the Month" calendars, or maybe a sexy, blue-collar-works-with-his-hands calendar, featuring only him in different poses for each month—shirtless with a leather tool belt slung low on his sexy narrow hips.

Tall, broad-shouldered and blond, his bluer-than-blue eyes crinkled at the corners as he ran his gaze over her. *Whoa.* Was he checking her out? The curls and waves of his too-long sandy locks looked as if they hadn't seen a brush all week.

She wanted to run her fingers through that mop, straighten it out for him. The flannel shirt he wore under the Carhartt canvas work jacket couldn't be any more faded, and the white, crew-neck T-shirt peeking out from underneath somehow made the entire scruffy ensemble endearing. The overall effect screamed, "I need someone to take care of me." He handed her a card.

She took it and slid it into her back pocket, too distracted to read. Flustered, she rolled her tongue back into her mouth and swung the door wide. "Are you here to do the estimate on the repairs to my house? You're the guy from the construction company, right?" *Oh, lord I hope so.*

"Yes, ma'am." He put little paper baggies with elastic tops over his work boots before stepping through the door. "If you'd like to show me what needs to be *done,* I'll get started right away. I wouldn't want to take up too much of your time on a Saturday night." He winked.

He winked at me? Once again those sexy blue eyes of his roamed over her. How could he make the word *done* sound like crazy-hot sex? Yikes. Where was this sudden surge of lust coming from? She hadn't been interested in anyone since . . . *Oh, for heaven's sake, Haley, you're not interested in him. He's just fun to look at.*

She led him through the living room, the small dining area and into the kitchen. Following his gaze as he studied the room, she knew it couldn't be called a kitchen anymore. Not since she'd torn it apart.

"Cripes." He turned around slowly, taking in the state of disrepair. "What happened here? Did you get this place through an auction? Was this a drug house or something, and a search and seizure led to this?" He gestured toward the walls.

"Hey." She glared at him. "I've been doing the tear-out myself, and you can't tell me your tear-outs look any neater. It's not the demolition that matters." She glanced at the holes in the old plaster walls where she'd begun to tear them down. "This kitchen needs to be rewired and the outside walls insulated. I was going to put up new sheetrock once that was done."

One side of the kitchen counter she'd managed to pry away from the wall, but the side with the sink she'd left intact. She had to brush her teeth somewhere. "I have stuff stored in the basement. A new sink and faucet I got on sale . . . light fixtures, insulation and drywall. I haven't picked out cabinets, countertops or flooring yet."

She stuffed her hands into her front pockets. "I'll need new appliances, of course. I think this stove is from the fifties, and the fridge is probably about twenty years old."

Moving over to the intact counter, she picked up the plans she'd had drawn up for her dream kitchen, along with the pictures she'd cut out of magazines of how she wanted the room to look. "This is what I had *planned* to do, only . . ."

He laid the plans on top of the aluminum clipboard he held in his hands, the kind that held a stack of papers inside and latched shut. She couldn't help noticing his hands. He had fine hands, long slender fingers that somehow managed to look entirely masculine. Maybe it was the roughness of the skin . . . Something about a man's work-callused hands just screamed *sexy* to her.

He studied the plans, and then he glanced at the magazine pictures. "Hmm." He lifted his gaze to hers, his expression incredulous. "You thought you could do this yourself?"

She nodded. An angry spark flared to life. She was intelligent and capable. Given enough time and a little direction, she could accomplish anything she set out to do, including installing a new kitchen. There had to be classes offered somewhere. She just hadn't had the time to look into taking one.

He gestured toward the entryway between her kitchen and dining area. Exposed fragments of framing from the wall she'd been knocking away stuck out at odd angles. "You do know that's a load-bearing wall, right?"

She had no idea what that meant. "Does that mean I can't widen the entry to the dining room? This house just feels so cut up. I want to improve the flow of movement from one area to the next. You know, open it up a bit."

"Sure. It can be widened, but you have to add support." He moved to the wall in question and stared up. Then he glanced at the arched entryway dividing her dining area from the living room. "You want it arched like that one?" He gestured with his pen.

"That would be nice," she said.

"If you don't mind my asking, what do you do for a living?" One side of his sexy mouth quirked up, rendering her weak in the knees. "I'm guessing you don't have a lot of experience in home repair."

"I'm a paralegal." How tall was he? Around six feet and some change, she guessed. Standing near him made her feel positively delicate. "Do you want to see the bathroom?"

"Is it in a similar state as the kitchen?"

She nodded. "'Fraid so."

He smiled and pointed with his pen. "Lead on, pretty lady."

He thinks I'm pretty? Her insides fluttered. She shook it off. He probably said that to all of his female clients. He's schmoozing, that's all. Her bathroom had puke-green, white and black swirly linoleum tiles covering the floor, and pink and black plastic tiles covering the walls halfway up. Hideous. She had no shower, and corroding chrome fixtures completed the dismal decor that hadn't been updated since the house had been built, and that had been 1947.

She'd ripped the rusting medicine cabinet and mirror off the wall, along with the matching fixtures for the toilet paper holder and the light switch cover. The vanity was cheap and the sink tiny. She'd shut off the water to the sink and had already torn the vanity away from the wall too.

Problem was, most of the things she'd torn out in her bungalow were too heavy or awkwardly large for her to carry out of the house by herself. As much as she hated to admit it, she did need help. "The only things working in here are the bathtub and the toilet." She backed away so he could move inside the tiny room. "I want a shower installed."

"I see," he said, making notes on his clipboard. "Give me about twenty minutes to do some measuring, and then we'll sit down and talk about an estimate."

"All right." She fought the urge to follow him around her house just to ogle. "I'll leave you to it. Just give me a shout when you're done."

He already had his tape measure out. His pen, now clamped between his teeth, and an expression of concentration on his ruggedly handsome face, he set to work. Haley moved down the short hallway to her bedroom. Might as well change for her night out. Her clothes were lying across the end of her bed. She closed the door, stripped and quickly dressed, and then she went to her closet to choose a purse—something small to carry the bare minimum so she could keep it slung across her chest all evening. She'd just finished transferring items from her larger bag to the smaller purse when the estimator called out to her. What was his name? His card was still in the pocket of her jeans. She'd look at it later.

His gaze traveled over her from head to foot again as she met him in her dining room. He sat with a bunch of papers spread out on her table. Was she imagining the look of appreciation he flashed her way? "So, what are the damages?" she asked, sliding into the chair next to him.

"Well, there are a couple of ways to go." He shuffled the papers in front of him. "We can get materials and appliances at wholesale, and our markup isn't nearly as high as the markups through retail stores. This estimate is for labor only," he said, pushing a page toward her. "If you decide you want to buy the materials on your own, keep in mind that's going to add quite a bit to the total. If you decide you want to purchase cabinets, countertops, et cetera through us, I'll point you in the right direction and give you a few catalogs to look through. Everything Lowe's, Home Depot and Menards carries, we can get for you at a good discount."

Haley glanced at the figure for labor, and a tiny gasp escaped. *Whoa.* "That much?"

"You want it done right, don't you? Your job is significantly more involved than just handyman services. This is a remodel."

"Of course I want it done right." Maybe she should insist that her parents get a few more estimates before deciding. But her mom had said they'd already hired this company, and knowing her dad, references and comparisons had already taken place. She stood up. "OK. I'll probably get materials and appliances through your company. At least that will save a little money." She'd pay for materials herself, no matter what her parents said.

He rose from his place and held out his hand. She rose with him and reached out to shake on the deal, stunned when she found herself being drawn closer. She peered up at him, confused. Alarmed. *Aroused.*

"I have some time on my hands. Would you like me to stay for a while?" he purred.

"What?" She withdrew her hand from his and took a step back.

"You know." He winked at her again. "I have time for a little of that *special touch* you requested. Although I have to admit, the touching part generally doesn't happen until after a job has been completed." He stepped closer. "In your case, I'll make an exception."

"I have no idea what you're talking about, and you need to leave. Now."

Confusion clouded his face. "When you called . . . when we made the appointment . . . *you* said you wanted my special touch."

"What are you talking about? I never called you." All the air left her lungs. "My *mother* is the one who set up this appointment." His expression went through a series of rapid changes, which would have been amusing under different circumstances.

He pointed his finger at her. "Your mother pimped you out? Why would she do that?"

Indignation swirled into the mix of mortification and shock freezing her in place. "No." She fisted her hands at her sides. "*You're* the one being paid here. My mother pimpled *you* out." Suspicion dawned, and more than anything, Haley wanted to be wrong. "What's your name again?"

"I gave you a card."

"I didn't read it."

"Sam Haney, with Haney & Sons Construction and Handyman Service."

Her eyes went wide, and her stomach dropped. "You're *him*. That guy from the radio show." Her humiliation was now complete. Her own mother had tried to set her up for a one-night stand with Sam the Handyman from *Loaded Question*. Her hand went to her forehead. "You're the man-whore who . . . you're a . . . a . . . ," she stammered.

"What *do* you call the male equivalent of a slut? There's a word for that; I know there is."

"Yep. It's *lucky*." He shrugged and began to gather his things.

"No. That's not it."

"Depends on your point of view."

"*Lothario*. That's the word, and you're fired," she bit out between clenched teeth. Her mother had gone too far this time, and Haley couldn't wait to have at her.

"You *can't* fire me. You didn't hire me. Your *mother* did."

"I certainly can fire you. This is my house." She jutted out her chin. "You can't be any good at what you do if you have to offer sex on the side to get jobs." She strode to the front door and threw it open. Cold air washed over her, but it did nothing to cool her anger . . . or her embarrassment.

"Whatever. Sorry for the misunderstanding. You can untwist your knickers, *Ms. Cooper*. I'm leaving."

Haley shut and locked the door after him, too dazed to move. She leaned back against the door. How should she deal with her mother? Her first impulse was to call her up and read her the riot act, but she knew better. When dealing with Trudy Cooper, it was always best to cool down first. Think rationally, even when the situation was anything but rational.

Her mom meant well, she just had no boundaries where her children were concerned. In her mother's mind, Haley was still a little girl whose life needed to be managed. "Argh! I can't believe my own mother tried to set me up with Sam the Handyman." Even worse, she couldn't believe how attractive she found him. Embarrassing, really. She really did need this night out with her friends.

Chapter Three

Sam made it all the way to his van before the implications of what had just occurred fully registered. *You can't be any good at what you do if you have to offer sex on the side to get jobs.*

"Ms. Cooper has no idea what she's talking about. I'm damn good at what I do," he grumbled. He opened his passenger side door and tossed his tape measure and clipboard onto the seat. He stared into the interior of the van—not moving, just thinking.

Why, oh why had he made a pass at Ms. Cooper? Maybe it was a rebellious reaction to all the abuse he'd suffered from his family about *Loaded Question*. He'd taken so much heat since the radio show. Had he simply wanted a bit of comfort from the curvy brunette he believed had asked for his attentions up front? Besides, she'd changed into sexier clothes while he was writing up her estimate. He thought about it . . . and shook his head. *Idiot.* This was *Saturday.* She was getting ready to go out, not trying to entice him.

Whatever prompted him to reach for her, it didn't explain the letdown at her rejection he couldn't shake. Haley Cooper was the cutest little brunette he'd *ever* laid eyes on. Petite, with a sweet figure, silky brown hair and a wholesome *girl-next-door* appeal. A man could get lost in those large brown eyes of hers. *Whoa.* Probably a good thing she'd fired him.

Still . . .

You can't be any good . . . Her words bounced around inside his head and churned in his gut. If Grandpa Joe got word of this . . . Oh, man, his rear end was going to be in the wringer for sure.

He scrubbed the lower half of his face with his hand and stared back at Haley's bungalow. The woman had exposed electrical wires in her kitchen. If they connected, arced, the place would go up in smoke. The house was a disaster waiting to happen. He shut the passenger door, circled around to the back of his van and fished out a few electrical wire caps from his tool box.

She'd dissed his skills as a carpenter. He couldn't let that fly. Then there was the mystery of why such an attractive woman's mother would feel the need to set her daughter up the way she had. He wanted answers. His feet started him back up the path leading to the front door.

He rapped his knuckles against the door and took a step back. The door swung wide, and Haley gaped at him in surprise. She was probably expecting some suit-and-tie guy come to take her out. Of course. She looked like a suit-and-tie kind of woman, not his type at all—not that he had a *type*. "Hey, I think we got off on the wrong foot."

"You think?" She arched a single brow and managed to look down her nose at him, even though she was a good six inches shorter. "Don't worry about it," she said with plenty of attitude. "I'm not going to complain about you to your HR department."

Haney & Sons didn't *have* an HR department. Far worse. They had Grandpa Joe and Grandma Maggie. Ms. Cooper's smugness annoyed him. "Obviously you have *mother* issues, and—"

"I don't have mother issues." A blotch of red blossomed on her collarbone.

Another red blotch appeared on her neck, and another on her cheek. Interesting. Ms. Cooper was not a woman who blushed. She blotched.

He bit the inside of his cheek to keep from smiling. Why hadn't he noticed that before? Oh, right. Probably because he was too busy trying to come up to speed on the whole mother-called-pretending-to-be-daughter thing and all. "OK, your mother has issues."

"I'll concede the point." Haley crossed her arms in front of her, lifting her breasts slightly.

Do not stare. Do not even glance in that direction. "I'm just as much a victim here as you are."

She snorted, and the smugness returned to her expression.

"Hey," he said, giving her his most charming smile. "I'm very good at what I do. Give me a chance to prove it to you."

Her brow rose, and one side of her mouth twitched up a millimeter. "I'm sure you're *very* good at what you *do*, Mr. Haney, but I'm still not going to have sex with you. Still not interested in your *special touch*." She made quote marks in the air, bracketing her words.

Well, *that* stung. Doggone it, not only had she insulted him, but now she wanted to rub salt into the wound? "I'm not talking about my skills in the bedroom, *Ms. Cooper*. I'm a skilled carpenter. The best." He straightened and crossed his arms in front of him, mimicking her stance.

"My brother is an excellent electrician," he informed her, "and my uncle is a plumber with years of experience. Haney & Sons can provide you with the very best tradesmen the Twin Cities has to offer." She seemed to be thinking about it. A good sign. "All I'm asking is that you give me the chance to prove to you that I . . ." *Don't need to offer sex on the side to get jobs?* Why did he feel the need to prove anything to this uptight little paralegal? "Look. Your mother already hired me to put your house back together. She's footing the bill, right? Let me do the job I was hired to do."

Sam reached into his jacket pocket and pulled out the electrical caps. "In the meantime, you have exposed live wires in your kitchen. At least let me cap them. I wouldn't want your house to catch on fire."

She studied him, her expression wary. "Free of charge," he muttered, "no strings or hands attached."

"That's very considerate of you." She opened the storm door wider to let him in.

Relief washed through him. "I'm a *very* considerate guy."

"You're a hound dog," she huffed.

"That's *horndog*." Another insult, and not even true. The worst anyone could say about his exploits was that he wasn't a man to let an opportunity pass him by. Why had he marched back up to her door again? "Haney & Sons is a highly rated company, and I'm a full partner in the business. If you want, I can give you a list of references to call, and we're on Angie's List. You can check out our ratings on that site."

"Whatever." She led him to her kitchen, her spine stiff. "*If* I let you do the work, there are a few ground rules that I must insist you follow."

"Of course." He put the caps on the exposed wires. "I'm guessing number one is to keep it strictly professional, which is unnecessary. I've *never* been the one to initiate first contact." *Until today, that is.*

"Good, because I certainly will not be initiating . . . anything." She lifted her prim little nose into the air. "I want to learn as much as I can about home repair. I'll try not to get underfoot, but think of me as your new apprentice. My involvement with the work being done means odd hours and working around my schedule. Are you OK with that?"

"When you say odd hours, what are we talking?" He glanced at her. "Evenings? Weekends?" This could seriously cut into his personal life, and the hockey tournament season was about to begin. "I do have other obligations."

"Oh, I'm sure you do. We can work around your other *obligations*."

Again with the smug. *Who does she think she is? Or rather, who does she think I am?* "I can do a few weeknights and maybe Saturday mornings, but it will take longer to get the job done. Will that suit you?"

"Yes. When do we start?"

"Can I call you once I know my schedule?" he asked. "I'm going to have to coordinate with my brother. He'll help me get the old stuff out of here, and he'll be the one taking care of the electrical work."

"Sure." Haley walked to her dining room table and tore off a corner of his estimate. She grabbed a pen and scrawled her name and number down. "You can reach me on my cell."

"I'll arrange for a dumpster to be delivered. If you have it placed in your driveway, we won't have to pay for a permit." Sam took the scrap from her. Their fingers touched, and his stomach flipped. The same thing had happened when he'd drawn her close, but then he'd blamed it on anticipation. This was nothing but a simple exchange. *Odd.*

He stared at her. More blotches appeared on her neck and crept up to her cheeks. Awkward seconds ticked by, and still he stood like an idiot with his stomach knotted and his tongue tied.

"Great." She broke eye contact first. "Let me know when the dumpster will be delivered, and I'll be sure to park in the street." She started for the front door, opening it wide again. "I'm expecting someone soon, so if you don't mind . . ." She gestured toward the outside.

"Oh. Right." He didn't like it. He didn't like the way she affected him one little bit. "I'll drop some catalogs off for you. If you're not home, I'll put them inside your storm door, and I'll give you a call next week."

"Do that."

The door closed behind him. Sam shook himself free of the annoying sensations she'd caused. The only reason he'd reacted to Haley Cooper the way he had was because she'd rejected him and insulted his skill as a tradesman. That's all there was to it. Wasn't it? He did admire her determination to learn, the way she set the ground rules, and he had to admit her quick wit appealed to him.

Still frowning, he climbed into his van and headed for The Bulldog. His brother and sister were waiting for him. A few cousins and friends were bound to show up too. He'd have a couple beers, a burger and call it a night.

Half an hour later, Sam settled himself into the high-top chair Wyatt and Josey had saved for him at their favorite watering hole. "You'll never guess what happened at an estimate I did this afternoon. I—"

"Let me guess," his younger brother quipped, his hoodie pulled up over his head as usual. "You *didn't* get laid on the job."

His sister laughed, and he scowled at both of them. "Ha-ha. Very funny." The server laid a coaster down in front of him. He smiled at her. She smiled back, and a spark of interest flickered in her blue eyes. He turned away. Not tonight. He wasn't even tempted. Couldn't she see he was just being friendly? "I'll have a Michelob Golden in a bottle, please. No mug."

"Coming right up. Anyone else need anything?" she asked, keeping her eyes on him.

Wyatt and Josey each ordered another beer, and Sam chewed on the Haley-and-her-mother puzzle.

"So?" Josey nudged him. "What happened on the estimate?"

"Huh?" Sam tore his eyes away from the tabletop. "Oh. You know that radio show fiasco last week?"

"Yeah." Wyatt sighed. "You're killing me, Sam. You know that, right? Ever since that stupid show, I've had women throwing themselves at me, thinking I must be like you because I'm a Haney." He pulled the hood of his sweatshirt lower over his forehead. "It's enough to make me think about changing careers. I should've gone into the accounting business. A small, quiet office somewhere in the back of a building would be nice." He glanced at Josey. "Women don't throw themselves at accountants, do they, Jo?"

"How should I know?" She frowned. "I've never met an accountant, since I do my own taxes. Besides, I wouldn't throw myself at anyone, no matter what they did for a living."

"Sorry, Wyatt. Didn't mean for my shit to spill over into your life, but at least now you know women aren't put off by the scars." Sam shot his brother an apologetic look. Wyatt grunted and scowled back at him.

His brother had been eight when he'd decided he needed to find out what would happen if he squirted lighter fluid onto hot coals. Their dad had been getting ready to barbeque, and he'd only stepped into the house for a minute to get the burgers. A minute was all it took for Wyatt to set himself on fire. Sam still remembered the screams, the smell and the shrill sound of the siren as the ambulance came to take his brother away.

He shuddered, and turned his mind away from the memory just as the server returned with their beers. The three of them placed their orders for food, and he waited until the waitress left before continuing. "Can we get back to my story?"

Jo shrugged, and Wyatt grinned. At least the mood had lightened. He launched into a brief description of the day's events from the time Haley's mother requested he do the estimate to what had happened at her house. "Why would someone do that? Do you think I'm the butt of some kind of sick joke here, or what?"

"Well." Wyatt smirked. "You're definitely a butt, and you're pretty much a joke as far as I'm concerned." Josey and Wyatt laughed.

Sam stared his brother down, far too used to his brother's teasing.

"Don't worry about it." Wyatt shook his head. "You're not taking the job, right? There were bound to be repercussions from the radio show. Just be prepared to let a few jobs go. Eventually people will forget about you and move on to other things."

"I'm doing the job, and you're going to help, Wyatt."

"What?" Josey leaned forward. "Did I hear you right? After a setup like that you're taking the job?"

He nodded, picking at the label on his beer bottle.

"Why?" the two said in unison.

"Because Ms. Cooper thinks I *have* to offer sex on the side to get work." He focused on peeling the Michelob label from the glass. "I'm good at what I do, dammit." He had his reputation as a tradesman to defend, and for some reason, he needed to prove to Ms. Cooper that she had him all wrong.

◆ ◆ ◆

Haley answered the door the minute Kathy knocked. "You'll never guess what just happened." Indignation still thrummed through her veins. She needed to vent, or she'd call her mom and give her a piece of her mind. Until she calmed down, that would be a mistake. Fighting with her mom never accomplished anything, and doing so would only make her more miserable. Talking it through with Kathy would help, and then she'd decide how best to deal with her meddling mother.

"OK. I won't guess." Kathy took off her coat and laid it over the back of Haley's couch. "Tell me."

"You remember that handyman from *Loaded Question?*" Haley paced around her living room.

"Sure I do. Why?"

"You'll never guess—"

"You already said that." Kathy stood in front of her, stopping her midpace. "Spill it, Haley."

"My *mother* hired Sam Haney to work on my house. He was here. He made a pass at me."

Kathy let loose a loud peal of laughter. "You're kidding."

"I'm not." Haley shook her head. "He's gorgeous, by the way. Dreamy, like that guy who plays Thor in all those Marvel comic book movies. Only Sam's hair is really curly."

"Sam looks like Chris Hemsworth?"

She nodded.

"Wow."

Haley nodded again. "My *mother* set me up for a one-night stand with Sam the Handyman from *Loaded Question*." She paced again. "Can you believe that?" It was pace or tear out her hair, and she didn't want to have to redo the hair before they went out. "She's really outdone herself this time."

"It could have been a coincidence, Haley. What are the odds that your mother heard about Hands-On-Haney?"

"Oh, this was no coincidence." She swung around to face her friend. "When Mom called to make the appointment, she pretended to be me. My mother told Sam that I wanted his *special touch*."

"Oh . . . wow." Kathy's eyes went wide. "Can we trade mothers?"

"Absolutely. Take her. She's yours." Haley paced again. "You have no idea what she's like. Once, when I was in the fifth grade, the most popular girl in my class was having a birthday party sleepover, and I wasn't invited." She arched a brow. "*My* mother called *her* mother and wheedled her into inviting me."

"What did you do?"

"I refused to go of course, but I suffered the mean-girl teasing and harassment for the rest of the school year. Thank goodness she and I ended up in different middle schools."

"That must have been mortifying," Kathy said.

"It was." Haley nodded. "Then there was the time my freshman year in high school when I was feeling down because I hadn't been asked to the homecoming dance. Trudy *paid* a neighbor boy to ask me to the dance. She swore him to secrecy, but he told me anyway." She snorted. "Those are only two examples out of many, many more. You still want her?"

"Um, no. I get it. She's over the top, but have you talked to her, asked her what she intended when she hired Sam?"

"Not yet." Haley stopped and tapped her chin. "I wanted to calm down first, give it some thought." She grinned. "You know what I'm thinking?"

"Again. I have no idea. Quit asking me questions I can't answer." Kathy threw her hands up. "What *are* you thinking?"

"My mother is going to go crazy wondering what happened here today. I'm going to let her stew in her own juices." Haley laughed out loud. "I'm not saying a word to her about Sam Haney and what happened today. That ought to fix her wagon."

"Haley."

"What?"

"You just laughed. It's been a while since I've heard you laugh, and I like the sound." Kathy put her hands on Haley's shoulders and gave her a shake. "It's good to see you happy, even if the cause is something so bizarre. So, tell me all about Handyman Haney."

"Oh, he's a tall piece of man-fluff." She flapped her hand in the air and paced again. "Nice to look at, but . . ."

"But?"

"I don't know." Sam had been considerate enough to walk back to her door with electrical caps. Plus, before he'd made the pass at her, she'd been all for having him do the job. He was efficient, professional and he clearly knew what he was about. He'd agreed to keep his hands to himself and teach her as they went. He wanted to prove his skills as a carpenter, and she appreciated his efforts. Still, he was a promiscuous hound dog.

"He's going to teach me stuff about home repair, and I get to watch him flex his muscles." She laughed again. "You should have seen the look on his face when he realized my mother pimped him out."

"Yeah?"

"Yeah. It was like watching one of those old silent movies on steroids. His expressions changed so fast I had a hard time keeping up. Poor guy." A car pulled into her driveway. "They're here."

Kathy put her coat on. "Why *poor guy*?"

"If everyone at our law firm's reaction is anything to go by, along with what we've seen on social media, he's been the butt of everyone's jokes since that radio show aired last Monday. And now my own mother is using him for . . . I don't know what. Who knows what Trudy Cooper is up to? I wouldn't want to be in Sam's shoes right now, but he *is* the one who stepped into them."

She shook her head and snorted. "Besides all of that, he doesn't strike me as the kind of man who gets rejected. Ever. I can see why women throw themselves at his feet." Haley grabbed her coat from the closet. She grinned at her friend. "Let's go get a little stupid and have some fun."

"I like this new attitude. I think maybe Sam the Handyman is good for you."

"He's not *for me* at all. Not my type. Definitely no dating potential there. He's done it with just about—"

"You know, Haley, it's all right to go out with a man just for fun. They don't all have to be husband candidates."

One guy. She'd had one man in her life. Period. And he'd broken her heart. "I've never done the casual dating thing."

"Maybe it's time you did. Play the field. Learn what it is you want in a mate, and what it is you don't want."

"I'll give it some thought, but I don't really know how to meet men. I don't want to go out with some guy I met at a bar or a nightclub though, that's for sure."

"Why not? We're nice, normal women, aren't we?"

"Yeah, so?" She opened her door and gestured for Kathy to go out first so she could lock up.

"*We're* going clubbing. Don't you think there are decent men out there who are doing the exact same thing we are tonight, and for the same reasons? Everybody needs to blow off steam and have a little fun now and then."

"Hmm. Hadn't thought of it like that." Her enthusiasm for their club crawl rose a notch. Maybe she would meet someone nice—or at least someone to dance with tonight.

"Sam said he normally doesn't do the touching part until after the job is finished, but for me he was willing to make an exception." Laughter spilled out of her again. "He is hot, and kind of sweet, in a messed-up way."

"Fling."

"We'll see." Did she have it in her? "We'll see."

Trudy added butter and milk to the ceramic bowl of boiled potatoes and started the electric hand mixer to mash them. She glanced at the clock. Haley hadn't called her after Haney & Sons did her estimate. How had things gone with Sam? The timer dinged, and she stopped the mixer and reached for the oven mitts. Pulling Sunday's pot roast out of the oven, she inhaled. "Mmm."

"Hey, Mom." Frank Junior poked his head through the back door. "Wow, it smells good in here."

"Thanks." She smiled at her youngest. "Did you pick up the rolls like I asked?"

He handed her the bag dangling from his hand. "I did, and I also bought a cherry pie while I was at Kowalski's grocery store. I hope that's OK."

"Oh, good. I didn't make a dessert."

Haley trailed Junior through the door. Trudy's heart leaped to her throat. Had she done the right thing? The wrong thing? She studied Haley. She didn't look any different.

"Hi, Mom." Haley set a casserole dish on the kitchen counter and unwrapped the scarf around her neck. "Yum, pot roast. I'm starving." She gave her younger brother a hug. "Good to see you, Junior. How's school?"

"Stressful." He hugged her back.

Her children took their coats off and hung them on the hooks by the back door. Trudy frowned. Had the handyman made a move on Haley or not? "Dinner's ready. Junior, go tell your father it's time to eat. He's in the family room watching the game."

"Dad," Junior shouted, "grub's on."

"Coming," her husband called back.

Trudy tsked and shook her head. "I could've done that."

Grinning, Haley wrapped her arm around her mom's shoulders. "Do you need me to do anything?"

"Take the potatoes to the table, and then you can pour the wine." Her hands full, Trudy gestured toward the fridge with her elbow. "The bottle is already open. It's on the bottom shelf of the door."

A few minutes later, her family was seated at the dining room table. Trudy passed the platter of pot roast to her husband. "How'd it go with the construction company yesterday?" she asked, forcing the burning curiosity out of her tone.

"It went fine, but you're not going to like the estimate. It's in my purse." Haley put a pile of potatoes on her plate and passed the ceramic bowl to Junior. "The estimator said it's a remodel and not really a handy-man job." Haley glanced at her. "I hope that's OK. I can foot some of the bill, and I'm paying for materials."

"Who did the estimate?" Trudy's heart pounded, and a niggling guilt stole her breath.

"A guy named Sam Haney." Haley took a spoonful of the spinach casserole she'd brought. "He seemed to know what he was doing. He's a journeyman carpenter, competent and professional. I'm sure Haney & Sons will do a great job, but it's going to take more than one person. That's partially why the labor cost is so high."

Professional? Sam the Handyman had *not* made a move on her daughter. Trudy had half a mind to fire him. How dare he not make a pass at Haley?

"Good. Good." Her husband nodded. "I'll take a look at the estimate after dinner, honey. You don't have to foot part of the bill. Your mother and I want to do this for you."

Not good. Not good at all. Her plan hadn't worked. Trudy pursed her lips. *Unless . . .* The divorcée on *Loaded Question* had said *after* the job was done. That was when she did Sam . . . *after.* Haney & Sons hadn't even started on Haley's house yet. There was time. It could still happen. "When will they begin the work?"

"Not for a couple of weeks. Mr. Haney has to coordinate things with the other workers. He said he'd call me to set things up." Haley passed her the spinach casserole. "This is a new recipe. Let me know what you think."

"Smells great," Trudy replied. Haley had called Sam *Mr. Haney.* Not at all personal, not at all what you'd call someone who'd flirted or made a pass at you. Didn't Sam find her daughter attractive? She took a spoonful of the spinach and passed the dish to her husband. "Haley, you're a lovely young woman."

Junior snorted, and Haley choked on her mouthful of potatoes and covered her mouth with her napkin. Her husband looked slightly puzzled.

"What?" Trudy's defenses surged. "She *is* a lovely young woman. Is there something *wrong* with a mother telling her daughter she's pretty?"

"No. Of course not, sweetheart." Frank senior sliced off a chunk of his beef. "Just seemed a little random is all." One side of his mouth quirked up.

Haley looked like she was struggling not to laugh, while Junior shoveled food into his mouth as if this might be his last meal. Trudy huffed. "Well, she is pretty." She lifted her chin. "You are, Haley, and don't let anyone convince you otherwise."

"I won't, Mom. Thanks." Haley kept her eyes on her plate. "Great dinner."

"Hmm-mm," Junior mumbled with his mouth full.

Trudy mulled. Her plan might still work. Perhaps Sam would make his move after the job was done. That must be it. He's waiting. She nodded.

"What are you nodding about, Mom?" Haley asked, her brow raised.

"I was just thinking about how much I love it when we're all together like this, that's all." She smiled lovingly at her family and crossed her fingers in her lap. "Eat up. Junior brought pie."

Chapter Four

Wednesday evening, Sam stood in front of the large Minnesota Wild calendar on his kitchen wall. He held a green Sharpie in one hand and the city league hockey schedule for his team in the other.

When his cousin Andrea's son and daughter, fraternal twins, expressed an interest in playing hockey, Sam had jumped at the chance to coach, especially since their dad's schedule with the National Guard prevented him from taking it on. Sam had started his coaching career with the twins when they were Mini-Mites, then Mites, and now they'd switched to a Saint Paul league for nine- and ten-year-olds. Their team would actually get to compete in the tournament this year, and he couldn't wait. Sam had played hockey as a kid, and still did occasionally. He really got a kick out of coaching, and spending time with his cousins was an added perk.

Sam wrote times and locations for their practices and games at various Saint Paul parks and indoor rinks. In no time at all, November and December were covered in green. Stepping back, he looked for open times when he could work on Haley Cooper's disaster relief project. What with the other jobs he had going on and hockey, he wouldn't be able to do more than complete the tear-outs before Thanksgiving.

He grabbed a pad of paper and wrote down a few possible openings. A tentative plan of action in mind, Sam grabbed his cell phone from the counter and searched for Haley's number in his contacts. He *had* looked up the meaning of lothario. No way was he a selfish seducer of women, nor was he sexually irresponsible.

Ms. Cooper had misjudged and looked down her nose at him. That got under his skin. Call it pride or whatever, it still bugged him. Of course, he hadn't helped matters by making a pass at her, and his reputation as the handsiest handyman in the Twin Cities had gone viral. He could see how she'd come to her conclusions, no matter how wrong she might be. He went a little breathless as he pushed Call. What was it about her that made him so nervous?

"Hello?" she answered after the second ring.

He had to clear his throat before he could speak. "Ms. Cooper, this is Sam Haney. Have you had a chance to look through the catalogs I left for you?"

"Why, yes I have, *Mr. Haney.* Thank you for dropping them off for me."

Was that a smirk he detected? Amazing. She managed to convey a facial expression through tone alone. "Did you find anything you like?"

"Yes, but I want to make a trip to Home Depot or Lowe's to take a look at everything before I decide, and I'd appreciate it if you'd do the measuring before we order. I don't want to mess up on anything."

"Of course." Her voice sounded ultra-feminine and slightly husky over the phone—when not smirking, anyway. He stared at his calendar, searching for another open spot. "Do you want me to go with you when you check out the products?"

"Hmm. I don't know if that's necessary, but thanks for the offer."

"It's up to you." Her rejection chafed, which made no sense. He wasn't pursuing her. He wasn't interested in pursuing anyone, for that matter. "If you'd like, I'm available to offer my professional opinion on materials. I'm familiar with the companies that produce quality products and those that don't."

"I'll think about it and get back to you."

In other words, no. "OK, it's fine either way," he said, pumping positive into his voice. "The reason I called is that I have some possible dates for the tear-outs, but we won't be able to get to the wiring, plumbing or installs until after Thanksgiving." He ran the dates by her. "It'll take a few weeks for the materials to arrive once we do the ordering, longer if they're custom."

"Just a minute," she said. "I have to get to my calendar."

They went back and forth about dates and times, finally arriving at a couple that worked for both of them. "Good." Sam added more green to his calendar. "I'll let you know when the dumpster will be delivered, and we'll begin gutting the bathroom next Saturday morning. I'll bring my brother along to help carry heavy items out of the house."

"I'm going to help," she reminded him. "Don't forget. I want to learn how to do this stuff. That's part of the deal."

"I haven't forgotten," he assured her. He'd be able to show off his knowledge and skill. That shouldn't excite him like it did. He shook it off. She'd mostly be underfoot. "Next Saturday then. Have a great week."

"You too."

He hit End Call and dialed his brother's number. *Have a great week?* When had he turned into a Walmart senior greeter?

"Hey, Sam," Wyatt answered.

"Hey. Are you free next Saturday morning to help with a tear-out?"

"Let me check." Wyatt sighed into the phone as he moved through his apartment. "Is this for the woman whose mother set you up?"

"Yes. Does that make a difference to your availability?"

"Nah, just curious. And yes, I'm free on the twenty-first. Can't wait to get a look at her."

"A look is *all* you're going to get." Now, why had that flown out of his mouth? His brother always clammed up and turned several shades of red in the presence of strangers—especially if those strangers happened to be attractive women. Wyatt posed no threat in the competing-for-women department, not that they *were* competing. Was it because Sam saw Haley Cooper as his own personal source of irritation? "That's all *either* of us is going to get," he tossed out for good measure.

"Oh, that's right. Gramps has you on a short leash." Wyatt laughed. "I heard you're on *personal* probation."

"Whatever." Sam dropped the Sharpie into the catchall basket he kept on his kitchen counter. "Just be here at eight on the twenty-first."

"No problem. What're you doing for dinner tonight? You want to go grab a burger?"

"Not tonight. I'm just going to hang out here." He scanned his apartment. The walls were a neutral shade of rental-white and unadorned. A very large smart TV and entertainment center took up an entire wall in his living room, with a nice comfy La-Z-Boy recliner couch against the opposite wall angled just right to play video games or watch sports with a few buddies. The couch even had beverage holders for their beer cans. "If you want, you can join me here for frozen pizza and a video game. Otherwise, I'll see you tomorrow."

"Nah, but thanks. That reminds me, Josey is up in arms again."

Sam frowned. His sister definitely had middle-child issues. "What about this time?"

"She says the name of our company is sexist. She wants Grandpa Joe to drop the 'sons' in Haney & Sons Construction and Handyman Service."

Josey had it rough in their business. There weren't many women carpenters or plumbers, and she was a Haney, though obviously not a *son*. She, too, was a partner in the family business. He could see her point. "Thanks for the warning."

He and Wyatt ended their call, and Sam headed for his refrigerator—Ms. Cooper coming to mind as he glanced at his calendar. What had Haley's mother been thinking? What had she hoped to accomplish by setting him and her daughter up the way she had?

That was the burning question, and it was like an itch he couldn't reach. Why on earth would such an attractive, intelligent and interesting woman need setting up, anyway? He wanted to get to the bottom of that mystery in the worst way.

Haley sat at her desk and twiddled her pen between her finger and thumb while staring into space. She should be typing up the brief she'd been given, but her mind . . . well, her mind was on kitchen cabinets and countertops, bathroom vanities, floor tiles and the hot handyman who would be installing everything.

What had her mom intended with her meddling, and how could Haley convince her to keep her nose out of her personal life? She had to find some way to make the whole setup backfire, that's how. To do that, she had to ferret out why her mother had done what she'd done. "Special touch, my ass," she muttered under her breath.

"Hey, you want to go out for lunch today? It's noon already." Kathy stepped into her office. Calling the closet-size room an office was stretching it, but at least she had her own space.

"Definitely." Haley's stomach gurgled in response to the prospect of food.

"I was thinking Panera or The Local. What are you in the mood for?"

"The Local." She opened her bottom desk drawer and pulled out her purse. "It's nice to have someone bring our food to us." Both restaurants were located on Minneapolis's Nicollet Mall and within walking distance via the skyway from Bremmer, Stevens & Schmitt, the law office where she worked. "Is Felicia coming?"

Felicia poked her head around Kathy's shoulder. "Right here."

"Good. We need to talk." Haley rose from her place and grabbed her sweater. "Let's go."

The three of them trekked through the crowded LaSalle Plaza skyway toward the US Bank lobby escalator down to street level. They dashed across Nicollet Mall through the cold and entered The Local, a popular Irish pub and restaurant. The delicious smells inside enveloped Haley, and her empty stomach rumbled again.

She gave her name to the hostess, who handed her a pager and told her there'd be a short wait. Haley pulled her sweater close and peered out the window at the overcast day. "It looks like we're going to get snow, and it's not even Thanksgiving yet." She huddled against the wall with her friends.

"Have you told Felicia about . . . er . . . Saturday's handyman fiasco?" Kathy asked.

Felicia's eyes widened. "Come again?"

"No. I haven't really had the chance." As she and Kathy had left her house on Saturday, she'd asked Kathy to keep it to herself during the club crawl. Haley hadn't wanted the new intern to hear about her latest humiliation. She glanced at the huddled crowd surrounding them. "Let's wait until we're seated, and then I'll bring her up to speed."

"You won't believe it." Kathy laughed. "Haley's mom hired a handyman to help put her house back together."

"OK." Felicia's expression clouded with confusion. "That's a good thing, right?"

"It's a weird thing," Kathy told her.

The pager in Haley's hand began to vibrate, signaling their table was ready. She handed the pager back to the hostess, and the three of them followed her to a booth. Once they were seated and had ordered, Haley told Felicia everything that had happened and how Sam had made a pass at her.

"He said he doesn't normally do the touching part until after the job is done, but he was willing to make an exception in my case." She leaned forward, her eyes wide. "Can you believe that?" Should she feel as flattered as she did? Probably not. "My own mother set me up for . . . for a one-night stand with the infamous Sam Haney."

Felicia sat back with a stunned look on her face. "Just how hot is this Hands-On-Haney?"

"Oh, he's definitely an eleven and a half on a scale of one to ten," Haley said. "But he's a total hound dog."

Kathy grinned. "I think you mean horndog."

"Whatever," Haley muttered.

Felicia's brow rose. "Can we trade mothers?"

"I asked the exact same thing." Kathy laughed.

"You're missing the point," Haley huffed. No matter what Trudy's intentions might be, her meddling hurt. Obviously she didn't believe Haley could get a date on her own. She bit her lip. Dammit, if she wanted to date, she could. She just wasn't *there* yet.

"I want to teach Trudy a lesson, but I can't figure out what she was thinking. What did she hope to achieve? If I knew that, I could come up with a plan that would end her meddling for good."

"Oh, that's easy." Felicia tapped the table with her finger. "Let's look at the facts."

"Right," Kathy said, leaning forward. "The facts, like it's been around seven months since Michael left. How many dates have you gone on in that time?"

"None, but—"

"Look, no dates in seven months, and that poor bungalow of yours has turned into your own personal punching bag." Felicia tapped the table again. "Mama bear sees you're not over Michael. She sees you're not moving on. She hears this radio show, and thinks to herself, baby bear needs a nudge in the right direction."

"Mama bear thinks baby bear needs to get laid." Kathy giggled.

"But . . . but . . . Trudy knows I'd never do a one one-night stand. It's just not in my nature." Haley frowned. "So, why do this? What kind of mother encourages her daughter to—"

"You're a grown woman, Haley, not a teenager, and I don't think Trudy expected you to act on Sam's offer." Felicia canted her head and studied her. "I think—and this is just my opinion—I think maybe your mom hoped you'd be flattered by the come-on, and that it might inspire you to get out there and date again. There's nothing like a hot guy's attention to make a woman feel desirable. Right?"

"That's it!" Kathy clapped her hands together. "Your mom is trying to nudge you into dating again, and Sam is her means to that end." She leaned forward and placed her forearms on the table. "You want to teach Trudy a lesson?"

"I do." Haley nodded. "I really do."

"Then date the handyman."

"What?" Haley blinked. "I . . . I can't do that. He's . . . he's not dating material."

"I'm not saying *marry* the handyman." Kathy shook her head. "Just ask him out. Date him, and let your mom know. The last thing she wants or expects is to see you with the Twin Cities' most infamous man-whore. She *hired* him to give you a spark, a jolt to your libido to get you moving forward again. As stereotypical as it sounds, mamas still want their daughters to marry and give them grandchildren. Thanks to that weasel Michael, you're stalled."

"At a complete standstill," Felicia agreed, nodding like a bobblehead.

"Your mother is expecting Sam the Handyman to *jump-start* your dormant hormones," Kathy continued.

"Exactly." Felicia waggled her eyebrows. "She's hoping Sam will give your love life a little mouth-to-mouth resuscitation."

Thankfully, their food arrived and Haley didn't have to respond. Absurd. Date the handsiest handyman in the state of Minnesota?

She couldn't. Nope. Absolutely out of the question. She shuddered at the thought of where his hands, mouth and man bits had been. Although . . . it certainly would give Trudy Cooper the shock of a lifetime, and it might make her think twice before plotting out Haley's life ever again. Just because she went out with him didn't mean she had to sleep with him. What was she thinking? She couldn't go out with him. She was way too attracted to him, and she didn't need to play with fire to know she'd get blistered. He was a complete man-ho. "Nope. Can't."

"Can't what?" Kathy asked.

"I can't date the handyman." She speared her fork into a piece of roast beef on her plate and swooshed it around in the gravy. How many women had Sam slept with? Was it a *Guinness World Book of Records* number? Another shudder racked through her. Her one lover to Sam's X number of partners. No. She was not the fling type, and she couldn't see herself getting involved with a man who saw sex solely as a recreational sport.

Felicia peered over her soda glass at Haley. "What are you afraid of, Haley?"

She bristled. "I'm not afraid. I just have an overabundance of common sense." She would have to come up with some other way to press home to her mother that her meddling was unacceptable.

"So." Felicia sipped her soda and put the glass down. "Did that cute guy you were dancing with at Ground Zero ask for your number?"

Her mouth full of food, Haley nodded.

"Has he called?"

She swallowed. "No. I told him I wasn't comfortable giving out my number, and he gave me his instead."

"*Are* you going to call him?" Kathy's fork stopped halfway between the plate and her mouth.

"Sure."

Her two friends exchanged a look.

"Maybe," Haley muttered.

Another look passed between Kathy and Felicia, this one involving raised eyebrows.

Probably not. Sighing, Haley focused on her lunch.

Sam parked his van in front of Haley's house and continued to grip the steering wheel. His heart should *not* be racing like this. Maybe something was wrong with him. He'd better schedule an appointment for a physical come Monday. That thought only made things worse. He hated going to the doctor.

"You gonna shut off the engine, or are we gonna spend the entire morning sitting in the van?" Wyatt asked, looking a little puzzled.

"What do you think?" Sam shut off the engine and glanced at Haley's front door. He drew in a long breath and let it out slowly, trying to slow his heart rate. "OK. I'm ready."

"Ready for what?" Wyatt frowned. "Since when do you need to get *ready* to step out of the van? Is there something you haven't told me? Does Ms. Cooper have a couple of badass Rottweilers ready to attack us or something?"

"No." Without further explanation, Sam opened his door and climbed out. Wyatt followed him to the back of the van, and they gathered the tools they'd need to work on the bathroom.

"You going to tell me what's up?"

"There's nothing to tell. I'm still not fully awake is all."

"Right."

The front door opened before he and his brother reached the front steps. "Good morning," Haley said, pushing the storm door wide to let them in.

She'd pulled her hair back into a ponytail, and she wore an old pair of jeans and a sweatshirt. Even without makeup she was cute . . . in an altogether too wholesome way. "Ms. Cooper, this is my brother, Wyatt.

He'll be doing the electrical wiring and helping with the heavy stuff. Wyatt, this is Ms. Cooper."

"Please stop calling me Ms. Cooper." Her brown eyes flashed annoyance. "I'm pleased to meet you, Wyatt. I'm Haley." She reached out to shake Wyatt's hand.

Wyatt touched her hand briefly and mumbled a greeting. Sam set the drop cloths and tools on the living room floor. "We're going to cover a path so we don't mess up your floors as we're hauling stuff out to the dumpster."

"OK. Good." Haley gestured toward the kitchen. "I made coffee. Would either of you like a cup?"

Wyatt, who had gone into silent shy mode, nodded and followed Haley to the kitchen. Shrugging out of his jacket on the way, Wyatt draped it over a dining room chair. He kept the hood of his sweatshirt up as usual. Sam followed, leaving his coat on the chair next to his brother's.

Did he want coffee? Seeing how his pulse was still elevated, caffeine would probably be a bad idea. "Water would be good," he told her as she took a couple of mugs from the still-intact cabinet. "I've already had enough coffee this morning."

"I have bottled water in the fridge," she said. "Help yourself."

Wyatt accepted a cup of coffee and scanned the kitchen. Sam grinned at his brother. "What do you think?"

"I don't know what to think," Wyatt murmured, his gaze darting to Haley. "You did this?"

A few red blotches appeared on her neck. "Yes. I did *this*. Why? Did I do something wrong?"

"Other than the load-bearing wall, no. You haven't done anything wrong. It's just that there are a bunch of random starts and stops," Sam said, opening the refrigerator. He reached for a bottled water. "Usually, when folks do demolition, they finish one area before moving on to the next. I figure you went at it the way you did because you lacked the know-how and the confidence to continue. You'd start, doubt yourself and stop. Am I right?"

She surveyed the wall, and her forehead creased. "Probably," she conceded.

"I'm curious." Sam unscrewed the cap on the water and took a fortifying gulp. "Why didn't you buy a nice little condo or a townhouse, something new that didn't need fixing up? Your life would've been a lot simpler. Houses are a lot of work for one person to maintain on their own."

A few more red blotches appeared on her neck. "Can we just get started?" she snapped.

"Sure." Her tone only piqued his curiosity more. Haley marched out of the kitchen, leaving him and his brother to follow in her wake.

Wyatt flashed him a look. "Way to go, idiot."

"What?"

"You asked me what I thought about this mess, right?" Wyatt said, his voice barely above a whisper. He gestured toward the scattering of holes in the plaster walls, and the segment of kitchen counter that had been pulled from the wall. "Looks to me like she was one pissed-off female when she did this. You're so dense."

"Well, at least I can talk to her."

Wyatt punched him in the shoulder as he passed. "It might be better for all concerned if you didn't."

"Ouch." What had he done to deserve such persecution? It's not like he'd insulted Haley. He'd just voiced an opinion and asked a question. Sam followed his brother to the living room, and they draped the floors with drop cloths, forming a path to the bathroom.

Haley waited for them next to her bathroom door, a crowbar in hand. "I turned off the water from the downstairs valve into the house," she informed them, all business. "I have a half bathroom in the basement. If you could leave the tub in here functional, I'll be OK for a few weeks."

"Will do." Sam slid by her and into the small space. He caught a whiff of her clean scent, sweet, like fresh laundry and floral shampoo. The bathroom was too small for three people. He turned to survey the walls. "It's tight in here. It's going to be hard to work safely with three of us wielding sledgehammers and crowbars. I promise to let you tear out whatever you want in the kitchen, but would you mind standing outside of the bathroom? I can explain what we're doing each step of the way."

"Oh," she said with a sigh. "I see what you mean."

He nearly jumped at the sound of her voice so close. Turning around, he found her right behind him. Now they faced each other. *Too close.* Way too close. Her scent wafted over him, and every little breath she took, every minute movement she made affected him like he'd stuck his finger into a live electrical outlet. His mouth went dry while his heart beat double time. It took Herculean effort to keep from staring at the two inches separating her breasts from his chest, and he was already against the wall with no room to back up. He gripped her upper arms and physically moved her *out* of his personal space and into the hall.

"Hey," she snapped. "We agreed. No touching."

"Hey," he snapped right back. "You were in my way. Watch and learn, but stay *out* of the bathroom. I don't want to be sued because you get hit by something."

Wyatt made a muffled snorting noise, and Sam scowled at him. Haley did one of those female tongue-sucking sounds of annoyance and crossed her arms in front of her, drawing attention to her chest again.

Dammit. Was she taunting him on purpose? "After we take out the vanity, sink and toilet, we'll tear out the walls. There have been a lot of improvements over the years in the materials used in bathrooms. We'll replace the old stuff with more appropriate mold-resistant materials." He kept his eyes trained on the ugly pink and black plastic tiles covering the walls. "After we put in the plumbing for the shower, we'll install the new ceramic tile surround."

"Sounds good." She leaned against the door frame, her arms still crossed.

Sam ground his molars together. He and Wyatt had worked together for years—ever since they were old enough to follow their dad and grandfather around on jobs. Once they settled into the routine, he'd be fine, because he'd be concentrating on what he was doing.

Wyatt disassembled and capped the plumbing, and Sam unbolted the toilet from the floor. Then, he and Wyatt hauled the stuff out of the small space and headed for the dumpster before starting on the walls.

Haley held the door for them as they carried load after load out of the house. By noon, her bathroom was gutted and stripped to the framing, with only the tub remaining intact.

He and Wyatt cleaned up as best they could, using Haley's Shop-Vac for the bits of particle board and dust left behind. Haley surveyed what had once been her bathroom, as he used a cloth to wipe the dust out of her tub. "You sure you don't want us to put in a new toilet today?" he asked. "We can pick one up at Home Depot. They aren't that expensive."

"I have the bathroom downstairs." She moved out of his way. "The basement is kind of semi-finished. We had planned to remodel that as well, only not until after the main floor was done."

"We?" His brow rose. Haley's lips thinned into a straight line. The inadvertent slip of the tongue only confirmed his suspicion. She'd gone through a bad breakup. Yep. Emotional involvement only leads to emotional stress. Who needs it? Still, he wanted to know what had happened.

"Sam," Wyatt called from the living room. "I have to get going. Let's get the tools and drop cloths to the van."

"OK," he called back. "We have the measurements. I'll get your materials ordered on Monday, and we'll put a rush on them, so you don't have to go too long without a bathroom."

She nodded, still tight-lipped, and he caught a glimpse of sadness in her eyes. That got to him. "Well," he muttered, gathering up his sledgehammer, stud finder and crowbar. "We'll be back on Wednesday night to start on the kitchen tear-out."

"Right." Haley followed him to the front door. "And I get to do some of the work this time."

He grinned at the determination in her voice. He liked that about her. "You bet."

"See you on Wednesday," she said.

Wyatt's head bobbed, and he mumbled his good-bye. "See you then," Sam said as he walked out into the brisk afternoon, more than a little satisfied that he'd managed to discover a small piece of the Haley Cooper puzzle.

He and his brother stowed their stuff in the back of the van and climbed in. Sam started the beast and shivered. "So, what do you think?" he asked, glancing askance at Wyatt.

"She's pretty. Nice." Wyatt shrugged. "Somebody broke her heart, that's for sure. Maybe she was married, and went through a nasty divorce. Maybe she caught her husband cheating on her."

"Could be." Sam fiddled with the temperature controls while the van warmed up. "Or maybe she lost someone in an accident." He remembered the sadness he'd glimpsed in her eyes, and his heart turned over. He knew the feeling, the utter devastation left in the wake of losing a loved one. "I didn't see any pictures anywhere of her with a man though. I'm thinking a bad breakup."

"Of course, none of it is our business," Wyatt said, sending him another pointed look. "She's a client. Period."

"Right." Sam drove the van away from the curb. His curiosity had not been satisfied—not by a long shot. He wanted to know more about Haley, but that wouldn't happen with his brother hovering close, ready to punch him in the shoulder whenever he crossed that personal boundary with her. "Let's meet at her house on Wednesday night. That way, you don't have to drive all the way to my place first."

"Works for me. Six thirty, right?"

"Right." He planned to get there early, give himself time to ask a question or two. Twenty minutes ought to suffice. Once his curiosity was satisfied, he'd be able to figure out the whole setup thing. Then he'd stop obsessing about Haley and move on with his life. "I'll place her order this afternoon. That way, the vendors will get the purchase order first thing Monday morning. I'd like to get this job done as quickly as possible."

"Can't blame you." Wyatt grunted. "What with Grandpa Joe getting on your case about your . . . er . . . extracurricular activities and all, I'm sure Haley Cooper must seem like forbidden fruit."

That bit. He had as much control as the next guy when it came to women. "Again. It was *not* me who started things with anyone. I'm never going to live that radio show down, am I? It's going to haunt me for the rest of my life."

"Probably, but Sam . . . it's not the *radio thing* that needs living down. It's what you were up to." Wyatt laughed. "And living *that* down isn't going to stop me from busting your chops every chance I get."

"Thanks, Wyatt. I know who *not* to go to when I need a sympathetic ear." Was his younger brother on to something with the forbidden fruit thing? Was he attracted to Haley simply because he *couldn't* have her? He'd give that some thought. In the meantime, he'd find out more about the *we* part of her life. He counted the days until he'd see her again. Five days was a long time to wait. Good thing he had plenty to do 'til then.

Chapter Five

Haley tried on one pair of jeans after another. Sam was due to arrive at six thirty—with his brother, of course. Tossing her most recent denim selection over her footboard, she huffed out a breath. Ridiculous. Who cared how she looked? They were tearing out her kitchen, for crying out loud, not going out on a date.

She snapped and zipped the jeans she had on and scowled at the evidence of her momentary lapse in sanity—several pairs of jeans piled on top of her bed. Well, if anyone—anyone being Sam—caught a glimpse of the pile on her bed, they—meaning Sam again—would likely think she was cleaning out her dresser.

Haley headed for the takeout meal she'd set on the dining room table. She had thirty minutes to relax and eat, and she'd best take advantage. Who was she kidding? Even thinking about being anywhere in Sam's proximity made relaxation impossible. Being around him gave her a bad case of the jitters.

Even worse, something about him had her itching to run her hands all over those broad shoulders, firm chest—and his butt. Especially his butt. Yep, Sam the handyman had great glutes, firm and nicely rounded.

Michael's butt had been pretty much nonexistent. Flat, as if someone had let out all the air from both cheeks.

"Enough already," she muttered. Haley took a seat and opened the bag containing her soup and sandwich. She'd told Sam there would be no touching. That *had* to be the reason why she wanted so badly to touch him. Plus, he was a very fine specimen of masculinity. All that hardness under sexy worn denim, soft flannel and white cotton T-shirts didn't help matters. Did he wear boxers or briefs?

Were those muscles a result of what he did for a living, or did he work out? She could see why some women threw themselves at him. She refused to be one of them. Is that why he insisted on calling her *Ms. Cooper*?

A flash of irritation burned through her. He was mocking her; she was sure of it. He probably saw her as uptight and prudish, just because she'd turned down his *special touch*. She grabbed the magazine she'd been reading. Not that she cared what he thought, but . . . if he could see what went on inside her head, then he'd know she was no prude. She grinned. Good thing he couldn't see the show-and-tell going on in there.

She finished her sandwich and turned the page of her magazine just as someone knocked on her front door. She checked her wall clock—it was only ten after six. She moved to the front door and peeked through the small window. Sam stood beneath the light, a crowbar and a sledge-hammer in hand. He smiled at her, and her stomach performed all kinds of acrobatics. She opened the door and let him in. "You're early."

"Am I?" He pulled out his phone and checked the time. "Oh. Sorry. I thought it was later than it is. The clock on the dashboard of my van broke years ago, and it gets dark so early now, what with the end of daylight saving time a couple of weeks ago and all." He gestured toward said van with his thumb. "Do you want me to wait outside for twenty minutes? Because I—"

"No. Come in. I was just having my supper."

"I don't want to disturb you." He followed her to the dining room and leaned his tools against the wall.

"Where's Wyatt?" she asked.

"He's meeting me here. Mind if I fill my water bottle before we tear out your plumbing?"

"Go ahead." While he was gone, she lifted her tomato soup and took big hurried gulps from the cardboard container. No way did she want to eat soup in front of him. She was way too self-conscious around Sam as it was, and with him watching, she'd likely dribble soup down her chin.

He returned and settled himself at the table. "Tonight you get to do a supervised tear-out. You excited about that?" His eyes lit with amusement.

Was she? "Sure." Haley lifted the plastic spoon, dipped and sipped the little bit of soup that remained.

"So . . ." Sam traced a finger along the wood grain of her table. "While we were doing the bathroom tear-out, you mentioned remodeling the semi-finished basement, and—"

"Are you angling for more work, Sam?"

"No." He shook his head. "I was just wondering. You said *we* that day, as in *we* planned to remodel the basement. Who is *we*?"

Her jaw dropped. "You came early to snoop!"

"No I didn't."

"Yes you did." Her eyes narrowed.

"OK, maybe I did." He shrugged. "I'm curious. The way your mother set me up, the whole situation, you have to agree it's weird. Can you blame me for trying to figure out why she did it? I thought maybe the *we* thing might be a clue."

She huffed out a breath. What difference did it make anymore? It's not like the whole mess was a big dark secret. In the entire history of weddings, she certainly hadn't been the only bride jilted. Besides, Sam had been pimped out by her mother. He had a good reason for wanting to know what Trudy had going on in her twisted brain.

"It's no big deal," she said. "Not anymore, anyway. I was supposed to get married last May. My fiancé and I bought this house together." She grabbed the paper sack from her meal and crammed the soup container, napkin and sandwich wrapper inside.

"And?"

She cringed inwardly. "And two weeks before the wedding, Michael moved to Indonesia without me. No explanation. Nothing. He just signed the house over and left."

"Oh, man. What an ass."

She nodded, her throat too tight to speak.

"See, that's why I never get involved." He arched an eyebrow and leveled a sharp look her way. "No involvement means no pain. You think I'm this big lothario—which I looked up, by the way, and you're wrong. I don't disrespect, abuse or exploit women. I'm completely up front, and I make it clear from the get-go that I'm not looking for a relationship. There are plenty of unattached females who feel as I do. They don't want to get close either, and—"

"Hold on." She canted her head. "Are you saying you've *never* been involved in a serious relationship?"

One side of his mouth quirked up. "Now who's snooping?"

"Hey, fair's fair. Have you ever been seriously involved?"

"Nope."

A shadow of something—was it hurt?—flitted across his face for a nanosecond and disappeared. The shadow was replaced by a glint of challenge. Clearly he intended to defend his position should she wish to argue the point. He'd probably had to do plenty of defending since *Loaded Question* had aired.

She studied him, searching for any hint of the pain she'd glimpsed, but he'd masked whatever it was, and only the cocky handyman remained. Someone must have broken his heart at some point, or he wouldn't have closed himself off the way he had. She ought to know. It took one to know one, as they say. "How old are you, Sam?"

"I turned twenty-nine a couple of weeks ago."

"Hmm. Almost thirty, and you've never had a serious relationship?" She frowned. *Curious.* She opened her mouth to delve deeper into his lack of involvement, but he beat her to the punch.

"Back to the original topic." He flashed her another one of his blue-eyed pointed looks. "What did your mother hope to achieve by setting us up?"

"Right." She shifted in her chair. "A couple of friends and I have figured it out. Trudy believes—"

"Trudy being your mother?"

"Yes. Trudy thinks—"

"You refer to your mother by her given name?"

"I do, but *only* when she pulls manipulative, definitely un-motherly shenanigans like this one." Haley gestured between the two of them. "My mother loves to meddle. Correction, make that she *lives* to interfere in the lives of her children. It's her only hobby.

"After my brother and I were born, she quit working outside the home, and by the time we started school, she'd discovered her true vocation in life—messing with our personal lives, which generally leads to excruciatingly embarrassing situations. Not for her, or course, but for us." Haley shook her head. "And here's the strange part. My mother is not a mean person. She *thinks* she's doing right by me and my brother."

Sam laughed, and tiny shivers of pleasure skipped down her spine. He really was gorgeous. "My friends and I believe Trudy hired you after hearing the radio show. She thinks I haven't gotten over what happened with Michael, and—"

"*Have* you gotten over what happened with Michael?" His gaze intensified.

"Who recovers from something like that?" She had to fight the urge to squirm. "I could've handled a breakup much easier than desertion.

If he'd told me he didn't love me anymore, or that he'd found someone else, I'd have gotten over it eventually. But the man just up and moved to the other side of the planet to get away from me, and I'll never know why. That's what I can't get past."

"He's gay."

Not the first time someone had suggested Michael was gay. Wouldn't she have known? They'd had a sex life. Plus, he could've told her if that had been the case. They'd been best friends since their junior year in high school. "You never met the man. How can you possibly make such an assumption?"

"No, I haven't met him, but I do have a gay cousin. I know how difficult it was for him to come out after hiding it for so long." He smiled. "We'd all figured it out years ago though, and it didn't matter to us. He's a great guy, and he's family."

Sam leaned back and crossed his arms. "There's still a lot of prejudice out there. Your fiancé probably freaked out. He realized marrying you would be colossally unfair—to you both. I'm guessing he didn't know how to handle the situation, so he disappeared. Disappearing probably felt far easier to him than coming out of the closet two weeks before your wedding."

"You have an active imagination."

"Maybe, maybe not. You'll never know unless you ask him."

"You think I should contact Michael and demand to know what his sexual preferences are?"

"When you put it that way, no. But you could ask him why he did what he did. Enough time has gone by that the two of you might be able to have a conversation without all the emotional drama."

"I'll think about it." He was right. She knew he was right, but even thinking about contacting Michael churned up the hurt she'd gone through. Still, getting the answers she needed might help her get past the pain once and for all.

"Regardless of his reasons, your ex is a selfish jerk. Nobody deserves to be treated the way he treated you, Haley. It's about him, not you."

Her throat closed up, and her eyes stung. "Thanks, Sam." She rose from the table, and a knock sounded on the front door, ending the conversation.

"That'll be Wyatt," Sam said. "You didn't tell me what you and your friends figured out. Why did your mom set us up?"

"Some other time. Your brother is here, and I'm ready to tear stuff up."

◆ ◆ ◆

Sam held his stud finder to the wall. "We're going to locate and mark the studs on this outside wall," he told Haley, careful to keep his eyes *off* the way the long-sleeve T-shirt she wore hugged her breasts and the curve of her waist. Talk about a challenge. "Once the studs are marked"—he penciled an X on one and moved to the next—"then you can hammer at the plaster *between* the marks." He called to his brother, "You about done down there, Wyatt?"

Wyatt, crouched under the sink to disconnect and cap the plumbing, backed out. "All done."

"Do you want to take out the counters first?" Sam asked. Haley grinned and nodded, and his heart skipped a beat. "OK. Remember what I told you. Have at it."

He and his brother set Haley loose and stood back to supervise. She wedged the crowbar between the remaining kitchen counter and the wall and put all of her muscle into separating the two. She made noises, grunts and groans that went right through him. And when the pieces finally came apart, she whooped and fisted the air with a look of triumph on her flushed—make that blotched—face.

Sam laughed. "Wyatt and I will haul this out, and you can start on the upper cabinets."

She stepped back and surveyed her work. "Yeah . . . how do I do that again? I didn't see any bolts or anything when I emptied them."

"Same way. Why don't you wait for us to return? It's best if we treat it as a two-man job anyway. You don't want to get hurt when the cabinets drop."

"I'll knock out some plaster while I'm waiting." She set the crowbar down and hefted a sledgehammer.

"She's really into this tear-out stuff," Wyatt said, taking up his end of the load. "It's a little scary."

"Good." Haley lifted the hammer and swung at the wall between the graphite Xs. "Every woman should have a scary side." Post-World-War-II plaster crumbled and fell to the floor in a pile. She let loose with a peal of feigned maniacal laughter.

"She *is* scary," Sam said, laughing again. "We ought to talk Grandpa Joe into hiring her for tear-outs." Haley truly was something to behold in demolition mode. All the prim and proper fell away, and he caught a glimpse of the passion she kept under wraps. She threw herself into the task of destroying her kitchen, no holds barred. Still grinning, he and Wyatt hauled the old kitchen counter toward the front door.

"What time did you get to Haley's house tonight?" Wyatt asked once they were outside. They set the counter on the driveway and lowered the tailgate of the dumpster.

"A few minutes before you got here."

"How many is a few in Sam time?" Wyatt asked as they hoisted the old counter and walked it into the dumpster. "Like, thirty or sixty?"

Sam frowned at his younger brother. "Why the third degree? Did Grandpa Joe or Grandma Maggie tell you to babysit me or something?"

"No." Wyatt shook his head. "Haley seems really nice, and I don't want to see you do or say anything that might upset her. I have a feeling she's in a vulnerable place right now."

"Look at you, using words like *vulnerable*. When did you turn into Mr. Sensitive?" Sam smirked. "I'm not going to cross any lines. Haley's mom did what she did for a reason, and I intend to learn what that reason is. I came a little early so I could ask Haley a few questions. I had hoped to get some answers. That's all."

"Did you get answers?" Wyatt asked, starting toward the house.

"Not entirely, but you were right. She went through a bad breakup. Two weeks before her wedding last May, her fiancé up and left the country without a word of explanation."

"What an idiot," Wyatt huffed out. "He could have at least written her a letter or something. To leave her hanging like that . . . wow." He shook his head. "Selfish prick."

"My thoughts exactly."

By the time they returned to the kitchen, they found Haley issuing battle cries at the wall as she swung her sledgehammer—the female equivalent of a Norse god with her mighty hammer of doom. "Keep doing what you're doing, Haley," Sam told her. "Wyatt and I will work on the cabinets."

"OK." She grinned at him over her shoulder, her face beaded with perspiration. "This is fun."

The way her eyes sparkled and her skin glistened weakened his knees. He imagined her in bed, sweaty and hot, writhing beneath him, wearing nothing but that same expression of passionate abandon. Swallowing the groan rising in his throat, Sam tightened his jaw and focused on tearing out the cabinets.

Wyatt had already moved the stepladders into place beneath the cabinets. Crowbar in hand, Sam joined his brother, determined to keep his mind out of the gutter and far, far away from images of Haley naked. Not easy. In fact, damn near impossible.

He cast a look at her as she shouted another battle cry and pounded the poor wall. He wanted to laugh and growl all at the same time. One thing for certain, he'd better get his answers and finish this job quickly or he'd be in serious trouble where Ms. Haley Cooper was concerned.

Haley clutched her Thanksgiving contribution in her hands and walked between the parked cars in her parents' driveway. Her aunt and cousins were already there, and so was Junior. All the lights inside were on, giving her childhood home a warm, cozy glow. She opened the front door and walked into the living room to find her mother waiting for her.

"Hi, Mom. Sorry I'm late," she said. "Here's the caramel apple crisp as promised, and I have a can of whipped cream in my purse."

"You're not late." Her mom took the dessert from Haley's hands. "Everyone else came early."

"Hey, sweetie," her aunt called from the kitchen.

She waved and inhaled the scent of roasting turkey, dressing and all the fixings. "Mmm. Smells delicious in here." She took off her coat and hung it in the front closet. "Where is everybody?"

"Everyone is in the rec room downstairs watching football on the big-screen TV. Nanci and I are getting the food ready to put on the table. Why don't you join us in the kitchen? We could use your help."

"OK." *Gulp.* The not-so-subtle probing and prying was about to begin, and Haley so wanted to confront her mother, but no. Not yet. Not until she came up with a way to make it count and end this kind of interference in her personal life for good. Instead of asking—How could you?—she rolled up her sleeves and followed her mom to the kitchen.

Aunt Nanci stood at the stove, whisking the gravy. "What's new, Haley?" she asked as she turned off the burner. "Seems like I haven't seen you for months."

"Not much, and it has been months," she replied. "What would you like me to do, Mom?"

"All the serving dishes are right there." Trudy pointed to the far counter. "Start loading them up and transferring them to the dining room."

"So," her aunt said, exchanging a surreptitious peek at her mom. "How're things coming along with your house? Your mom said she and your dad hired a construction company for the remodel."

Ah-ha. Her aunt was in on the setup. Haley should've known. Trudy and Nanci were cut from the same cloth, after all. "It's going great. The Haney brothers are teaching me a lot. My muscles are still sore from last week's tear-out."

"*You're* doing the work?" Trudy frowned as she scooped the dressing from the turkey and added it to the serving dish in front of her. "What are we paying them for if *you're* doing the work?"

"I'm helping because I want to learn how to do things myself. Both the kitchen and the bathroom are completely gutted." She grabbed the pot of mashed potatoes from the stove and moved to the opposite counter to transfer them into one of the china serving dishes. "Saturday, their uncle Dan is coming over to install the shower in the bathroom, and Wyatt will be doing some rewiring. I'm having an additional electrical outlet added, and he'll also install the new light fixture. Then, once their uncle is done, Wyatt and Sam are putting up the new walls and starting on the ceramic tile work around the tub."

"Sounds like you have an entire crew there," Aunt Nanci remarked, sharing another look with her mom.

"Yep. Pretty much." She smiled. "Things are really coming along." It was obvious the two still hoped something would happen between her and Sam. *Unbelievable*, Haley thought. *They're probably going nuts right about now, speculating and watching for my reaction.* But she wasn't about to give any hint that she knew what they were up to. Even without a plan, at least she could take pleasure in having thwarted them by keeping the two in the dark.

Having her mom and aunt stew over what they didn't know wasn't the only plus in this bizarre situation. So far, working with Sam and Wyatt had been fun, and the three of them had cut loose a little while destroying her kitchen. The two brothers had talked a lot about their huge extended family, and how they all gathered at their grandparents' house for the holidays. She imagined Sam was there right now, enjoying a feast surrounded by family.

She straightened as it occurred to her that neither one of them ever mentioned their mom and dad. It was always Grandpa Joe this, or Grandma Maggie that, uncles, aunts and cousins, but never Mom and Dad.

Was it because his parents weren't involved with Haney & Sons? Maybe they didn't even live in the same state. Well that certainly bore looking into, especially given the way Sam had pried into her personal life. He owed her. "Humph."

"What, Haley?" her mom asked.

"Hmm?" Haley set the lid on the serving dish of mashed potatoes and carried the empty pot to the sink.

"You humphed. Something on your mind?"

"Always, Mom." Haley grabbed the green bean casserole. "I was just thinking about work and something I forgot to do yesterday. I won't get to it until Monday now, and that'll back up everything else on my pile, that's all."

"Oh."

Good save. "I'm starving, and this all looks so good. You've outdone yourself this year." In more ways than one. She sighed. At any rate, she'd managed to thwart her mother's scheme. She'd still come out on top. She and Sam had a deal—the no-hands-involved clause. She ignored the ping of regret that thought caused and focused on transferring the green bean casserole into a serving dish.

"Humph," Haley grunted again just for the hell of it, grinning at her mother and aunt.

"Good morning," Haley greeted the receptionist as she walked into Bremmer, Stevens & Schmitt on Monday. "Did you have a nice Thanksgiving, Julie?"

"I did. How about you?"

"It was great." Haley unbuttoned her coat and slipped it off.

"Brent wants you to stop by his office first thing," Julie told her.

"Thanks." The front desk phone rang then, and Haley headed down the hall toward Brent's office. He was one of the lawyers she was assigned to, and they'd become good friends in the three years she'd worked for the firm. He walked out of the employee lounge just as she reached the door. "You wanted to see me?"

"I do." Brent nodded toward his office. "Put your things away first." He held a napkin-wrapped treat in one hand, and coffee in the other. "Somebody brought doughnuts this morning. If you want one, you'd better get it now. You know how fast sweets disappear around here."

"I couldn't. I'm still full from Thanksgiving." She grinned and continued on.

A few minutes later, she walked into his office. "What have you got for me?"

He handed her a sheet of paper with notes scrawled on the front. "I have some research I need you to do for me."

"When do you need it by?"

"End of the week?"

She scanned the sheet. "No problem."

"Say." He straightened the notepads on his desk. "The firm's Christmas party is coming up."

"I know. I got the same e-mail you did," she teased.

"You want to go together?"

The firm always had their party early because the senior partners took vacation time over the holiday. They also allowed their staff to bring a significant other or a date. Her heart gave a painful squeeze.

This would be her first Bremmer, Stevens & Schmitt Christmas party without Michael. "Wait." Haley frowned. "I thought you were seeing someone? Josh, right? I thought he was the love of your life?"

"Yeah, well, so did I." He shrugged. "It didn't pan out like I'd hoped. We didn't want the same things."

"Oh, I'm sorry. Do you want to talk about it?" Haley moved to sit on one of the chairs in front of his desk.

"Not here. Maybe over drinks after work sometime."

"Plan on it," Haley said with a sympathetic smile. Like her, Brent wanted a life partner and a family, and yet they were both still single. Brent was nice looking and had so much to offer, and he was such a wonderful man. She couldn't understand why someone didn't jump at the chance to be with him. The two of them had bonded over their thwarted dreams shortly after Michael had dumped her. "Sure. Let's go to the Christmas party together. It'll give us a chance to get caught up."

"Great. I'll pick you up at seven."

"Brent, do you mind if I ask a question?" She fidgeted with the sheet of paper in her hands.

"Not at all. Fire away."

"You met Michael more than once."

"Yes?"

"Is he . . . Do you think Michael is gay?" she asked. "Did you get that vibe from him?" Sam popped into her mind. Where Michael had been slight and more brain than brawn, Sam was broad, rugged, with callused hands and a scruffy, totally masculine attractiveness. He had the kind of physique to make a woman drool. She forced him out of her head and focused on Brent.

"Oh. I don't know, Haley. My gaydar has never been all that reliable. In fact, in my case, I suspect my perceptions are more wishful thinking than anything else." Now it was his turn to give her a sympathetic smile. "All I can offer is a maybe. It makes sense though, given what happened. Sorry I can't be more certain."

"That's OK." She rose. "I have a brief to finish this morning. Once that's done, I'll start on this research."

She walked down the hall to her tiny office, her mind on anything but work. Would getting over Michael be any easier if she went with the *he's gay* theory? Probably not, because it would only be conjecture. Before she could move on, she needed to know why Michael bailed on her the way he had.

His parents would know how to reach him. Would they be willing to share his contact information? Of course they would. She'd been close to the entire family once upon a time. She'd gone on vacations with the Swensons and spent as much time with them as she had with her own folks.

After Michael had bolted, she'd been too emotionally wrecked to reach out to him and demand the answers she so desperately needed. Maybe it was time she did. Her heart pounded at the thought. She'd been so devastated and humiliated. Even if her life had depended upon it, she couldn't have faced Michael's parents at the time. Could she face them now? She had to. If she really wanted to move on, she had to.

Chapter Six

The homeowner, an attractive blonde with a lush body, stood too close behind Sam. She'd been brushing against him all morning. He tried to ignore her and set his level on top of the wall rack he'd installed for her pots and pans.

"Perfect," he declared. He'd done a few other repairs for her, and the rack had been the last item on the list. He placed the level into his tool box and took the invoice from his clipboard, placing the paper on her granite-topped center island. "Anything else you need done before I leave?"

She sidled up close and waved a check between her fingers. "Absolutely. I have a few things in need of . . . attention, if you catch my drift." She traced the check down his chest to his tool belt and tucked it inside. "Stay a while?"

Whoa! His pulse kicked up, and he backed away. "Uh . . . sorry, can't. I have hockey coaching in . . ." He checked the time. Geez, he didn't have to coach for another four hours. The kids probably hadn't even had their school lunches yet. "Look, you're really attractive and all, but I can't do this kind of thing anymore. I'll lose my job."

"You're a Haney." She looked askance at him. "Isn't the company called *Haney & Sons*?" She took a step closer and walked her fingertips up his torso. "Come on, Sam. It's early."

He tensed, but not with the usual sexual anticipation. This time, it was more like . . . irritation with a pinch of alarm. *What the hell?* "Nope. Sorry. Can't." He threw his things into his tool box, grabbed his coat and bolted for the door. When had he ever left a job so fast? Never.

He started his van, drove a few blocks and pulled over again to get himself together. He got out and removed his tool belt, retrieving the check to stow in his wallet. Wow. He'd turned her down, and she was a nice-looking woman—a friendly, recently divorced, uninvolved woman.

Sam climbed back into the van and ran his hands over his face. He frowned, not because he'd rejected her, but because of the way he'd reacted—the irritation, the mad dash without a backward glance, the shaking hands. Had she hired him based solely on his reputation as the handsiest handyman in the Twin Cities?

It had only been a handful of years since Haney & Sons had started offering handyman services, and in the entire history of his life, being the object of women's fantasies had been a mere blip on his timeline. Admittedly, he'd enjoyed being used. So what was different about today? The adrenaline rush, the fight-or-flight response—definitely a new and unusual response, and he'd been thrown for a loop.

There had to be a logical explanation. Of course, he *had* taken a lot of flak from his grandparents lately. Plus, Grandpa Joe *had* ordered him to cease and desist with the above-and-beyond services he'd been providing to some of his female clients. Wyatt and Josey had been teasing him relentlessly too. Especially Wyatt, whose comments were barbed more often than not. What was his brother's deal, anyway? Then there were the social media attacks on his character, not to mention the insinuations about his lack of skill as a carpenter.

Clearly he was under way more stress than he'd realized. "Yep. It's stress. That's all there is to it," he muttered, tossing his tool belt onto the passenger seat. "What else could it be?"

Eventually, everyone would forget about *Loaded Question*, including his family. He couldn't go back to the way things had been on the job, but that was OK. There were plenty of places to meet women who wanted the same thing he did, no strings, no involvement. And once he'd proven to a certain brunette that he wasn't lacking in carpentry skills, he'd be fine.

Thinking about that certain brunette started a slide show playing through his brain: Haley attacking her kitchen walls with her face all cute and blotched from her efforts; the way she crossed her arms and looked down her nose at him. He recalled the hurt he'd glimpsed in her eyes when she'd talked about her idiot ex, and his heart wrenched for her.

He had another job to do today. An elderly couple needed some caulking done, a shelf installed and a few things tightened around their home. He put his van into gear and headed for the office. Lunch, job and then coaching—all things he could handle, and none of them involved women.

Twenty minutes later, Sam pulled into his parking spot at Haney & Sons. Familiar surroundings and family, that's what he needed right now. He climbed out of the van and headed for the kitchen, stomping his feet against the concrete steps before entering. His grandmother was there, taking something out of the oven. He inhaled. "Mmm. Smells amazing in here, Gram. What's for lunch?"

"Turkey pot pie." She set the pan on top of the stove to cool and turned off the oven.

Jerry entered the kitchen, and Sam grinned at him. "How's my favorite cousin?"

"G-good. We coaching today?" Jerry walked to the sink and washed his hands.

"Not tonight, Jer. Practice is on Tuesday and Thursday this week. I'll pick you up here after work tomorrow." He joined his cousin at the sink. "Be ready."

His Uncle Dan, Uncle Jack and Gramps appeared deep in conversation about the Vikings and the Green Bay Packers. Sam dried his hands and waited for a break in their debate. "Grandpa Joe, all I've been doing lately is handyman work. Can you put me on a construction crew for a few months?" Sam asked. "I don't want my skills as a carpenter to get rusty."

If he worked construction, he wouldn't have to deal so directly with clients, especially the female variety. He'd have a crew with him as a buffer, too, just in case. There were drawbacks, though. His time would be way more constrained, and he'd be doing pretty much the same thing every day. On the pro side, working construction would give him time to weather the *Loaded Question* storm until the debris settled.

"If you want." Grandpa Joe's bushy brows rose slightly. "Smells delicious in here, honey," he said, pouring himself a cup of coffee. Gramps kissed Gram on the cheek and took a seat before turning back to Sam. "Next Monday I'll put you on the crew with Josey. We're doing the interior finishing work on a custom house we're hoping to complete by Christmas. Can't guarantee I can keep you busy all winter without handyman jobs, but I'll do my best."

"Great. Thanks." The tightness in his neck and shoulders eased. Sam grabbed the caddy holding utensils and napkins from the counter and set it on the table, just as Wyatt, Josey and two of his cousins stomped in through the kitchen door, and lunch commenced in earnest. Sam relaxed into the welcome, familiar routine, exactly what he needed after this morning's fiasco.

The chatter went on around him, and his mind drifted to Haley again. He really ought to stop that, but . . . what would his grandparents think of her enthusiasm as a destroyer of walls and cabinets? He conjured a mental picture, Haley in a skimpy superhero costume, swinging her magical sledgehammer and shouting out battle cries at her plaster and sheetrock enemies. He chuckled.

"What's f-funny, Sam?" Jerry said around a mouthful of Gram's pot pie.

"Just thinking about something I saw a few days ago that made me laugh." He grinned. "It's stuck in my head."

Wyatt peered down the table at him. "Care to share?"

"Nope. It's one of those you-had-to-be-there things." Sam turned his full attention to the flaky crust and steaming turkey and vegetables before him. Wyatt *had* been there. His brother would really give him a hard time if he knew how often Haley popped into his mind. *Forbidden fruit?*

What would Ms. Cooper think about being viewed as forbidden fruit? What would she be? A peach? A ripe plum? He conjured another image of Haley in some kind of fruit costume, like those old Fruit of the Loom ads. He could see her as a juicy peach, and he definitely wanted to take a bite. He almost chuckled again, but checked himself.

Haley was interesting, likeable, and she made him laugh. That's all. No reason why he couldn't enjoy her company while on the job. Their personal boundaries were well drawn and intact. Sure, he was attracted to her, but he had control, and the job would be done soon enough.

Haley watched the muscles of Sam's forearms as he positioned the two four-by-six wooden beams in the entry between her kitchen and dining room. He'd pushed up the sleeves of his sweatshirt. How could she not ogle his flexing muscles? And his hands. He had great hands. She stood close enough to catch a whiff of him. Was that Irish Spring soap? Mixed with a hint of aftershave or body spray and his own unique smell, the mixture went straight to her head. *Mmm.* "Where's Wyatt tonight?"

"A few Monday nights a month he plays basketball with a bunch of friends. We don't need him for this anyway," he said, tapping the beams into place with a mallet. "See how I made a V with these two joists to support the load-bearing crossbeam?" He pointed to the exposed horizontal beam above their heads. "Now we can *safely* widen the opening without fear that the second floor will come crashing down on us."

"Ahh, I see," she muttered, because he looked at her as if he expected some kind of response. She leaned against the exposed wood and continued to watch.

"We're going to use a bit more finesse than . . ." He straightened, his expression serious and—was that condescension? "See, we don't widen entryways by attacking them with sledgehammers, Haley. The first thing we need to do is make sure there aren't any water pipes, gas lines or electrical wires behind the drywall we plan to take out." He placed his hand on the wall in question.

"As much as you love to wield that thing, no more sledgehammers for you, Ms. Cooper. We're going to use a drywall saw"—he held up a tiny hand saw with a blade only about five inches long—"to carefully cut out a beveled rectangle so we can check what's behind the plaster before we start."

"Why beveled?"

"So if you change your mind, or we find an obstruction behind the wall, the piece we cut out will fit back into the hole without falling through." He used a straight edge to draw a rectangle and started cutting. "See how I have the blade positioned to create the beveled edge?"

She nodded. He was so dang earnest, so serious about teaching her how to go about carpentry the *right* way. Adorable. Her poor heart melted into a glob of marshmallow cream. She placed her hand on the exposed mess she'd made of the entryway and pushed off to get a closer look. Her palm slid down the wood. "Ouch! Cheese and crackers." She shook her hand.

"What'd you do?" Sam put his saw on top of the stove and grabbed her hand.

"Sliver." Haley bit her lip. A huge splinter, at least an inch long, had embedded itself into the fleshy mound at the base of her thumb.

He chuckled. "Cheese and crackers?"

"My mom says that instead of cursing or taking the big guy's name in vain." She shrugged. "I guess I picked it up over the years."

"Well, come on. Let's get you patched up." He kept hold of her hand and tugged her toward the bathroom. "Where's your first aid kit?"

"It's in the linen closet."

"Here you go." He flipped on her brand-new light fixture and guided her to the edge of the bathtub. "Sit."

While Sam went after the first aid kit, Haley forced her attention to something other than the stinging sliver. She admired her new shower with its ceramic tile surround, the fresh walls, already primed and ready for paint, and the new light fixture she'd picked up on sale months ago.

Her sink, vanity and mirrored medicine cabinet, along with the toilet, were going to be delivered and installed this coming Wednesday. She'd have a fully functioning up-to-date bathroom by next weekend. Could she afford to have Sam help her remodel the half story upstairs? An office, or a nice guest bedroom with a bathroom would be perfect.

Sam returned, first aid kit in hand. He sat beside her on the edge of the tub, opened the kit and set it on his lap. "How are you holding up?"

She rolled her eyes. "It stings, but I'm pretty sure I'll live."

"I'm going to take out the sliver, then we're going to wash your hand and apply some of this"—he held up a tube of antibacterial cream—"generic brand stuff."

"You're still in instructor mode." Haley grinned. "This is what I'm going to do, because it's the correct way to remove splinters," she said, mimicking him in a deep voice.

"Is that how I sound?" He took the tweezers from the plastic box and clamped onto the end of the piece of wood stuck under her skin. "I'm going to remove the sliver now. This might hurt a bit, so I want you to brace yourself."

She giggled. "See?"

"Mm-mm." He bent over her palm, concentrating on his task.

"Ouch," she whispered as the piece of wood came out.

Sam dropped the sliver into a plastic bucket filled with construction debris, put the tweezers away and set the medicine kit on the edge of the tub next to him. He leaned close and reached for the tub faucets. She turned her face up to thank him just as he tipped his head down, and . . . somehow, their lips met in the middle. *Whoa. How'd that happen?*

He kissed her, or . . . did she kiss him? A pleasurable shock wave washed through her. His touch was so achingly tender, so sweet, and his lips were perfectly warm and soft, she scarcely dared to breathe. His arm came around her, and he drew her closer. Surrounded by his heat, scent and hardness, she sizzled. Where had she put her fire extinguisher, because she was about to go up in flames.

Hadn't they agreed to no touching? Did she *care*?

He pulled back, his breathing labored. "I . . . uh . . . I didn't mean to—"

"A sympathy kiss?" She slid away and turned toward the faucets. Her hands shook as she washed them.

"Right. You were hurt, and I . . ." He cleared his throat and picked up the first aid kit. "Here's the antibacterial cream."

"I won't fire you this time, Sam, since the kiss had more to do with compassion than passion." Ha! What a crock. Especially since she may have been the one who kissed first, though she'd never admit that to him. Worse, she wanted to throw her arms around his neck, straddle his lap and demand more.

"You can't fire me, Haley. I thought we already established this."

"Yes I can. It's my house." She dried her hands on her jeans and applied the cream.

"No you can't. You didn't hire me, and you're not paying me." He arched an eyebrow and his eyes filled with amusement. "You'd have to get Trudy to fire me. Do you want to have your mother do that for you? What would you give her for a reason?"

"I'm not going to *have* you fired, then," she conceded. "You do good work, Sam."

"I do my best." He stood up, a Band-Aid at the ready in his hands.

Haley rose and lifted her palm, expecting a quick application. Instead, he brought her hand to his lips and kissed away the sting. Could hearts sigh? Because that's what hers did the moment his lips touched her skin.

He applied the Band-Aid and grinned sheepishly. "It's a Haney tradition to kiss the hurt away."

"Yeah?" What else could she say? Hey, there's a spot right between my shoulder blades that hurts, or . . . remember when I hit my funny bone against the wall? She could easily come up with a long list of hurts for Sam the Handyman to kiss. Not good. Not good at all. *Remember all the other women those lips have pressed against?*

"Thanks, Sam. Let's get back to work."

"Right."

She followed him back to her kitchen, her eyes drawn to his perfect butt. *Gah!* Maybe her mother hadn't been as far off the mark as Haley wanted to believe. Sam had definitely reignited her dormant libido. In fact, he'd ignited libido she didn't even know she owned.

"All right," he said, all businesslike again. He used a putty knife to pry out the bit of wall he'd cut, setting the rectangle on the stove.

"We're going to check behind the wall now." He picked up another tool from his box.

She stifled the urge to giggle. *Nerves?* Sam the instructor cracked her up. He took himself way too seriously, and he was so sexy in his faded jeans, old, paint-splattered sweatshirt and scuffed-up work boots. At least he wasn't wearing his tool belt tonight. Sam in a tool belt just about did her in. She sighed, and focused on what he was doing. She did want to learn after all. He used a mirror affixed to the end of a long thin handle to check inside the wall for electrical wiring, a gas line or plumbing pipes.

"We're good. Put on your work gloves. I don't want you getting another sliver, and I'm going to need your help soon." He put the mirror thingie away.

"Right." She crossed the room and fished out her gloves from yet another one of the plastic buckets strewn around her house. By the time she returned to Sam's side, he had a larger electrical saw in hand.

He glanced at her. "Now we're going to use a rotary saw to cut the wall, and then a reciprocating saw to remove the studs on either side to widen the opening."

"By *we,* I'm assuming you mean *you,*" she murmured, way more interested in watching him work than in learning how to do the job herself. A few hours later, with her help, they'd created the widened entryway she'd wanted, complete with additional support joists for the load-bearing crossbeam.

"Wow. I'm impressed." She stood back to admire the way the alteration opened up her kitchen and dining room. Sam lit up at her praise, and her insides melted in response.

"We still have to do the finishing work, and we need to get a few new replacement planks for the floor." He began putting his tools away. "If you don't mind leaving a key, Wyatt and I will be back on Wednesday morning to install the bathroom, and if we have time, we'll start on the finish work then."

"That'll work. I'll leave the key under the mat on the breezeway."

"Great." He turned to her, his expression . . . vulnerable? "We're good?"

"Are you referring to the job or the kiss?" She turned her attention back to the perfect frame they'd installed together. She crossed her arms around her midriff, feeling a bit exposed herself.

"The kiss," he said, his voice gruff. "I *know* my work is good, Ms. Cooper. I'm an experienced, skilled craftsman, one of the best in the Twin Cities."

Oh, right. She'd accused him of not being very competent at carpentry since he had to offer sex on the side to get jobs. Regret pinched at her conscience. "Hey, given the circumstances, can you blame me for—"

"That reminds me." He scrutinized her. "You never did finish telling me what your mom wanted to accomplish by pretending to be you, and—"

"Suggesting I wanted your special touch?" She huffed out a shaky laugh. "I'm pretty sure Trudy was hoping if you made a pass at me, I'd somehow want to get out and date again. Like, if you wanted me, so would someone else. She was hoping you'd restore my shaken confidence."

"I see." His brow furrowed, and his jaw tightened. He averted his gaze and busied himself with gathering his things.

What was running through his mind? Was he as insulted as she was at the way her mother had manipulated them both? "See why I want to find a way to end her scheming once and for all?"

"Yep." He hefted his tool box. "See you Wednesday if we're still here when you get home."

"Thanks, Sam. See you then," she said, following him to her front door. *Talk to me.* He'd gone quiet and his shoulders had slumped after she'd told him what had motivated her mother. It was almost as if he felt defeated. Insulted, more like it. That she could understand. She knew the feeling. Poor guy.

Haley watched Sam put his things in the back of his van, and before he circled to the driver's side door, he glanced her way. She waved. He waved back, and her heart skipped a beat. She closed her front door, reliving the kiss they'd shared and the tenderness he'd shown while taking care of her sliver. Never before had she reacted to a kiss the way she had to Sam's, and there hadn't even been any tongue involved. She sighed and raked her fingers through her hair. She wanted Sam in the worst way. "Dammit, Trudy Cooper!"

Sam drove off into the night, hardly able to get hold of a single thought or emotion before another jumped into the fray. That kiss with Haley had him rattled. His entire being had centered upon the sweet sensation of Haley's lips against his, as if that point of contact had become *the* center of his universe. He groaned, aching with frustration.

And what about the big reveal? Haley's mother wanted to use him, as if *he* were the right hand tool to rev her daughter up and send her back out into the dating world. He was supposed to fix her. What about him? Who was going to fix him? "I don't *need* fixing, and that kiss was just a kiss." He grunted. "Great. Now I'm talking to myself." He clamped his mouth shut.

All the way home he cursed the radio show and his own stupidity. Why had he felt it necessary to defend himself? If he hadn't picked up his phone and hit speed dial, nobody would've known he was Yvonne's handyman. His life would've continued on as it had, and he never would've laid eyes on Haley Cooper. "I am not a tool, dammit," he muttered.

He had to do a better job of fighting his attraction to her, make sure he didn't show up at her house alone. And for crying out loud, he needed to stop engaging her in conversation. Now that he'd gotten to the bottom of her mother's motives and Haley's breakup, he didn't need or want to know her any better.

Did he?

No. He did not. Sam shook his head, all the while fighting against the truth. Where Haley was concerned, what he wanted and what he actually did were two different animals entirely, and that scared him. There was absolutely nothing strings free or uninvolved about the woman, and letting her get to his heart would only lead to loss and pain.

By the time he parked his van in his apartment building lot, he'd managed to get a grip. His phone rang. He fished it out of his coat pocket and climbed out of the van. "Hello?"

"Hey, whose name did you draw for Christmas this year?" his sister asked.

"Yours."

"Yeah? What are you going to get me?"

"I don't know, and even if I did, I wouldn't tell you. That kind of defeats the purpose, Jo."

"You sound cranky."

"I am cranky." He stomped toward the front door. "Did you need something?"

"I hate this time of year," she said in a small voice. "Christmas always makes me think of Mom and Dad, you know?"

"I know." Man, the wind was so bitter tonight, it made his eyes sting.

"Remember how it was? Christmas was the best. Mom and Dad always made it so much fun, and Grandpa Joe would show up at our door dressed up as Santa with presents and candy. Like we couldn't tell it was him." She chuckled. "Remember how we'd sneak downstairs really early Christmas morning, before Mom and Dad were up?"

"Of course I remember." The familiar ache filled his chest, and that panicky sense of helplessness he always got when talking about his parents sent his heart pounding. "How could I forget? We had a great childhood, and Mom and Dad were great parents. But, Jo, we're lucky. We still have Grandpa Joe and Grandma Maggie. Right?"

"Of course."

He swallowed the panic and pushed the ache aside. "Christmas is still good. Isn't it? All the cousins, uncles and aunts getting together at Gram and Gramps' house . . . we have fun."

"I know. You're right." Josey sighed. "I just miss what we had. I miss Mom and Dad. You'd think I'd be over it after all these years, but I'm not." She paused, as if trying to pull herself together. "Anyway, I called to see if you need help with your Christmas shopping, and now that I know you drew me, I'd be happy to tell you what's on my wish list."

"I don't need help, but thanks."

"You say that every year, but then it gets to be a few days before Christmas Eve, and you come around begging for help."

He laughed as he walked into his building, grateful she'd distracted him from thoughts of Haley. "And every year you call weeks in advance and offer your unsolicited assistance."

"Accept it early this time. I have a vested interest."

"All right. What do you want?" He climbed the stairs to his second-floor apartment while his sister ticked off a list. "Got it. I'll see you tomorrow. Let's hang out after my team's hockey practice."

"Sure. We can meet at The Bulldog. Wyatt too," she said. "Being together helps."

"I agree." Plans made, he ended the call. Christmas, like most holidays, got to him for the same reasons it got to his brother and sister. Could it be the season was affecting how he reacted to everything else going on in his life? Along with the stress *Loaded Question* had caused, missing his parents, all the nostalgia . . . Yeah, he needed a vacation, somewhere warm. Maybe he'd go to the Bahamas or Mexico. Things were off-kilter, and he needed to set his life back on an even keel again. That's all.

Kissing Haley Cooper sure hadn't helped matters. *She* was the reason the ground he stood on no longer felt solid under his work boots. Haley, with her big brown eyes, soft curves and that kissable mouth of hers . . . He strode into his apartment, kicked off his boots and tossed his keys into the basket on his kitchen counter. A beer and then bed. He'd work on his defenses against cute brunettes tomorrow. He was way too tired to fight the good fight tonight.

Chapter Seven

Showered and wrapped in her bathrobe, Haley stood in front of her new medicine cabinet mirror and applied her makeup. Brent would pick her up for the Christmas party in an hour, and boy was it bliss to have a fully functioning, updated bathroom in which to get ready.

She couldn't keep the smile off her face. The bathroom had turned out way better than she'd imagined. The brownish-copper paint she'd chosen really set off the dark-cherry-stained vanity. Plus, she loved the sleek, contemporary look of her bronzed fixtures. They'd installed a travertine tile floor, and it really complemented the shower tiles. She still needed to find accent pieces and something nicer than the plain white shower curtain she had up, but for now, everything was perfect.

Her cell phone rang, and she hurried to grab it from her bedroom dresser. "Hello."

"Hey, it's Sam."

Surprise stole her breath, and she immediately recalled the kiss they'd shared. *Wait. It's Friday night. Shouldn't he be out carousing?*

"Haley, you there?"

"Yeah. Sorry. What's up?"

"Did I leave my cordless drill at your house on Wednesday?"

Her heart dropped, almost as if she'd been hoping he'd called just to talk to her, which he hadn't. "You did. It's sitting on a dining room chair."

"I'm going to need it this weekend. Would you mind if I stopped by in the next hour or so to pick it up?"

"I don't mind as long as you get here before seven. I'm going out." Seconds of silence stretched between them. She checked to see if the call had been dropped. Nope. "You still there, Sam?"

"Uh . . . yeah. Lost you for a minute. What did you say?"

"I said it's fine to pick up your drill, but it has to happen before seven."

"I'm on my way. I'll be there in ten or fifteen minutes."

He hung up before she could respond. Great, she was still in her robe and slippers. Haley tossed her phone on the bed and dressed. She tugged at the zipper of her dress on her way back to the bathroom to finish putting on her makeup. Part of her wanted to see the expression on his face when he saw her all dressed up. "I've lost my mind," she muttered, applying mascara to her already lined and shadowed eyes. She checked her hair one last time and reached for her lipstick.

Her pulse hit the charts. "Yep. I've definitely lost my mind."

Regardless of the state of her mind, she added the finishing touches: garnet earrings and a matching pendant. She padded back to her bedroom to check herself in the full-length mirror on the back of her closet door. Turning this way and that, she surveyed the results of her efforts and slipped her feet into her sleek black pumps. She loved the sexy new crimson-and-black cocktail dress, and the lacy black hose she'd chosen pulled the entire ensemble together. Exactly the right amount of cleavage showed, and the dress clung to her in all the right places. She picked up a bottle of her favorite perfume, spritzed some into the air and walked through the fragrant mist.

A knock on her door sent electric currents tracing along her nerves, and her mouth went completely dry. *Don't sweat.* She'd have damp spots under her arms if she didn't get hold of herself. She shook out her hands, walked to the door and swung it open. "Hi, Sam. Come on in. I'll get your drill."

"Holy hotness, Batman. You are dressed to break hearts tonight, Ms. Cooper." His razor-sharp gaze traveled over her, taking her in. "Where are you off to this evening?"

Pleased beyond reason, she sashayed to the dining room—was he watching?—to fetch his drill. "I have a date," she answered. He didn't need to know her date was gay, or that it was a company holiday party. She simply wanted to bask in a man's heated perusal and appreciation for a brief moment, all right? No, not all right. Not just any man's appreciative looks would do. She wanted Sam's heated looks, but she chose to ignore her motives for the time being.

"Wait," he rasped out, too close behind her. "I'll get the drill. I'd hate for any oil or dirt to ruin . . . Damn, Haley. You look positively edible." He looked her over again, his blue eyes darkening.

"Thank you." She clasped her hands together. No need to embarrass herself by fanning her face.

"Who's the lucky guy?"

Did she detect a hint of jealousy? "He's a lawyer."

"Ah." He nodded. "I kind of figured you for the suit-and-tie type."

"I don't have a type." She bristled.

"Oh, really." He smirked.

"Really."

"Then you and I should go out."

"What?" Her eyes widened. He looked as stunned as she felt by the words that had fallen from his mouth. "Oh, Sam, I don't think—"

"Oh, Haley, I know what you think. You don't see me as *dateable*." He flashed her a pointed look. "You think I'm this promiscuous horn-dog who—"

"Wait a minute. I'll admit in the shock of the moment I did call you a few names, but I never said you weren't dateable. You're completely date worthy. But, Sam—"

"Damn right I'm date worthy." His voice rang with challenge. "Spend some time in my world, and I'll prove it to you."

"Proving to me you're dateable is important to you?" Taken aback, she stared at him. "Why?"

"I guess it's because I'm competitive, and because you misjudged me from the start."

He shrugged, as if it didn't matter one way or the other, but again she caught a glimpse of something pass through his eyes. Vulnerability? Her heart turned over. "I—"

"Knock, knock," Brent called, opening the front door to let himself in. "Oh, wow, Haley." He placed both hands over his heart. "That dress. *You* in that dress . . ." He noticed Sam, and sent her a questioning look.

"Brent, this is Sam. His construction company is doing some remodeling work on my house." She crossed the living room, opened her closet and took out her coat. "Sam, this is Brent."

Brent took a step toward her. Sam strode to her side and took the coat from her hands. He held it up for her to slip into. "Brent," Sam said, settling the coat on her shoulders. "Nice to meet you."

Utter confusion clouded Brent's face. She could relate. Haley had her own mess of confusion to deal with. "Thanks," she muttered, stepping away. "Sam stopped by to pick up a drill he left here the other day." She gestured toward dining room.

"Guess I'd better get that drill and head out," Sam said in a tight voice. "You two have fun."

"You too," Haley said. He must have plans. Men who looked like Sam did not sit at home on Friday and Saturday nights, especially not men who had the kind of reputation Sam had admitted to on the radio. He grabbed his hand tool and stomped out of her house. Guilt knotted her stomach. The sashaying in front of him had been over the top. She'd provoked him.

"What did I miss?" Brent frowned at her.

She bit her lip. "I might have teased him a little, but I didn't *invite* him over. He called me. Can I help it if I just happened to be all dressed up for a party when he stopped by?"

"I see."

"Do you? Because I'm not sure I do."

"You're feeling a tiny bit guilty because you took pleasure in strutting your stuff in front of a man you're obviously attracted to, and he—poor heterosexual drooler that he is—took the bait. In fact, I'm pretty sure he swallowed the hook." He laughed at his own joke. "He reacted exactly as you hoped he would. Am I right?"

"Yes." She had strutted her stuff, and she'd reveled in his reaction. "Let me get my purse."

Brent was grinning when she returned. "What now?" she demanded.

"You should've seen the way your blue-collar stud glared at me while he helped you into your coat."

She sucked in a breath, gaining a new understanding of the expression *guilty pleasure*, only in this case, the expression should be *pleasurable guilt*. She rolled her eyes. "I even swayed my hips in front of him, and then he asked me out. I've *never* done this kind of thing before in my life."

"Maybe it's time you did. You poked the bear. What hot-blooded male can resist the occasional poke?" He winked and gestured her through the door. "Besides, what's the problem? You're single, and I'm assuming he is too, or you wouldn't have laid the hip-swaying move on him. Did you say yes?"

"I didn't really have the chance to say yes or no. You walked into the living room in the middle of the discussion." She locked the deadbolt behind them, and they walked to his car. "It's complicated. He's already told me he doesn't get involved. Ever. He's twenty-nine, and he's never been in a serious relationship."

"He told you that, huh? Hmm, there are two ways to look at this situation."

He opened the car door for her. Haley slid into the passenger seat and waited for him to climb in behind the wheel. "So, tell me."

"All it takes is the right person to change someone's mind about getting seriously involved. Most of the time, it's not even a conscious choice. We fall into involvement before we realize what's happening, whether we want to or not. That's scenario number one."

"Yeah, I doubt I'm the one who will change Sam's mind, and I don't think I want to become involved with him either, which is why I feel guilty about sashaying in front of him the way I did." No way did she want to join Sam's long line of lovers past and present—not even lovers—more like brief encounters of the sexual kind. Her heart would not take that well at all. "What's the second way to look at this?"

"The attraction the two of you share is palpable. If he isn't interested in a relationship, and neither are you, then he's safe. Have some fun. Spread those sexy wings." Brent grinned at her. "You could do a lot worse as far as rebound guys go. The man is *steamy*."

Haley grinned back. "I know, right? You should come over some time when he's working. Whew." She fanned herself with her clutch. "You have no idea. All those muscles flexing, and that tangled mess of thick blond hair . . . The tool belt. You should see Sam in his tool belt."

Brent laughed and she joined him, until that niggle of uncertainty reasserted itself. "I'm not a terrible person, am I? I did tease him. A little." She had poked the bear, but the bear had been the one who had called her, not the other way around. Come to think of it, why had he called on a Friday night? Surely he had more than one drill, or he could borrow one from his brother. *Wait a minute.* She knew he had a spare, because he'd loaned it to her while they were working together to install her medicine cabinet.

Her breath caught. Sam didn't need the drill. He'd left it at her house on purpose, so he could check up on her. Stunned, she leaned back against the expensive leather seat of Brent's Mercedes. He'd also shown up early to pry into her personal life that one night. And, he'd asked her out. Kind of. It had been more like he'd issued a challenge, and judging by the vulnerability she'd glimpsed, he obviously believed being turned down had been a foregone conclusion. A defense mechanism? She didn't know what to make of Sam Haney anymore.

After what she'd heard about his responses on the *Loaded Question* radio show, she'd expected him to be shallow and narcissistic. He wasn't either of those things. Instead, he was complex, endearing, considerate and tender. She ran a finger over the spot where the splinter had lodged itself in her palm. So far, everything she'd believed about him had been wrong.

Brent patted her hand. "You're not a terrible person, Haley."

"Huh?" Startled out of her jumbled thoughts, she had to scramble to remember what she'd asked. "Oh. Thanks." She cast around for something to say to change the subject. "I hope the food at this party is better than last year's."

"Me too. I've heard good things about this place, though."

Haley nodded, and Brent went on about different restaurants in Minneapolis he'd tried, while she only half listened. Sam the handyman surprised her at every turn. He was way more complicated than she'd given him credit for, and she was way too drawn to him. She didn't know if that was a good thing, or a very, very dangerous thing. He'd asked her to spend time in his world in order to prove to her that he was date worthy. Could she get to know him better and have her heart remain unscathed?

To dare or not to dare? Either way, deciding would rob her of sleep and occupy her every waking moment. She bit her lip. How would that be any different? Sam seemed to pop into her head all the time anyway. Her heart had already been scathed.

Sam had driven away from Haley's with no particular direction in mind. His lame plan hadn't turned out at all like he'd hoped, that's for sure. He'd intended to drop by for his drill, the drill he'd left there on purpose, and find Haley home alone on a Friday night. Then, being the great guy he was, he would've suggested they hang out together. They'd go somewhere, have a beer, play some pool or darts—not a date, just hanging out. Like friends.

When was the last time he'd allowed a new friend into his life?

His jaw clenched so hard, it ached. He should've backtracked the minute she'd told him she was going out, but curiosity had gotten the better of him. He'd always thought of her as cute, but in that dress and all done up like she was? She was the prettiest woman he'd ever clapped eyes on—not to mention sexy as hell.

Then, just as he and Haley had been discussing spending time together, Mr. Expensive Suit walked in. Damn. He scowled and gripped the steering wheel of his SUV, still in the grip of something that felt an awful lot like *jealousy*. Which was ridiculous, because he never got jealous or possessive. Both emotions had everything to do with relationships, and relationships weren't something he did. Ever. He just wanted . . . What? When it came to Haley, he couldn't quite name what he wanted. If only she hadn't made that crack about him needing to offer sex on the side to get jobs.

Haley's date had been the metrosexual type, and the guy drove a Mercedes. While he—Sam checked himself in the rearview mirror—hadn't even bothered to have his hair cut in six months. At least his jeans weren't faded or torn tonight, and he'd chosen a nice sweater to wear. He stopped at a red light and knocked his head against the top of his steering wheel.

What the hell had he been thinking? That he wanted to see her and maybe kiss her again? And once he had seen her, kissing took a backseat to wanting to peel that sexy dress off her a few inches at a time, tasting every luscious bit of her bare skin along the way. He'd bet his paycheck she wore a lacy black bra and matching panties underneath. He groaned.

Sam shifted uncomfortably in his seat. The light had gone green, and the driver behind him honked. Sam stepped on the gas and then pulled into the parking lot of a mini-mart. He grabbed his phone, hitting his brother's speed dial number.

"Yeah?" Wyatt said, sounding distracted.

"You doing anything tonight?"

"Right now I'm working on the graphics for a new comic book idea I'm developing. You?"

At least Wyatt had a hobby, something he was passionate about. His comic books were really good, too. One of these days, his brother would find a publisher, and his work would go viral. "Not a thing. You feel like meeting me for a game of pool and a few beers?"

"Sure. Give me an hour."

"I can do that. I'll call Josey and see if she wants to join us. Mad Jack's or Casper's?"

"Casper's. It's easier to get a pool table there. See you at eight thirty."

"See you." Sam hit Josey's speed dial number. She didn't answer, so he left her a message. Either she'd show up or she wouldn't. Somewhat relieved, he headed to Casper's, figuring he'd get something to eat while waiting for Wyatt and Jo.

Sam strolled through the busy bar and grill to the back room and put his name down on the waiting list for a billiards table. Then he moved to the bar and found an empty stool. Once he'd ordered food and a beer, he settled in to wait. The seat next to him emptied, and he draped his jacket over the back to save it for Wyatt.

"Say, you look like you could use some company." A nice-looking woman came to stand beside him. "Mind if I join you?" She leaned closer, and her breasts touched his arm. He jerked it away from any possibility of further contact.

"Uh . . ." Again he felt nothing but annoyance. He hadn't made eye contact with her, or smiled at her across the room. He'd been eating his meal and minding his own business. That's all.

"I saw you put your name down for a pool table. We could play a few games, have a few beers and see where it leads," she said, her tone seductive.

"Look, I appreciate the offer, but I'm waiting for someone." He placed his hand on the back of the barstool next to him so she wouldn't sit in it. "And here she is." He nodded toward the door and waved. Nothing but relief surged through him at the sight of Josey walking through the door. The woman gave Josey the once-over, huffed and moved off. Jo made her way through the tables and joined him at the bar.

"Sorry I missed your call. I had my hands full."

He took his jacket from the empty stool. "No problem. I'm glad you made it."

"Did I scare off the pretty lady hitting on you?"

"Yes." He sighed. "And thank you." This had been the second time this week he'd rejected advances. Stress, he reminded himself, but he couldn't deny the truth. He'd felt no interest in either of the women making passes at him. None.

She laughed. "You're thanking me? That's a first."

Frowning, Sam chose not to respond. He nodded toward the door. "There's Wyatt."

"Hey, you two." Wyatt dragged an empty barstool from a high-top table and positioned it next to Josey. He signaled the bartender. "How long before we get a billiards table?"

"We're up next." Sam pushed his empty plate away. How many weekend nights had he spent with his brother and sister? "Do you think it's weird that we're all in our twenties, and yet none of us are dating?"

"Speak for yourself," Josey said. "I date."

"You do?" Sam gaped. "How come we never hear about it or meet any of your dates?"

Josey swiveled around on her stool, beer in hand, and leaned against the bar. "Because they don't last long. That's why."

"Why not, Jo?" Wyatt asked. "Even though you're my sister, I can tell you're kind of pretty, and you're easy enough to get along with." He grinned. "Most of the time, anyway."

Frowning, she shook her head. "Once a guy I'm interested in finds out what I do for a living, I get put into a box labeled *possibly a lesbian*. When I finally convince him I'm straight, and we go out a few times, the insecurities creep in and cause problems."

Sam studied her for a moment. Josey had always possessed a boldness and self-confidence he admired. "I've never seen you as insecure."

"Not *my* insecurities." Josey shot him a wry look. "It's tough to find a man who can handle the fact that I know more about tools than he does, or that I'm way better at fixing things—including his car." She lifted her arm and flexed her biceps. "Or that I might be as strong, or in some cases, stronger." She sighed again. "Still, I keep trying, which is more than can be said about you two knuckleheads. I *want* a husband and a family."

That stung. He didn't need to be married or have a family to be happy. His life was exactly how he wanted it to be. He frowned. Somehow, he no longer felt as convinced by his convictions as he once had been. "Wyatt, you should get out there and find someone." Sam surveyed the busy bar. "Your burn scars bother you far more than they bother anybody else. There are a couple of nice-looking women over there." He gestured toward two blondes in the booth three away from the front door. "You could go over there right now and say hi, see if they want to join us for a game of pool."

"I don't think so." His brother's face turned red, and he tucked his head deeper into the hood of his sweatshirt. "Why are you focusing on me? What about you? Your scars don't even show."

My scars? He blinked a few times. After his mom and dad had died, he'd closed up shop as far as his heart went, sure, but . . . His chest tightened. Sam swallowed the rising anic, the hurt and confusion that had never completely left him since that day. Or the guilt.

"Why don't you get out there and date, Sam?" Wyatt glared. "Quit screwing total strangers. Find a nice girl and settle down. You're the oldest. You first. How about giving commitment and monogamy a try for a change?"

"Ouch." Sam glared back.

"Well this evening certainly has taken an unhappy turn." Josey laughed. "I thought this was the season to be jolly."

The group at one of the billiard tables put their cues away and gathered their things. Sam heaved a sigh of relief. "Sorry I brought up the subject of dating. Let's forget it. We're up." He nodded toward the back of the bar and grill. "Let's go shoot some pool."

"Good idea," Wyatt said, grabbing his beer from the bar and hopping off his stool.

"Do you want to play Cut Throat, or would you two like to take turns seeing who *can't* beat me at 8 Ball?" Sam smirked, eager to get things back to the way they'd been before he'd attempted to communicate about anything deeper than burgers, beer and billiards. He should've known better.

"Cut Throat." Josey slipped off her bar stool. "Don't count on winning."

"Back at you." Sam grinned. The three of them headed toward the rear of Casper's and set up the table for Cut Throat. *Find a nice girl and settle down.* That's exactly what Grandpa Joe had said. He cringed at the thought. Commit? Him? No thank you.

Seeing Haley, all dressed up and sexy as hell, had thrown him. That's all. He wanted her, all right. But . . . did he want to *date* her? He almost tripped over his own feet at the thought. Hadn't he asked her out, challenged her to spend time in his world? What about the lame plan he'd concocted just to see her tonight? He got a little light-headed. The room began to spin, and he couldn't draw enough air into his lungs. "It's stuffy in here," he griped, grabbing a pool cue from the rack.

Haley Cooper had him messed up, and that was a fact. He didn't like the way she made him feel one bit. All confused, conflicted . . . jealous. Her date tonight, would that lawyer lay his hands on her, hold her in his arms and kiss her? Pressure banded his chest, and he put down his cue. "I gotta get some air. I'll be back in a few."

"Are you coming down with something?" Josey put her hand on his forehead, like his mom used to do. "Is your throat sore, or—"

"No." He jerked away. "I just need air." He strode toward the back door, flung it open and walked out. A few hardy, coatless smokers stood around, and the smell of cigarette smoke filled his nostrils. Sam moved out of their range and hauled in a lungful of cold air, and then another.

He'd been with some gorgeous women, and they'd had no effect whatsoever on his heart. How had one petite, uptight paralegal managed to get under his skin the way Haley had? He growled, closed his eyes and rubbed his temples. He was in serious trouble.

Chapter Eight

Haley poured herself a cup of coffee and meandered into her living room. Was it weird that she'd miss working with Sam today? Definitely. Especially since she'd just seen him last night when he'd stopped by for his not-so-needed drill. Heat filled her face as she remembered how she'd behaved. What had gotten into her?

Oh, she'd known what she'd been after all right—she'd wanted to feel desirable, to be looked at the way Sam had looked at her. Probably a good thing he and his brother weren't coming today. She needed the weekend to get her head back on straight.

Speaking of being on her own, now would be a good time to get Michael's contact information. She set her mug on the coffee table, right next to her phone, and checked the time. Virginia and Greg would be up by now. Haley took a seat and ran her palms over her flannel-clad knees. She could do this. She had to, because it was way past time to stamp *paid* on that box of emotional crap labeled ex-fiancé. She took a deep breath, picked up the phone and punched in their number.

Virginia answered, and Haley's mouth went dry. "Hey, Ginny. This is Haley Cooper. How are you?"

"My, it's good to hear from you, Haley," Virginia said. "Greg and I are fine, just fine. How are you? How's your family?"

"We're all doing well, thanks." She bit her lip, unsure how to proceed. "The reason I'm calling is—" She tried to catch her breath. "—I was hoping you could give me a way to contact Michael."

"Oh, Haley. We feel so bad about what happened. Greg and I are so very sorry things turned out as they did. We both feel terrible that we didn't reach out to you after Michael left. We—"

"It's OK, Ginny." At the time, she couldn't have handled their sympathy anyway. Affection for Michael's parents overcame her, along with a flood of good memories. The tension she'd been holding eased. "What happened wasn't your fault, or Greg's." She cleared her throat. "Speaking of Michael, is he still in Indonesia?"

"Yes. He's teaching English at a private school." Virginia paused for a moment. "He hasn't been home since . . . Well, since the abrupt way he left. Michael has international phone service. Would you like his number?"

"What about e-mail? Does he have an e-mail address?" No way did she want to *talk* to the man who'd jilted her. She could deal with writing him a letter, but hearing his voice? Did she really want to listen to him refuse to give her the answers she so desperately needed? No thanks.

"He does. Hold on a moment, and I'll get it for you."

Haley waited; a sense of calm and rightness settled over her. She should have done this months ago.

"Do you have a pen and paper, Haley?"

"I do." She picked up a pen and an old envelope sitting on the table. "Go ahead." Virginia gave her the e-mail address and his phone number, and they chatted for a while before ending the call. Haley went to her second bedroom and sat down at her desk. She stared at the dark screen of her computer. How should she ask her ex what had been running through his mind the weeks before he'd bolted? *Keep it light, nonconfrontational.* She touched a key, and her computer sprang to life. Words began to form in her mind and she opened her e-mail. She began to write, tweaked it in the places where the anger leaked out, and finally she was satisfied.

> *Hey Michael,*
> *I hear you're teaching English at a private school these days. I hope that's going well for you. I'm writing because I believe you owe me an explanation for the way things ended between us. I deserve to know, as I'm sure you would agree. I'm not angry anymore, just puzzled. If for no other reason than the close friendship we once shared, I'm hoping you'll respond. I want to put the entire experience behind me, and I can't without knowing what happened. Thanks.*
> *~Haley*

Her finger hovered over the Send button. She was doing the right thing, wasn't she? In the days after Michael left, she'd racked her brain, going over every moment they'd spent together, looking for clues. Had she said or done something to drive him away, or had he simply fallen out of love with her?

Haley leaned back in her chair. Sam had defended her. He'd called Michael a selfish jerk. Smiling, she recalled the tender way he'd taken care of her splinter, the way he'd taken such pains to instruct her on how to be a carpenter. Her heart fluttered as she thought about the unexpected, mind-altering kiss they'd shared. He really was a sweet guy.

Sam had given her the impetus to finally reach out to Michael for closure. She needed to thank him, and she would. The more she thought about how Sam had invited her to spend time in his world, the more curious she became. What was he like with his family and friends? How did he spend his time away from work? Plus, she hadn't yet asked him why he never spoke about his parents.

Her kitchen counter and cabinets would be delivered this coming week. Her new kitchen floor would be installed Monday evening. She could hardly wait. *To see Sam?* Her house would be finished soon. No more working side by side with the hottest handyman in the state. A sinking feeling lodged itself in the pit of her stomach. She'd miss him.

Her phone rang. Sighing, Haley hit the Send icon on her e-mail and hurried to the living room where she'd left her cell. "Hi, Mom. What's up?"

"Hi, sweetie. Nanci and I are going to the Albertville Outlet Mall to do some Christmas shopping, and we were hoping you'd join us."

"I'd love to. I need to shop." Wow. Christmas was a few weeks away. Usually, she had gifts purchased and wrapped by now. She hadn't even put out any of her holiday decorations yet.

"Great. We'll pick you up around ten thirty. That way we can take a look at what's been done to your house."

"Sounds great. See you then." A wave of protectiveness came out of nowhere, hitting her squarely in the heart. The work she'd done with Sam suddenly seemed intimate. She didn't want to share the changes they'd made to her house with anyone quite yet, especially not with the two women who'd set her up for a one-night stand with her handyman. *My handyman?*

Since when did remodeling and construction work have anything to do with intimacy, and when had Sam become *her handyman?* Shaking off the ridiculous notions, she headed for her new bathroom to take a shower. Unfortunately, every single tile and fixture reminded her of Sam. "Argh. I need professional help, some kind of therapy."

"Frank, I'm leaving," Trudy called down the basement stairs. "Do you need anything before I go?" She slipped into her coat and slung her purse over her shoulder. He kept his workbench and tools on one side of the basement, and nothing made her husband happier than creating gadgets or fixing things around the house.

"Nope. I'm fine," her husband called back from his man cave. "Have fun, and don't forget, we're meeting the Meyers for dinner at the club tonight."

"I won't forget." Trudy rolled her eyes. Did he think she was going senile? They'd been meeting their best friends for dinner once a month for as long as she and Frank had been married. "I'll be home by four." She left him to his puttering, walked outside to their driveway and climbed into her sister's Jeep. "Haley is joining us."

"Good." Nanci backed her SUV out of the driveway. "We'll get to see the progress on her remodeling. Has she given you any clue about whether or not the handyman has done the *real* job you hired him to do?"

"No," Trudy muttered. "I'm kind of thinking the whole idea is a bust, but at least I won't have to worry anymore that her house will fall down around her ears."

Nanci turned onto the parkway leading to Haley's bungalow. "The job isn't finished yet. Since Haley insisted on learning how to do things from him, she and Sam have been spending quite a bit of time together, and Haley is attractive. It could still happen."

"Haley spending time with him isn't what I had in mind." Trudy scowled. "According to what we heard on *Loaded Question*, Sam Haney is extremely promiscuous, an opportunist. I just wanted him to make a pass at her. A pass she'd turn down, of course. That's all."

Guilt turned her breakfast into an uncomfortable lump in her stomach. She shouldn't have set her daughter up the way she had. What if the handyman tried to take advantage of Haley somehow? After all, she was in a vulnerable place. Other than Michael, she hadn't dated much in high school. What did she know about men like Sam? Nothing. Trudy frowned. Maybe she should confess, tell her daughter what she'd done and why. Then she wouldn't have to worry about Haley being taken in by the sexy handyman.

By the time she and Nanci parked in front of Haley's house, Trudy's hands were shaking and she couldn't seem to get enough air into her lungs. "Do you think I ought to tell her what I did?"

"No." Nanci narrowed her eyes at her. "If you're right, and the whole thing failed, then why does she ever need to know? And, if by chance Sam does make a pass once the job is finished, Haley still might come out of her funk." She opened her car door. "Take a wait-and-see approach for now."

Trudy nodded, though doubt still gnawed at her. Haley waved at them from her front door. Her daughter really was a lovely young woman, and she deserved every happiness. Perhaps she'd think of some other way to help her get past her heartbreak. There had to be someone who knew someone who had a great single son. She'd ask the Meyers at dinner tonight.

"Can't wait to see what's been done to your house," Nanci said as she walked into the cozy bungalow. Trudy followed.

"I can't wait to show you," Haley said. "Are you going to take off your coats, or do you just want a quick look before we head to the mall?"

"I think a quick look," Nanci suggested. "When everything is finished, you can have us all over for dinner."

"That's a great idea." Haley's eyes lit up. "We'll be done right after Christmas. I'll have a New Year's Day open house for family and a few friends."

We'll. Haley had said *we'll be done*, as if she and the handyman were partners on the job. Trudy pursed her lips. What did that mean?

"Come see my new bathroom." Haley led them through her house toward the room and stepped back so they could enter.

Curious, Trudy leaned in and scanned the remodeled bathroom. She gasped. "Wow. It's—"

"Perfect," her sister finished the sentence for her. "I love the colors in here. I can't believe your old bathroom has turned into *this*."

"I know." Haley grinned. "I love it. I might try remodeling the downstairs bathroom by myself now that I know how. Sam has taught me so much, and he's really good at what he does. He's a great teacher. Very patient and thorough."

Trudy's eyes widened, and she had to force herself not to gape at her daughter. The warmth and pride in Haley's voice when she talked about the handyman had her stymied. She snuck a peek at her sister to see if she'd noticed too. Nanci raised an eyebrow and canted her head ever so slightly. Yep. She'd noticed.

"Look at the new entryway between the kitchen and dining room." Haley gestured toward her kitchen, leading them away from her completely new and stylish bathroom.

"Oh," Nanci exclaimed. "It's arched." She looked from the curved entry between the living room and dining room, back to the identical arch separating the kitchen and dining room. "This really opens things up, and I like how it's the same style as the other entryway."

"I know." Haley walked into her bare kitchen. "Creating the matching arches was Sam's idea. We've insulated the outside walls in here, added some much-needed electrical outlets, and we're laying the floor Monday night. Not long now, and I'll have my dream kitchen."

Haley turned a slow circle on the sub-flooring. "Thank you so much for hiring Haney & Sons to do the job, Mom. I couldn't be happier with their work or with Sam."

"You're welcome." Trudy scanned the room. "Looks like they do good work, all right."

"Why are you frowning?" Haley asked, a puzzled look on her face.

"I'm not." Trudy's frown deepened.

"Yeah, Trudy. Why are you frowning?" Nanci snorted. "I can't wait to see your kitchen when it's finished, Haley, but let's hit the road, you two. The outlet mall awaits, and I have gifts to buy."

"I wasn't frowning," Trudy insisted, following Nanci and Haley to the front door. "I was *concentrating*. There's a difference." Of course she'd been frowning. Her daughter seemed happier than she'd seen her in months, and obviously Sam Haney was to blame. Haley actually liked and respected him, which meant her daughter had no clue about what kind of man she was dealing with. *Oh, this is not good—not good at all.*

Haley dropped all of her shopping bags on the living room floor, shrugged out of her coat and hung it up. It had begun to snow heavily on the drive home from the outlet mall, and her nerves were on edge. Her aunt always drove as if everyone else on the road should get out of her way—and snow didn't slow her down one bit. Haley should've offered to do the driving today.

At least she'd finished most of her Christmas shopping. Only a gift for her mom remained on her list, and she'd already ordered her present online. Her mom made shopping for her a no-brainer. She always told both her children exactly what she wanted and exactly where to get it.

Haley transferred the gifts she'd purchased to the closet in her office. She'd wrap and tag them tomorrow. Right now, she needed a few minutes to recover from her day of shopping—especially the harrowing drive home part. She glanced at her computer, and her stomach lurched. Had Michael answered her e-mail? She'd fix herself a mug of tea and a frozen dinner in the microwave, and then she'd check.

Haley dropped a tea bag into a cup and added bottled water. She placed it in the microwave, and then she watched the snow outside her dining room window. Fat white flakes were falling thick and fast, and the wind had picked up, sending the snow careening against her house. Her backyard motion light had switched on, turning the precipitation into a bombardment of tiny diamonds against the windowpane.

Her mind drifted to Michael. Did it snow in Indonesia? She didn't think so. How would he react to her e-mail? Would he respond at all? Her phone rang, jolting her out of her thoughts. She grabbed it from her dining room table just as the microwave dinged. "Hello?"

"Hey . . . It's Sam."

Her nerves pinged, and her pulse raced. "What's up? Did you leave another hand tool here I don't know about?"

"Nope. No missing tools. Some weather we're having, huh?"

"When are we not having *some* weather in Minnesota?" She grinned. "Did you call me to discuss the weather?"

"No, just thought I'd mention it's snowing."

"I can see it's snowing." Haley took her tea from the microwave. Still grinning like a fool, she slid onto a chair before her knees gave out. "I was just watching out my window. It's hypnotic."

"It is," Sam agreed. "Like a wood fire burning in a fireplace."

"Is there a reason you called, Sam, or did you just want to chat?" She heard him draw in a breath, and her stomach did that fluttery thing it always did with him.

"That guy . . . Brent. Are you two involved, or . . ."

"No. We're just friends and coworkers. He and I went to our company holiday party together, that's all."

"Ah." A few quiet seconds ticked by. "If you'll recall, I issued a challenge."

"I haven't forgotten." Self-doubt, curiosity and attraction churned through her. Dammit, she wanted to spend time with him. "And I accept."

"Good. I coach a Pee Wee Hockey team with my cousin, and we have a practice scrimmage scheduled for Wednesday evening at Highland South Arena. It starts at six. Would you be interested in watching a bunch of eight- and nine-year-olds play hockey?"

She could hear the smile in his voice. "Sure. Sounds like fun," she said. Given the way he taught carpentry, he was probably an excellent coach. The fact that he gave up his time to coach sent tendrils of warmth wrapping around her heart.

"What time do you get home from work?" he asked, his voice slightly gruff.

"I can be flexible. What time do you need me to be home?"

"Five would be good. I'll pick you up then. Jerry and I need to be at the rink before the practice is scheduled to begin, because a few kids always show up early." He paused for a few seconds again. "After the practice, I thought we could maybe go get something to eat."

"All right." Her mind swirled like the snow outside her window. Exhilaration and nervousness cascaded through her all at once at the thought of spending time with Sam in a place that didn't involve remodeling her house.

"Wear warm clothes," he cautioned. "It's an indoor rink, but it's still cold."

"I will." She did a mental inventory of her closet. Had she kept the pair of flannel-lined jeans her mom had given her for Christmas a couple of years ago? "We're still installing the floor on Monday, aren't we?"

"Of course. Well, OK. I guess we're set. I'll see you on Monday, and you'll join me and my cousins on Wednesday."

"Cousins? I thought you said you coached with your *cousin*, as in only one."

"I do. My cousin Jerry helps with the coaching, but two kids on my team are my first cousin's twins. Not sure what that makes them. Second cousins? First cousins once removed, thirds or something?"

"Oh." She frowned. "I couldn't say without looking it up."

"Me either, which is why I just call the whole bunch *cousins*."

He chuckled, and more tendrils of warmth wove around her heart.

"I'll let you get back to what you were doing, Haley."

"All right. See you Monday."

"Monday."

With that, the call ended. Haley stared into space, sipped her tea, and attempted to corral her racing thoughts. Sam had called her for a purely social reason. He could've waited until he was at her house on Monday night to ask her to join him for the hockey scrimmage. Why hadn't he? Obviously she'd been on his mind—like he was so frequently on hers.

She rose, picked up her mug of tea and walked into her office. Still standing, she hit a key on her computer to wake it up and checked her e-mail. No reply from Michael. She calculated the time difference. Maybe he hadn't read her letter yet.

On the other hand, he might have read it and opted not to respond. What else could she expect from a man who'd chosen to run away rather than face her? "Coward," she huffed, returning to her kitchen for a frozen dinner.

Scanning the empty space, she grinned. Two weeks from now her dream kitchen would be complete and fully functional. She and Sam would install the floor Monday evening, and she'd also see him on Wednesday *and* Thursday. Why waste time thinking about her really lame ex, when she had so much more to look forward to? Wow, who knew all it took to change her outlook was getting her house put back together?

Yeah, right. It's the house, and not the handsome handyman.

Chapter Nine

Sam poured himself a mug of the coffee he'd made and settled into a seat at Haney & Sons' kitchen table, waiting for Josey's arrival. He and his sister had been van-pooling to the job since he'd moved to the construction crew.

Wyatt walked in, bringing a blast of cold air with him. "Morning," Sam said.

Wyatt, never a morning or a Monday person, grunted and headed for the coffee.

"Say, seeing you reminds me," Sam said. "I don't need you at Haley's tonight. We're laying the kitchen floor, and she wants to help. Not exactly what you'd call a three-man job."

Wyatt folded his lanky frame into a chair and slouched forward. Nodding in response, he rested his forearms on the table and gripped his coffee cup like it was all that was keeping him upright.

Sam played with the handle on his mug, bracing himself for Wyatt's reaction, but hanging with his siblings was a big part of his life. If he wanted Haley to see him in his world, that meant including Wyatt and Josey. "Do you want to meet at The Bulldog Wednesday night after my hockey scrimmage? Haley will be with me."

Wyatt's brow lowered, and a look of confusion suffused his sleepy features. "What did you just say?"

"Haley is coming with me to my team's hockey scrimmage Wednesday evening. Afterward, I'm going to bring her to The Bulldog for something to eat. Would you care to meet us there?" He pointed to Wyatt's coffee. "Drink up. You need the caffeine."

Josey walked in then, and Wyatt turned to face her. "Jo, are you free Wednesday night?"

"Yeah, why?" She too made a beeline for the coffee and filled her thermal cup.

"History is about to be made," Wyatt quipped, significantly more alert now. "Sam is bringing Haley Cooper to our favorite bar and grill Wednesday night. Our brother has a date."

Heat surged up Sam's neck to fill his face. "It's not a date."

"OK." Wyatt shrugged. "What are we calling it then, and how do you plan to explain fraternizing with a client to Grandpa Joe?"

"Wait." Josey leaned against the kitchen counter. "Isn't that the woman whose mother—"

"Yes." Sam shot up. "Forget I said anything. I just thought it might be fun to include her at our favorite hangout place this once."

"But . . ." Josey frowned. "You never include anyone in anything— not anyone outside of family or people you've known for years, anyway." She gaped. "After the way her mother set you up, don't tell me you want to *date* her."

"Let's go, Josey." Sam snatched his jacket from the back of his chair and thrust his arms into the sleeves.

"Hold on. Hold on." Wyatt straightened. "Of course we'll meet you and Haley at The Bulldog, but first you need to tell us what is going on."

Sam raked his fingers through his hair. "It's hard to explain. Haley accused me of having to offer sex on the side to get work. Remember? She thinks I'm this big *lothario*, and she looked down her nose at me. I—"

"She's all of five feet five, Sam. She's not tall enough to look down her nose at you, or anybody else for that matter." Wyatt smirked.

"You know what I mean. She passed judgment. I've proven I'm a skilled craftsman, and now I'm going to show her that I'm a decent guy." He scowled. "She made assumptions about me that are patently false and entirely unfair. She and I were going back and forth about the whole thing the other day, and I challenged her to spend time in my world. It just kind of came out."

He blamed it on the dress. Yep, the dress, her curves and those legs of hers. And her kissable mouth. "It's not like I planned to ask her to spend time with me, but I did. Anyway, like I said before, it's wrong to make assumptions." Who was he trying so hard to convince? He grabbed his gloves from the table and stuffed them into his jacket pockets. "I was completely up front with her about my reasons. That's all there is to this Wednesday night thing."

Not exactly. There was way more to this Wednesday night thing than he cared to admit. Haley Cooper invaded his thoughts and his dreams far too often. He made up excuses to talk to her, to see her. Not good, but he couldn't seem to stop himself. Wyatt and Josey gawked at him like he'd taken a one-way trip in the wrong direction—around the bend.

"Oh, Sam," Josey said, her eyes full of pity. "You really believe what you're saying, don't you?"

"Yes." He set his empty mug in the dishwasher. "Are you going to meet us at The Bulldog, or not?"

"Of course," Jo said.

"Oh, I wouldn't miss this for anything." Wyatt grinned. "What time are we talking?"

"The scrimmage will be over by seven. Let's say between seven thirty and eight. That'll give me time to wrap things up at the rink."

"It's a *date*," Wyatt teased as he rose from his chair. He chuckled his way down the hall toward Grandpa Joe's office.

"Ready?" Sam asked his sister. She nodded and grabbed her mug. He strode out of the building with Jo trailing him. Sam climbed into his van, stuck his key into the ignition and glared at his sister as she buckled her seat belt. "I don't want to talk about Wednesday or Haley Cooper anymore today."

"Fine by me." One side of her mouth quirked up.

Thankfully, his sister sipped her coffee without another word, and he drove them to the custom house they were finishing. A few of their contracted workers were already there—a painter, and the company putting in a gas fireplace in the downstairs family room. He and Josey were working on window frames and the trim around closets today. Nothing too challenging, and that was the problem. The day would drag by, and he wouldn't have enough going on to keep his mind off Ms. Cooper. Nope. He'd be counting the hours, minutes and seconds until he could see her again.

Haley peered into the office Kathy shared with Felicia. "Can you go to lunch today?" She glanced at the empty desk beside Kathy's. "Where's Felicia? I haven't seen her all morning."

"Yes, I can go to lunch, and Felicia is out in the field today." Kathy took her purse from her desk drawer. "What's up? You sound tense."

"I had a very strange weekend, and I need to vent," Haley said. "Why weren't you at the Christmas party Friday night?"

Kathy smiled. "I had a date." She joined Haley in the corridor, and they headed down the hall.

"You could've brought him along, you know," Haley said.

"I didn't want to. We've only been out a few times, and we're just getting to know one another. Bringing him to a company party at this point didn't feel right, and he'd made plans for us already. Maybe you remember him. I met him at Ground Zero the night we went clubbing."

She glanced sideways at her. "He and I danced a few times, and he sat with us for a while."

"The tall dark-haired guy?"

Kathy nodded, her grin growing wider. "His name is Blake, and he's a Saint Paul firefighter."

"Wow."

Kathy sighed happily. "Wow is right. He's a great guy."

They decided to go through the skyway to Rock Bottom Brewery on Hennepin Avenue, hoping the popular spot wouldn't be too busy since it was a Monday. No such luck. Even though it was only eleven, a line had already formed at the door. Kathy gave the hostess her name and took a pager, and the two of them moved to the mall area outside the restaurant's entrance.

"So, what's up?" Kathy asked.

"Sam the handyman is what's up. He asked me to go out with him. He says he wants to prove I've misjudged him."

"Perfect." Kathy laughed. "Did you accept?"

A pleasurable shiver sluiced through her as she remembered the awkward, endearing conversation she'd had with Sam about the weather. "I'm going to watch his Pee Wee Hockey team play a practice scrimmage on Wednesday, and afterward we're going out for dinner." She turned to face Kathy. "That's not all. We kissed."

"Say what?" Kathy's brow rose.

Haley told her all about what had led up to *the kiss*. "He was so sweet when he took out my sliver." She held up her hand. "He even kissed my palm before he put on the Band-Aid. I don't know what to think, or what to do. Is spending time with him a huge mistake?" Haley asked. "I need help."

"Well, you already agreed to go out with him. Seems to me you're killing a few birds with one hot hunk."

"The hot hunk part is right," Haley grinned, "but, how do you figure?"

The pager went off. "Come on. Let's get our table." Kathy handed the pager to the hostess. "Has it occurred to you Sam might be right?"

"About what?" She trailed Kathy through the crowded restaurant and took a seat. "You heard the radio show."

"I did." Kathy slid into her chair. "Isn't it possible the radio show blew everything way out of proportion? Isn't it also possible you've been a little hypercritical?"

"I doubt it." Haley took her seat and opened her menu. "He admitted on the air that women throw themselves at him on the job. If Yvonne was anything to go by, he doesn't turn them down. Would *you* trust a man like that with *your* heart?"

"Uh-oh." Kathy's brow creased. "We're talking hearts here?"

"I don't know," she said with a groan. "He's so sweet, considerate, patient, fun to be around. He's also complex and sexy as hell. But Kathy, he's completely promiscuous. I shudder to think how many women he's been with. I don't know if I could get past that part of his history. I'm not sure I could ever trust him."

"First of all, it's just one date. Aren't you kind of jumping ahead? And second, just because a person is promiscuous while they're single, that doesn't mean they'll continue being promiscuous when they're in a relationship with someone. Haven't you ever read any Regency romances?"

Haley laughed. "What do Regency romances have to do with anything?"

"In all the Regency romances I've read, the matrons always tell the heroines that reformed rakes make the best husbands." Kathy shrugged. "There has to be a kernel of truth to that, or the theme wouldn't be so frequently repeated."

"Regency romances are *fictional*. You do know that, right?" Exasperated, Haley flashed her friend an incredulous look. "Are you suggesting I base my decisions on works of romantic fiction?"

"Look, do you still want to end your mother's meddling? Because, as you might recall, I suggested the best way to go about it would be to date the handyman. Lo and behold." She waved her hand. "Look who asked who out. Here's your chance to teach Trudy a lesson."

"Oh." Haley sat back.

"How does Sam feel about your mom's reason for setting the two of you up the way she did? I'm assuming you've discussed it with him."

"I have, and he didn't take it well at all." Her heart ached, recalling how he'd gone silent, the way his shoulders had slumped and his jaw had tightened. "I *did* tell him I wanted to find a way to end Trudy's interference in my personal life once and for all."

"Well there you go. He knows. Did he object?"

"No, but . . . don't you think it would be wrong to use him to get back at my mother? I mean . . . won't I be lowering myself to Trudy's level of manipulation?"

Kathy shrugged. "Not if Sam knows you want the setup to backfire, which he does. And not if he doesn't object, which he didn't."

"Hmm. True, but when he and I talked, I wasn't planning on using him to teach Trudy a lesson." Haley tried to look at it from all angles. "On the other hand, he might appreciate the chance to give my mom a spoonful of her own medicine."

"Exactly," Kathy crowed.

Haley went back to studying the menu. "I'll think about it."

"You do that." Kathy laughed. "It's perfect, you know. Trudy never expected you to date Sam."

"That makes two of us."

After rushing home to shower and put on clean work clothes, Sam climbed back into his van and drove to Haley's house to install flooring. He pulled his truck into her driveway, and his pulse kicked into high gear. He shouldn't be this eager to see her. Torn between smiling and thumping himself in the head with a hammer, he climbed out and went to the rear of the van for supplies. Haley had the front door open for him by the time he'd gathered everything.

He couldn't decide which he liked better: Haley in old jeans and a sweatshirt, or Haley all dolled up and ready for a night on the town. "Hi," he said as he approached, his smile winning the battle against the head thumping. "Ready to work?"

"I am." She smiled back. "I've already diagrammed the floor and done the math exactly the way you showed me when you put in the bathroom floor."

"Good." He handed her the chalk line. "Let me check it over once I put this stuff down." He'd dropped off his power tile cutter the same day he'd delivered the boxes of tile. Sam followed her to the kitchen, hyperaware of the way she moved. Her clean, sweet scent drifted back to him, and he was glad he'd showered before coming over. Something he never did between jobs until today.

Haley took the diagram she'd made from under a magnet on the fridge and handed it to him. He'd already measured and marked off the place on the floor where the new cabinets would go. "The new tiles are twelve-by-twelve, and you've got us cutting the end tiles to three inches."

"Is that a problem?"

"Well, this is where experience comes in. As a general rule, we don't want to cut a ceramic tile under half. So we're going to borrow a twelve-inch tile, add it to your remainder, and divide that total by two. That way, we'll have end tiles of nine inches instead of three. It'll look better, and there's less chance of breakage when we cut."

"Makes sense." Haley leaned over and studied the diagram, looking adorable as hell.

Sam fought the urge to haul her into his arms. "Find the middle points for the length and width of the floor and mark them, and then we'll use the chalk line to create our grid." He gestured toward the pile of equipment. "While you're marking off the center points, I'll mix the mortar."

The two of them went to work on their tasks, and fifteen minutes later, they were side by side, ready to lay tile. He loved how Haley wanted to know how to do things on her own, and he couldn't help but appreciate how quickly she learned and the meticulous way she did everything. She was smart lazy—like him and Grandpa Joe. "If it's OK with you, Haley, I'll stop by tomorrow sometime in the early afternoon to do the grout work. That will give the mortar time to dry."

"OK. I'll give you a spare key before you leave tonight. Just leave it on the dining room table and lock the doorknob when you leave."

A warm, fuzzy feeling swelled in his chest. He sat back on his heels, trowel in hand, and watched Haley set a tile, and then place the spacers. "You do good work, Ms. Cooper."

"Thanks," she said, looking pleased. "Can I ask you a personal question?" She set another tile and kept her eyes on her work.

The warm fuzzy feeling disappeared. Ever since he'd asked her out, he'd been afraid this would come up. "I know what you're going to ask, and it's not as many as I'm sure you imagine."

Haley peered at him over her shoulder, her expression puzzled. "I have no idea what you're talking about."

"Never mind." *Damn.* "What were you going to ask?"

"Oh, no you don't, Sam. You said the words, and now you have to explain them."

"That's a rule?" He cocked an eyebrow.

"It is in this house."

He scooped up another glob of tile mortar and spread it over the next patch of floor to be tiled. "I thought you were going to ask me how many women I've been with. You know, because of the radio show."

"Oh." Haley seemed to ponder that for a minute. "Not that many? Really?"

"Really." He grunted. "The whole thing started a few months after Haney & Sons added handyman services to our business. Believe it or not, before that, I was pretty shy with women. Nothing like Wyatt, mind you, but not all that active." He troweled more mortar onto the floor.

"Haney & Sons was strictly construction, remodeling and contracting before the recession. Plus, not all clients are young, available women, and not every woman is the sort to throw herself at a guy who's there to fix a leaky sink." He stared into Haley's soft brown eyes. "So . . . no. Not as many as you probably think, and it's over with now, anyway."

She laughed. "In trouble with the boss?"

"Something like that." More like no interest, but he wasn't about to let that slip. "What were you going to ask?"

"You never mention your mother and father, and I'm curious about why that is. If it's too personal, you don't have to answer."

"They died on my fifteenth birthday." He hadn't meant to blurt it out like that. Dread tightened his gut. He wouldn't be able to handle it if she went all sentimental and sympathetic on him.

"I'm sorry," she said, her tone matter-of-fact. "You don't have to talk about it if you don't want to." Her eyes met his in a steady gaze. "I know it must be difficult for you."

"I don't mind," he lied and went back to work. "My dad had his pilot's license, and he loved to fly. He and my mom owned a single-engine plane, and every now and then, they'd have Grandpa Joe and Grandma Maggie come stay with us so they could fly away for a weekend."

"Oh," she murmured. "What happened?"

He swallowed a time or two. "Their anniversary and my birthday were only a few days apart. They flew to Grand Marais to celebrate on a Thursday, planning to be back in time for my birthday party on Sunday. On the flight back, they were caught in an unexpected ice storm, and their plane went down in Lake Superior. We got the call during my party." His jaw tightened.

"That must have been horrible for you." Haley placed her hand on his forearm and gave it a squeeze. "Your grandparents raised you after that?"

"Yep." He never talked to anyone about what had happened to his parents. He'd never needed to, since his family and friends already knew. "It all happened a long time ago."

"Hmm."

Sam sat back on his heels again. Haley's brow had creased, and she looked like she might be puzzling through something. "What are you thinking, Haley?"

She shrugged, kept her eyes anywhere but on him. "I'm just wondering."

Waiting patiently for her to continue, he marveled at the fact that telling her had been so easy. For some reason, he'd wanted her to know. "Wondering?" he prompted.

"Do you think losing your parents the way you did at that critical point in your life might have something to do with why you've never *allowed* yourself to become seriously involved with anyone? Maybe you have"—she cast him a furtive glance—"a few unresolved issues surrounding your loss." A few blotches bloomed on her neck and cheeks.

"Perhaps." He waited for the defensiveness to kick in, but it didn't. Instead, her tentative attempt to psychoanalyze him made him want to drag her into his arms and kiss her breathless. Again. Pretty much everything she did elicited that same response. He grinned. "Are you going to bill me for this session, Dr. Cooper?"

"I might." She smiled back. "Thanks for telling me what happened, Sam. I can't imagine what that must have been like for you and your family."

"It's no big deal," he said.

She studied him for a few seconds, and then went back to laying tile. A companionable silence settled between them, and they fell into a rhythm. Trowel mortar, lay tiles, move on, repeat. "You're easy to be around, and you work hard. If you ever get tired of being a paralegal, you can come work for Haney & Sons. We're always on the lookout for good workers."

"Good to know." She smiled. "Kind of makes you feel guilty for charging me so much, doesn't it? I mean, I'm working as hard as you are." She nudged him with her shoulder. "How about we trade what you owe me for the psych session and my labor, and you reduce my bill?"

"Uh, no. You're paying for my expertise, which I am"—he placed his hand over his heart—"graciously sharing with you at no *additional* charge."

"Well, it was worth a try."

"I will agree to buy you dinner on Wednesday, though. How about that?"

"That depends. Where are you taking me?" Her eyes filled with a mischievous glint.

"The Bulldog."

"Do they have lobster on the menu?"

He chuckled. "Not even close."

"Yeah, that's what I figured. Expect my bill for your session within the week."

He laughed again. When had he ever felt this comfortable with a woman before? He'd just told her about his darkest moment, and doing so had left him feeling relieved, closer to her. Before he knew what he intended to do, he dropped the trowel and swept her into his arms, his lips finding hers for a scorching kiss.

Haley gasped and put her arms around his neck. They were both on their knees, and he maneuvered them around so he could hold her against him. His tongue delved into the sweetness of her mouth, and he cradled the back of her head with both hands to deepen the kiss. She groaned and pressed herself closer. Intense longing overpowered him, and it wasn't just for sex. For the first time in his life, he yearned for more—more moments involving closeness and sharing. He burned for her, only for her. *Dangerous.* Where women were concerned, he never lost control. With Haley, he *had* no control.

Much to his regret, she ended the kiss. Her pupils were dilated, and her breathing came in ragged puffs. "Whew." She placed her hands on his wrists where they rested on her shoulders and drew a long breath. Her gaze roamed over his face, and befuddlement clouded her expression. "I don't know what to make of you, Mr. Haney."

A few strands of hair had come loose from her ponytail, and he tucked them behind her ears. A wave of tenderness nearly knocked him on his ass. "I don't know what to make of you, either, Ms. Cooper, and that's the truth."

She nodded and they continued to stare into each other's eyes. He didn't know how to break the spell, or if he even wanted to, but they couldn't keep this up for much longer without falling back into each other's arms. Why was that a bad idea again? Oh, yeah, because Haley was not a one-night stand. She deserved more, and he wasn't sure he was prepared to step up to the plate for what that would entail. He forced himself to break the eye contact first.

"We have a floor to finish, and we don't want this mortar to dry up on us. We should get back to work."

"Right." She crab-walked back to where they'd left off. "I've been meaning to tell you about what I did this past weekend."

"Oh?" Concentrating on bringing his breathing back to normal, he scooped up mortar from the plastic bucket. "What's that?"

"I e-mailed my ex and asked him why he bolted the way he did— only not in those words. Talking to you about him made me realize I need closure. I wanted to thank you for that."

"You're welcome." Her ex was the last thing he wanted to hear about. What if the guy had a change of heart after hearing from her? "Have you heard back?"

"No. I might not ever, but at least I feel better for trying. Either way, I did what I needed to do, and it feels good."

"Would you take him back?"

"Huh?"

"If Michael showed up at your door this week, begging for your forgiveness and a second chance, would you take him back?"

"Absolutely not." She grunted. "I may not be over how it all went down, but I'm definitely over him."

"Good for you, Haley." Grinning, he went back to troweling cement. *Good for me.*

Chapter Ten

Sam would arrive any minute, and she didn't want to keep him waiting. He had a team of children to coach, after all. Haley hurried to change her clothes, doing up the zipper of her flannel-lined jeans on the way to the bathroom to freshen her mascara and lip gloss.

She headed to her living room, the heavy leather boots she'd put on making a clomping sound on her maple floors. She tugged at the waistband of her slightly large flannel-lined jeans. The bulkiness would take some getting used to. Surveying the interior of her front closet, she chose a down parka, scarf, hat and gloves.

The second she closed the closet, Sam knocked. Haley's heart danced around her ribcage as she let him in. He wore a newer—as in not at all his usual scruffy and torn—pair of jeans. And wow, did they fit him well. He also had on a navy sweater under his jacket that made his eyes a darker shade of blue. "Hi," she said a little too breathlessly.

"Hi." The corners of his eyes creased, and his smile was every bit as wide as hers. "Here, let me help you with your coat," he said, taking the parka from her hands.

"Thanks." She slid her arms into the sleeves. Sam lifted her hair out of the collar, and the graze of his knuckles against her skin sent a current of heat curling to her toes. Flustered, she busied herself with stuffing her gloves into her pockets.

"Ready?" he asked, leaning close to her ear.

"Yep." Haley grabbed her scarf and purse and reminded herself to breathe. She followed him outside and locked the front door. "It's going to snow again tonight." Small talk. That's all she could manage until the internal flurry settled.

"I heard," Sam said, taking her elbow as they crossed an icy spot on her sidewalk, kicking up the butterfly riot inside her again, just as she'd begun to settle down.

"Not more than an inch or so, though. My SUV has four-wheel drive, Haley. We'll be fine."

"I wasn't worried." She glanced at his car, noting his cousin sitting in the back.

He led her to the passenger side and opened the door. "Haley, this is my cousin Jerry. Jerry, this is Haley."

"N-nice to meet you," Jerry said, leaning forward.

"Nice to meet you, too, Jerry." Sam hadn't mentioned his cousin had Down's. Haley climbed in, and Sam crossed around the hood to the driver's side. Was he testing her reaction, or was it because it was no big deal to him? It wasn't a big deal to her, either. Her nervousness must be why she was overthinking everything.

"Are you g-gonna coach hockey with us too?" Jerry asked.

"No." Haley twisted around to face him. "I wouldn't know the first thing about coaching hockey. I'll just watch, but if you need me to do something, let me know."

"OK." Looking relieved, Jerry settled back.

"How long have you two been coaching?" She fastened her seat belt.

"This is our third year, right Jer?" Sam turned around in his seat to back out of her driveway.

"R-right."

"The twins are in the Pee Wee League now. The past two years it's been mostly about skill development and learning the game. This is our first year playing actual games and participating in the tournament."

"Oh. How's your team doing?" she asked.

Sam and Jerry shared a comical look, and Sam chuckled. "As well as can be expected for our first year in the association."

"That m-means we s-suck," Jerry blurted. "B-but Jacob and Angie are really g-good. They're my n-niece and n-nephew."

Sam glanced at her. "Other than my cousins, it's an entirely new group of kids, and an entirely new system. We're coming along."

"Y-yeah. We're c-coming along," Jerry echoed.

It only took twenty minutes to arrive at the arena, a squat, concrete building in Highland Park. Sam parked, and turned to her. "We have a bunch of stuff in the back to unload. It'll just take a minute. You can stay in the SUV if you want. It's warm."

"No, I'll help." Haley climbed out and followed them to the back of Sam's SUV. He opened the tailgate and began handing things to Jerry. A big canvas bag full of hockey sticks, a plastic crate holding pucks, and another canvas sack of equipment. "Most of what's in this bag are things our kids left behind." He grinned. "Do you own ice skates, Haley?"

"Of course," she said, hefting the crate of pucks. "And cross-country skis, though it's been a couple of years since I've used either."

"We'll have to skate at Rice Park sometime during the Saint Paul Winter Carnival," he said, closing up the SUV. "I get a kick out of seeing all the ice sculptures and the ice castle."

The winter carnival didn't start until the end of January. He was thinking that far ahead? How long did he think it would take to prove she'd been wrong about him? "Sounds like fun," she said, not exactly committing, but not exactly turning him down either.

"Do you search for the medallion?" she asked. Every year, the carnival organizers hid a medallion somewhere in the city, usually at a park. Throughout the carnival, clues were announced about its whereabouts.

Whoever found the medallion won a bunch of money or a huge prize, like a house.

"No. I don't have the time or the patience for that kind of scavenger hunt." Sam threw one of the sacks over his shoulder and placed his hand at the small of her back. "Lead the way, Jerry."

"OK, S-Sam."

By the time they got all the equipment situated by the rink, kids on both teams began to trickle in.

"Hi, D-Dad," Jerry called, waving enthusiastically.

Haley glanced over her shoulder to find Sam's Uncle Dan coming toward them. He had two children with him, and both wore hockey gear and carried skates. "Are they your niece and nephew, Jerry?"

"Yep. The t-twins."

"Hello, Haley. Nice to see you again." Dan's eyes were fixed on her, and his brow rose slightly in question as his gaze shifted to Sam. "How's the remodeling coming along?"

"The bathroom is completely finished, and we're starting the kitchen install tomorrow," Sam told him. "I'm taking half the day to do the work, and so is Jo."

"Good." Dan handed his grandchildren their helmets. "All right, you two. Mind your Uncle Jerry and Sam, and do your best. I'll be right here in the bleachers." He turned to Haley. "I'm taking Jerry and my grandkids out for pizza after the scrimmage. Would you and Sam like to join us?"

"Thanks, Uncle Dan, but we already have dinner plans." Sam sat the twins down beside the growing number of children on the bench and supervised as they put on their skates. Then he checked the rest of their protective gear.

"I see." Dan glanced from her to Sam. "Well, another time perhaps." He gestured toward the bleachers. "I'm going to go sit down. Play hard. Have fun," he said before leaving.

"Should I go sit in the bleachers too?" Haley asked. "Am I allowed to stay here?"

"You can stay with us, so long as you're behind the plastic." He straightened and surveyed his team. The boys and girls fidgeted and chatted with each other. "Ready to warm up?" Sam asked, his tone going all authoritative. A chorus of assent filled the air. "Helmets and mouth gear on, and let's hit the ice." With a flurry of activity, all the kids left the bench and headed for the ice, taking hockey sticks and pucks as they passed. "Jerry, see that the stragglers are checked in, and then send them out on the ice. Scrimmage starts in fifteen."

"OK, S-Sam." Jerry, clipboard in hand, stood at attention and searched the arena for stray hockey players.

Haley settled herself on the bench and watched Sam put the kids through a number of drills at one end of the ice, while the opposing team's coach did the same at the other end. After the warm-up, the scrimmage began, and Sam turned into Coach Haney on the sidelines.

He used the same *instructor* tone with his team that he used with her when teaching carpentry. He was patient, even-tempered and incredibly focused, encouraging when one of his kids made an error, and redirecting when a few of his team members distracted each other by playing around on the ice. She couldn't take her eyes off him or keep her grin in check.

Haley leapt to her feet and cheered when either team scored a goal. She groaned along with everyone else when either team missed making a goal, or when one of the players fell down on the ice. She knew how time-intensive hockey was, because Frank Junior had played for a couple of years. Coaching took a lot of time, and she found it endearing that Sam was willing to volunteer his free time to coach his cousins' team. He'd make a great dad. Where had that come from?

He'd made it clear he had no interest in ever getting serious, which probably meant he had no interest in becoming a parent. Coaching his cousins might be as close as he ever intended to get to fatherhood, and she'd best keep that in mind.

Her heart wrenched. She should say no to skating at Rice Park or any other outings, or she'd have one heartbreak on top of another to deal with. It would be so easy to fall for Sam. So easy and such a huge mistake. She continued to watch, swallowing against the tightness in her throat. Sam Haney was a great guy. He was considerate, intelligent, fun to be with and good looking. More than good looking, actually.

Too bad, too, because they didn't want the same things at all. A family of her own, sharing her life with one man worthy of her complete trust . . . she wanted the whole package. A fierce yearning rose up to engulf her, followed by a pang of regret.

Maybe it was time she took steps toward finding that elusive happily-ever-after for herself. She could sign up for an online dating service, or at least go out more. Sitting home alone wasn't going to get her where she wanted to be. Unfortunately, where she wanted to be was not part of Sam's life plan, and didn't it just figure *he* was the one she wanted?

Sam placed the canvas bag of hockey sticks into the back of his SUV. "So, what'd you think?" He cast a sideways glance at Haley. He'd been aware of her eyes on him during the entire hockey scrimmage, and he couldn't deny the pride buzzing through him.

"I think watching eight- and nine-year-olds playing hockey is way more fun than watching the Minnesota Wild play professionally."

He raised an eyebrow. "You've been to a Wild's game?"

"Several." She shrugged. "I've also been to baseball games—minor league and major league—and football. Although it's been a while since I've gone to any sporting events, I like team sports."

"What about the Timberwolves and the Lynx?" A brand-new item went on his list of things to like about Ms. Cooper. He'd have to lay his hands on some hockey tickets. If the way she'd cheered for the Pee Wees was anything to go by, they'd have a blast.

"Basketball isn't my favorite. What about you? What's your favorite sport to watch?"

"I'd have to say hockey. I played as a kid and all through high school. I was offered a college scholarship to play for the University of Minnesota."

She flashed him a look of surprise. "Did you take it?"

"Nope." He opened the passenger side door for her, and helped her climb in. Not that she needed help, but it was another excuse to touch her. He crossed around the hood and climbed in.

"Why not?"

He buckled his seatbelt and started the SUV, then maneuvered the truck into the line of vehicles leaving the arena. How would she react to the choice he'd made? *Why do I care?* Ah, but he did.

"Sam, are you going to answer my question? Why didn't you accept the scholarship and play for the Gophers?"

"A couple of reasons," he said, edging his Chevy toward the exit. "One, hockey is a game I love to play. It's strictly a recreational sport for me. Playing college hockey, and perhaps professionally, would've made it something altogether different. It would've become my job. And two, playing professional hockey would've involved lots of pressure to win. Contracts, always on the road, never knowing when I'd be traded off to some other team." He shook his head. "I didn't have any interest in turning something I love into that kind of grind."

"I get that, but what about the college part? You could've gotten an education for free, and you wouldn't have had to go on to play professionally."

"I went to school to become a carpenter." Had he given her another reason to look down her nose at him? He was strictly blue-collar, and always would be. "I didn't have any interest in a four-year degree."

"But—"

"Look, I love what I do and who I do it with. I'm part owner of a thriving business, and I don't ever have to worry about being out of work. I have skills." His grip on the steering wheel tightened, and he kept his eyes on the road. "Maybe what I am doesn't seem like much to you, but I'm happy. I earn a good living, and I get to work with my family." He shot her a challenging look. "As far as I'm concerned, that makes me one hell of a lucky man."

"It's enough, Sam." Haley placed her hand on his forearm, her grip firm. "What you do, who you are . . . it's . . . *you* are definitely more than enough. I'm just trying to figure out what makes you tick. I didn't mean to upset you. You challenged me to spend time with you, so you could prove to me that I was all wrong about you."

Haley bit her lip, and her face blotched up with red patches. "I knew I'd misjudged you weeks ago." She peeked at him through her lashes. "Those things I said when we first met . . . I was embarrassed and feeling defensive. You get that, right?"

His brain was still stuck on *you are definitely more than enough*. Did she mean he was enough for her, or . . . He managed to nod. It took a while for the rest of what she'd said to get through the fog. "Wait." His brow rose. "Did you just say you knew weeks ago that you'd misjudged me?"

"Did I say that?" One side of her sexy mouth turned up.

"I'm pretty sure you did, which means I don't really have anything to prove after all," he teased.

"Ha. That's what you think." She huffed. "I was referring to carpentry, Sam, not your personal life. Remember? I accused you of being incompetent. After working with you a few times, I could see you are very skilled."

Once again she managed to look down her pert nose at him, but the sparkle in her eyes clued him in. "Good save, Ms. Cooper." He chuckled.

He found a parking spot about a block away from The Bulldog. "Wyatt and my sister are meeting us. The three of us hang out here a lot after work, and since I'm giving you a glimpse into my life, I figured this is typical for a Wednesday evening." He unfastened his seatbelt. "I hope that's OK."

"I'm always happy to see Wyatt, and I'm looking forward to meeting your sister." Haley opened her door and climbed out. She joined him on the sidewalk as he entered his information into the parking meter. "I've never been to The Bulldog," she said.

"They have excellent tater tots." He took her elbow to move her away from the curb, placing himself between her and the street as they walked.

She laughed. "Tater tots?"

"Dipped in buffalo sauce." A surge of happiness shot through him at the sound of her laughter, and for some reason, having her beside him made him want to stand taller.

"You're kind of a throwback, Sam." Haley took his arm and nudged him.

"Hmm? A throwback as in catch-and-release?" he teased. "Like a walleye?"

"No, silly." She gave his arm a squeeze. "As in you're a gentleman. You open doors for me, help me with my coat, put yourself between me and the curb. It's really sweet. I want you to know how much I appreciate the effort."

His chest swelled at her praise. "My grandparents' influence. Speaking of opening doors, here we are." He reached ahead of her to open the door to the bar and grill.

Haley scanned the interior. "It's so spacious inside, and I love all those windows. I'll bet there's a great view of Mears Park when it's light out."

"Wyatt's here. I don't see my sister, but I'm sure she'll show up in a few minutes." Sam led her to the high-top table where Wyatt waited.

"Hi, Wyatt," Haley said as she slipped out of her parka and draped it over one of the chairs. "It's good to see you again."

"Good to see you too, Haley. How was hockey?"

"Hockey was great." She took a seat. "The kids were cute, and it was fun to watch Sam in coach mode."

"Where's Jo?" Sam asked as he settled into the chair next to Haley's.

"She should be here any minute. I just got a text from her."

The same waitress who'd given him the I'm-interested-in-you vibe several times in the past few months approached their table, making eye contact with him. Sam tensed. What if she gave him the same vibe in front of Haley? Before the waitress got to them, he leaned close to Haley and put his arm around her shoulders. "What do you feel like tonight? The burgers are good."

Haley shot him a what-just-happened look. "I don't know. I haven't even picked up the menu yet."

"Can I get you something from the bar?" The waitress asked, her expression nothing more than friendly.

Just in case, Sam ran his hand up and down Haley's arm. "I'll have a Michelob in a bottle, and start a tab for the two of us," he told her, nodding toward Haley. "What would you like, Haley?"

"Do you have hard cider?" she asked, glancing at their waitress.

The blonde launched into a list of the hard ciders they carried, and Sam heaved a quiet sigh of relief. Wyatt studied him for a second before ordering a beer for Josey and another for himself.

"Jo's here." Wyatt jutted his chin toward the door.

Josey wended her way through the bar and grill toward them. Her face was flushed from the cold, and her eyes were bright with curiosity. "You must be Haley. I've heard a lot about you."

"And you must be Josey." Haley smiled. "I've heard a lot about you, too. You're installing my dishwasher, disposal and kitchen sink tomorrow."

"I am." Jo shrugged out of her jacket and sat at the empty spot at their table. "And I'm connecting the gas to your new stove."

"I ordered your beer, Jo," Wyatt told her.

"Thanks." She picked up one of the menus. "I am starving, and it's been a long day. I'm ready for a beer and food."

"I told Haley about the tater tots. Do you want to share a couple of orders? Maybe one with the buffalo sauce and another with ranch?"

"Sure." Josey peered at Haley over her menu. "Have you been here before?"

"No, but I've heard about The Bulldog. Didn't somebody drive through the front windows last year?"

"Yeah." Wyatt chuckled. "Just so you know, none of us had anything to do with that."

Sam checked the menu, which he pretty much knew by heart. "We should play darts after we eat. Me and Haley against you two."

"Are you sure you want me on your team, Sam?" Haley asked. "You don't know if I'm any good at darts or not."

"I noticed the dartboard hanging on your wall in the basement when I was bringing up some of your building supplies." He returned her look. "I have confidence in you."

"Hmm." Haley studied her menu, but not before he caught the pleased expression his words elicited.

The waitress came back with their drinks, and they placed their orders. Conversation flowed easily between Haley, his sister and Wyatt, who had gotten over his shyness around her. Sam settled back in his chair, content to observe the interaction between her and his siblings. Haley fit in. She was easy to be with, pretty, smart, funny. Plus, he wanted her in the worst way. Maybe Wyatt was right. Maybe it was time he gave commitment a try.

Gulp. Did he really want commitment? When his parents died, he'd lost the two people most important to him in the entire world. Did he really want to set himself up for the possibility of another painful loss?

Haley laughed at something Wyatt said, and Sam's heart tumbled. The air left his lungs in a whoosh and he couldn't tear his eyes from her. Dammit. His heart had stopped buying what his head had been selling weeks ago—the minute he'd laid eyes on Haley Helen Cooper.

It was nearly eleven when he, Haley and his siblings finally left The bulldog. They stopped on the sidewalk. A light snow had begun to fall, dusting everything in sparkling white.

"This was so much fun," Haley said, a happy grin lighting her features. "I guess I'll be seeing all of you again tomorrow."

"Right," Wyatt said. "Tomorrow is the kitchen install. I'll bet you're eager to have a kitchen again."

"You have no idea." Haley laughed. "I feel like a seven-year-old on Christmas morning."

"Well, I should get you home so you get a good night's sleep," Sam said before turning to his sister. "Where are you parked, Jo?"

"In the same ramp as Wyatt. He'll walk me to my truck."

"OK. Good night. See you tomorrow." Sam steered Haley toward his SUV.

"Night," Wyatt called, moving off in the opposite direction, with Josey beside him.

Sam's mind jumped ahead to good-night kisses with Haley. Would she invite him inside? His blood rushed at the possibility. He drew her close to his side. "So, you had a good time tonight?"

"I did." She peered up at him. "Thank you, Sam. Dinner and darts, a Pee Wee hockey scrimmage . . . tater tots. Who could ask for more?"

"Good." A snowflake landed on her cheek, and he brushed it away. He wanted to kiss her so badly. He couldn't remember ever wanting a woman the way he wanted Haley. When they reached his SUV, he drew out his debit card and paid for the parking before helping her into the passenger seat. "Brrr. Cold tonight," he murmured once he was behind the wheel. "It's supposed to be a nice weekend though."

"Hmm-mm." She rested her head back against the seat.

He started his SUV and pulled onto the city street. "Do you have any plans for Sunday morning?"

She turned his way, a dreamy half smile drawing his attention to her kissable mouth. "No, why?"

"Would you like to go snowmobiling with me?" he asked. "We can take the Lake Elmo Park Trail. It's close."

"Oh." She sat up. "I've never been snowmobiling. Don't I need a helmet?"

"I have an extra. Do you have snow pants?"

"Of course I have snow pants. I'm Minnesotan, born and bred."

"What do you say? I'll pick you up early, and we can go out for breakfast first."

"Sounds like a lot of fun, but . . . Do you think this is a good idea, Sam?"

"I think it's a great idea. You agreed to spend time in my world. Snowmobiling, hockey, hanging out with Wyatt and Jo, this is what I do."

"I know, but . . ." A crease formed between her eyebrows.

"But what?"

"You don't get involved." She shrugged and peered out her window. "If we spend a lot of time together, won't things get complicated? Aren't you worried that I'll want more. I mean—"

"More?" He snorted. "With me? The handsiest handyman in the Twin Cities?"

"No. Not *that* guy." She shifted in her seat. "More with the man who opens doors for me. The man who removes my slivers and kisses away the hurt." She glanced at him for a second. "More with the hockey coach, affectionate brother and excellent carpenter. The *you* I've gotten to know is completely at odds with what I believed about you after that stupid radio show."

He had to swallow a few times before he could respond. "I see what you mean, and I did say I don't do *involved*." Seeing himself through her eyes did a number on his head. And his heart. Taking a risk suddenly seemed . . . worth it where *she* was concerned. "How about we take things one day at a time? I enjoy snowmobiling, and I'd love to share that experience with you. We're friends, aren't we?"

"Friends whose kisses are downright combustible. I don't know, Sam."

So she did feel what he felt. His groin tightened and his blood rushed. "We're adults, Haley. We can—"

"Have strings-free casual sex?" She shook her head. "See, that's what I'm trying to tell you. You don't do *involved* and I don't do *casual*. Things are bound to—"

"I wasn't going to suggest strings-free casual sex, Ms. Cooper. What I was *going* to say is that we are both mature, responsible adults well able to control ourselves." He tossed her a wry look. "Right?"

"Oh. Sorry."

"See? This is exactly why I challenged you to spend time with me, and obviously I have not yet proven to you that I am not the total horn-dog you believe me to be. Hence, snowmobiling on Sunday."

"You win." She chuckled. "I'd love to try snowmobiling."

Sam pulled into her driveway. Now that he'd convinced her they could control themselves in a mature, adult manner, how receptive would she be to making out with him on her living room couch? Not very, he guessed. Talk about painting himself into a corner. He shut off the engine. "I'll walk you to your door."

"You don't have to." She fished her keys out of her pocket.

"Yes, I do." He got out of his SUV and hurried around to her side. Opening her door, he held out his hand for her. "Grandma Maggie would give me an ear-beating if I didn't, and somehow she'd know. She's witchy about stuff like this."

"I think I'd like Grandma Maggie." She took his hand and climbed out.

He led her toward her front door. "I know she'd like you, Haley." He spoke the truth. His entire family would like her. She was a genuinely nice person. Now that he'd ruined any chance of making out with her, he wasn't sure how to end the evening. He stood behind her while she fit her key in the lock.

"I had an amazing time tonight, Sam. Thanks for including me." She turned to smile up at him.

"Thanks for joining me." Sam placed his hands on her shoulders and pressed a chaste kiss on her forehead. "Good night, Ms. Cooper."

"Good night, Mr. Haney." She opened her door and disappeared inside.

Sam strode back to his SUV, adjusting the tightness in the inseam of his jeans. Once again he wondered what it was about Haley that had him jumping through hoops and trying so hard to prove he was . . . what? Dateable? What did that even mean, and why did he want to be dateable? "Control is highly overrated," he muttered.

Chapter Eleven

Haley's alarm buzzed, and she reached out to turn it off before sliding out of her warm cozy bed. Yawning, she stood and stretched. "Better get moving." Her cabinets and appliances were going to be delivered between eight and eleven. Sam and his sister would arrive at noon. She had an hour to bathe, dress and have a toasted bagel before the window of possible delivery opened. "Coffee first."

She padded into the dining room and pushed the Start button on her coffeemaker. Thank goodness she'd had the foresight to set it up last night. *Last night.* A bittersweet smile broke free. No doubt about it, she could fall hard for Sam. She shook her head and sighed. Why had she agreed to go snowmobiling with him?

While she waited for the coffee to brew, she got her old work clothes ready to go for today's kitchen install. Signing up on one of those online dating services suddenly sounded like a really good idea. She needed the distraction. In fact, once she had her coffee, she'd go check out a few sites.

A steaming mug in hand, Haley headed for her office and took a seat at the desk. She sipped her coffee and brought her computer to life. May as well check her e-mail, although at this point, she no longer expected an answer from Michael. She hit the e-mail icon, and her lungs seized. "Oh, God." He'd responded.

Staring at her laptop screen, she wasn't sure whether or not she wanted to know what his reasons for leaving were anymore. She didn't need new wounds. Haley took a fortifying gulp of coffee and forced herself to click on the e-mail.

> *Hi Haley,*
> *Good to hear you're doing well. I know I owe you an explanation. I'm sorry I handled things so poorly, but the closer our wedding got, the more I realized marriage wasn't what I wanted. We started dating so young, and neither of us really ever played the field or spread our wings. It's not that I didn't love you anymore, but it was the way a friend loves a friend. Our relationship was more habit for me than anything else. I didn't feel any passion, and I realized I wasn't ready to settle down. I wanted adventure, to travel and have as many life experiences as I could before taking on the responsibilities of marriage and family. To be honest, I also wanted to date other women. I hope you can find it in your heart to forgive me for ending things the way I did, but it was for the best. I hope we can be friends again one day. I wish you all the best, Haley.*
> *Your Friend, Michael*

It took going through his letter twice before Michael's words hit home. "Adventure? After all the years we were best friends you couldn't talk to me about what you wanted? You just . . . left? Of all the immature, self-centered, stupid . . ." Her hands formed fists in her lap. She was better off without him and his skinny, flat butt.

She blinked back the angry tears and stormed to her bathroom. A nice hot bath, that's what she needed, a good soak to calm her nerves.

She started the water to fill the tub, her hand resting on the very place where she'd sat next to Sam while he removed her sliver—the place where they'd shared their first kiss.

What would Sam have to say about Michael's response? She could hardly wait to tell him. Another hot tear slid down her cheek. When had Sam become her go-to guy?

◆ ◆ ◆

Sam surveyed the newly installed maple cabinets and white granite countertops with flecks of black and gold. Haley had done a fantastic job on the design, and he looked forward to seeing the finished product. She'd chosen a turquoise paint for the walls and black accent pieces. Josey and Haley were moving the new gas stove into place. "You done with everything?" he asked.

"Yep. Everything's been tested, and it's all good to go." Josey gathered her tools and tossed them into their wooden crate.

"Thanks, you two. Everything looks wonderful," Haley said, her hands stuffed into her front pockets.

"Would you mind taking this load to the van, Jo?" Sam asked, putting his drill on top of the pile of tools. "I need to wrap up a few things here before we go."

He'd waited all afternoon to have a minute alone with Haley. Something was bothering her, and that bothered him. She'd been quiet and withdrawn throughout the installation of her kitchen cabinets and counters. Not like her at all, and he missed the sledgehammer-wielding superhero. He needed to find out what had put a damper on her enthusiasm.

"Yeah, sure." Josey slipped into her jacket, eyeing him intently before taking up the crate full of tools. "I'll wait for you in the van. I have a phone call to make, anyway."

"Thanks. I'll be out in a few." The second the door closed, Sam turned to Haley. "Tell me what's bothering you?"

"I'm OK. Really." She brushed some debris off the new granite countertop. "It's just that I heard back from Michael this morning, and it's been on my mind."

Her gaze rose to his, and the hurt he glimpsed in her pretty brown eyes went straight through him to pierce his heart. "What did he have to say for himself?"

"You can read it for yourself if you want." She shrugged.

What he wanted was to haul her into his arms. She needed comfort, and more than anything, he wanted to be the one to make everything in her world all better. He should probably think about that before he got in any deeper than he already was, but this was Haley. Seeing her so dejected scrambled his insides. "Josey drove me here today. Can you give me a ride home? We can read the stupid e-mail together, and then maybe go out for pizza somewhere where we can talk."

She nodded, her eyes bright.

Aw hell. If she cried, he'd lose it. Sam pulled his phone from its halter and texted Josey. She answered right away with an emoticon smiley face and a thumbs-up. He blew out a breath. Clearly she mistook what was going on here. His sister didn't know Haley well enough to have picked up on her unhappiness. Putting his phone away, he moved closer to her. "Let's go see this e-mail."

He followed her to the second bedroom. Haley crossed the room to the desk where her laptop sat. She opened it up, went to her e-mail and stepped back. "Have a seat if you want," she said, gesturing toward the desk.

Sam gave her shoulders a squeeze before he sat down. Then he read. "He walked out on you because he wanted *adventure*? What an ass," Sam barked out. Haley stood next to him. He glanced up at her. "Do you want me to delete this?"

"Please do."

He hit the delete icon and rose from the chair. "He's an idiot."

"A lot of what he says is true." Her mouth turned down. "He and I were friends all through high school. We started dating our senior year. We *were* really young, and—"

"No. He's an idiot." Sam drew her into his arms. "And do you want to know why?"

Haley laid her cheek against his chest and wrapped her arms around his waist. "Sure. Tell me why."

Sam ran his hands up and down her sides. Her sweatshirt had tugged up a bit when she put her arms around him, and his fingers grazed a narrow strip of soft warm skin. Need slammed into him, setting his blood on fire. "Because he was blind to the truth," he whispered, kissing her temple. Her sweet scent enveloped him, and he tightened his hold.

Haley leaned her head back, and her gaze roamed over his face, stopping at his mouth before staring into his eyes. "And what truth is the truth, Sam?"

"The fool didn't realize . . ." He shook his head. "Haley, you *are* the adventure. You're beautiful, brilliant, funny, gutsy and sexy as hell." Her sudden breathy intake shot straight to his groin. "And with a sledge-hammer in your hands, you're a goddess."

"*That's* how you see me?" She smiled. "A sexy goddess with a sledge-hammer, huh?"

"You have no idea." He cupped her perfectly rounded bottom and pressed her against his raging erection. "See what you do to me?" He crushed her to him and kissed her with all the longing that had been coursing through him since the first day she looked down her nose at him.

Her arms came up to circle his neck. He deepened the kiss, his tongue plunging in and out of her luscious mouth. He couldn't resist the temptation and slid his palms to the exposed skin at her waist. Running his hands under her sweatshirt and up along her sides, he grazed the undersides of her breasts with his thumbs. Desire weakened his knees—and obliterated his good sense.

She moaned, her breath mingling with his. She was perfect in his arms, so feminine, soft and small. He wanted to protect her, make her smile. Hell, he wanted her writhing and naked beneath him, and to hear her call out his name as she came apart in his arms. Her warmth seeped into the deepest recesses of his soul, imprinting herself there.

His heart pounded, and he could hardly draw enough breath to keep himself upright. Could wanting someone this much cause a man's heart to explode? Because his might be close. The way she responded to him had him throbbing and aching to completely lose himself in her.

What was he doing? If he took this any further, would she think he'd taken advantage of her vulnerability in the wake of her ex's e-mail? Of course she would, and he wouldn't blame her. She'd slap that lothario label right back on his ass, and he'd worked so hard to get her to see him as more than his reputation. *Damn.*

It took every ounce of willpower he possessed to remove his hands from her silky skin. Ending the kiss, he gripped her upper arms and pressed his forehead against hers. "I can't lie to you," he rasped. "I want you, Haley. I've wanted you from the moment I first laid eyes on you, but . . ."

"But you don't do *relationships.*" She sucked in a long shuddering breath, her forehead still pressed to his. "I get it." She moved out of his arms. "It's OK, Sam."

"No." He shook his head slowly. "Trust me on this—you don't get it at all."

She turned away from him. "Don't I?"

"Nope."

"Care to enlighten me?"

"Nope."

"Well . . . thanks for being my shoulder to cry on tonight." She looked everywhere but at him. "Do you mind if I take a rain check on going out for pizza? I'm really tired. It's been a weird day."

"That's fine." He'd hurt her. That's the last thing he'd wanted to do. "Haley . . ."

"Come on, Sam. Let's get your things." She walked out of the room, heading for her kitchen.

He followed, racking his brain for the right words to say to make the tension disappear. "We're still on for snowmobiling and breakfast Sunday." He didn't dare leave it open to discussion. "I'll pick you up at eight."

Haley grabbed his coat from where he'd dropped it over a five-gallon bucket. She handed it to him, still avoiding eye contact. "I'll be ready."

He took his coat and put it on. "Monday evening we'll install the tile backsplash. Tuesday and Wednesday I'm tied up with hockey, and Thursday is Christmas Eve. I won't be able to paint the kitchen or do the cleanup until the following week. It'll take an entire day to finish things up here."

"I know. You already told me."

"Haley . . ."

Finally her eyes met his. "What?"

"You're wrong," he said, his voice raspy. "Whatever you're thinking right now? You have it all wrong." One side of her mouth quirked up, but all he saw in her eyes was uncertainty and sadness.

"Well." Her chin came up a notch. "I guess that makes one more thing you'll have to prove to me then."

He hauled her into his arms and kissed her. Hard. He couldn't bare his soul, couldn't admit to her the feelings he hadn't yet dared admit to himself. "Sunday." Sam let her go and strode to the front door. "Be ready."

"Sam," she called.

But he kept walking, too emotionally churned up to hash things out with her right now. He got all the way to her driveway before he remembered—*she* was his ride home. *Dammit.* He stomped his foot and turned around.

Her garage door rose. He groaned and scrubbed his face with both hands. His balls ached, and he didn't know if he was coming or going. Haley Cooper was driving him crazy. Why oh why had he felt the overwhelming need to prove himself to her in the first place? She didn't just confuse him—hell, she terrified him.

"Were you planning on walking home?" Haley grinned and dangled her car keys in the air.

"I was thinking about it." He threw his head back and stared at the starless sky. "It's awfully cold out though, and it looks like it might snow again." He heaved a sigh. "Sure could use a ride."

Haley laughed. Dropping his head to glare at her, he walked toward her car. "You say a word about this to Wyatt or Jo, and I *will* get even."

"I was afraid I was going to have to chase you down the street in my car."

"Ha, ha. Very funny."

"I thought so." She laughed again and slid into the driver's seat of her car.

His tension eased, and he grinned. Maybe crazy wasn't such a bad place to be after all.

New snow sparkled under a cloudless sky, and the air was crisp, fresh and cold. Good thing the helmet Sam had loaned her had enough room for sunglasses. Haley fastened the strap under her chin and put her mittens back on. The crunch of boots on snow behind her made her smile.

She'd been teasing Sam all morning about the way he'd stormed out of her house the other night forgetting she was his ride home. It hadn't surprised her to learn he lived in a large, nondescript apartment building. The man couldn't even commit to a place of residence. Sad. A carpenter as good as he was should have a home of his own, a house custom built with his own two hands. There wasn't anything he couldn't do when it came to construction. Except the electrical maybe, but he had Wyatt for that.

"Let's go." Sam came to stand beside her. "Looks like we're the first ones to ride this morning."

"Are you going to let me drive that thing?" She followed him to his snowmobile.

"Umm." He lifted his helmet from where he'd hung it on the handle and swung his leg over the machine. "Probably not today. Climb on and put your arms around me."

She did as she was told, snuggling close enough that her thighs caressed his perfect backside. "So this is why you suggested we go snowmobiling," she teased, circling her arms around his waist.

He twisted around, his grin visible behind the plastic visor of his helmet. "Busted."

How many women had he taken snowmobiling? *Don't go there.* Why had he stopped kissing her Thursday night? She'd definitely been willing, and wasn't he the man who never passed up an opportunity? She wanted Sam, even knowing being intimate with him would only lead to heartache. He wanted her too. He'd made that perfectly clear. And what had he meant when he said she had things all wrong?

The snowmobile jerked forward, and he steered down the marked trail at a sedate speed until they'd passed the first distance marker, then he accelerated. Haley squealed and tightened her hold. His laughter flowed back to her, as snow sprayed up around them. Trees and fields flew by, and they bounced and raced over the trail. "This is great," she shouted. He nodded. They went over a rise, and for a few glorious seconds they rode nothing but air. Her cheeks ached from smiling so hard. Why hadn't she ever gone snowmobiling before?

The trail didn't make a loop like she'd expected, but veered away from the regional park onto another trail. They had to cross a road, which took them to another path leading them through farm fields. Haley surveyed the gorgeous landscape, rolling hills, fields and forest. They passed a couple of small frozen lakes along the way. She poked Sam's shoulder to get his attention. He slowed, and leaned his ear closer to her. "Do you ever ride on the lakes or rivers?" She had to shout to be heard over the sound of the engine.

He called back, "All the time. Just to be on the safe side though, I don't ride on ice until I'm sure it's safe. January, usually."

They raced on, but then he slowed and pointed across a pond. Three white-tailed deer stood together, their eyes and ears turned toward them, alert to any danger. He pointed again, and she scanned the area he'd indicated. A large bald eagle sat perched on the branch of a pine. The raptor paid no attention to them and continued to clean its wing feathers. She squeezed him to let him know she'd seen, and he patted her hands.

As cold as it was, her insides warmed. It touched her that Sam wanted to share this with her. Shortly after their view of the eagle, he turned the snowmobile around and headed back the way they'd come. All too soon they were back in the parking lot.

Haley helped him load the machine onto the trailer hitched to his SUV, and then set her helmet in the cargo space beside Sam's. "*That* was great. I might have to buy myself a snowmobile." She frowned. "But then I'd have to buy a new vehicle, one with towing capacity."

He fastened the last strap holding the snowmobile in place. "Toys are expensive." Once the machine was secure, Sam unzipped his snowmobile suit, worked it off and stowed it in the back of his SUV. He grabbed his jacket and put it on. "I enjoy getting out of the city and seeing the wildlife. St. Croix Park is another great place to go snowmobiling. We can go there next time if you want, and I'll teach you how to drive."

There he went again, making plans. What were they doing? Haley opened the passenger side door and sat sideways to take off her boots so she could get out of her snow pants. She settled herself in her seat and tossed the snow pants in the back, her mind crowded with questions.

Sam started the SUV and leaned back. "You liked snowmobiling, I take it."

His face was ruddy from the wind, and he had a bad case of helmet hair. His lopsided smile gave him a boyish appearance, and her heart skipped a beat. "I loved it," she said, and he rewarded her with a kiss. His lips were cold, and he smelled like the outside, fresh. Clean. She shivered, but not from the temperature.

"I knew you would," he murmured against her lips. He moved away and steered the car out of the parking lot.

"Sam . . ." She tugged at her seatbelt.

"Hmm?"

"Why did you stop Thursday night? You know, when we were kissing."

He shot her a sideways look. "You were hurting, Haley."

"Ah," she said, nodding slowly. "You didn't want to take advantage. You were being a gentleman."

"Something like that," he muttered.

"I wasn't hurting *that* badly." She huffed out a breath. "Mostly I was angry. Anyway, I'm over it."

He chuckled low in his throat. "Good to know."

What did that mean? If she invited him in, would they take up where they'd left off? Should she invite him in? By the time he pulled into her driveway, her mouth had gone completely dry. *Be brave.* "Would you like to come in for coffee?"

"I'd love to, but I can't." He opened his door. "I've got stuff I need to do today." He climbed out and came to her side of the SUV to help her out. "This was fun, Haley. We'll have to do it again sometime." He walked with her to her door.

Confusion and horniness had stolen her ability to speak. He'd turned her down again. She nodded. Sam waited while she put her key in the lock. "Thanks," she managed to mumble. "I had a lot of fun." Pushing her door open, she took a step.

He turned her around by her jacket. His eyes bored into hers for a second, and then he hauled her into his arms. All the air left her lungs the minute his mouth met hers. Wrapping her arms around him, she kissed back, desperate to get closer. Much, much closer. The sound of his heavy breathing sent curls of heat spiraling to her very core, causing an answering throb. Just as quickly as it had begun, Sam ended the kiss and set her an arm's length away. Damn his long arms.

"I'll see you on Monday," he said, his voice husky. He turned from her and strode to his car.

She nodded again, but he wasn't looking. Wasn't he the guy who saw sex as his favorite recreational sport? The guy who didn't turn down women who threw themselves at him?

Frustrated, and even more confused, she tromped into her house, slammed the door shut and let out a loud roar. Sam Haney was making her crazy. "Enough with the *proving yourself* crap already," she muttered. What the hell did he want from her?

Yawning, Haley leaned away from her desk and checked her phone for the time. She had half an hour to go before she could leave work without getting disapproving looks. It was all Sam's fault she was so tired. She'd tossed and turned all night trying to figure out whether he was toying with her, or if he really was trying to prove he wasn't a total hound dog.

Her stomach flipped. She'd see him again in a few hours. They were installing the tile backsplash tonight. She needed advice, and she needed it badly enough to embarrass herself to get it. Haley dragged herself down the hall and knocked on Brent's office door.

"Come in," Brent called.

"I need help. Do you have a minute?"

"Sure." He closed his laptop. "Have a seat."

She dropped into a chair. "You remember Sam, the blue-collar stud you met the night of the Christmas party?"

"Yeah, what about him?"

"I want him."

"Of course you do." One side of his mouth turned up. "I'm guessing the feeling is mutual."

"He says he wants me, too, but . . ." She threw up her hands. "Every time we . . . start . . . things, *he's* the one to stop them. Why would he do that, Brent?"

He laughed. "I'm going to need more to go on than that."

"Don't laugh." She glared. "This is hard for me."

He crossed his heart and squelched his grin. "OK. Talk to me."

"Remember I told you he asked me out that night?" She waited for his nod. "Well, what I didn't tell you is that he has this need to prove to me that I'm all wrong about him, that I misjudged him because of that radio show, *Loaded Question*."

"Wait." Brent's brow lowered. "Are you telling me he's the guy every single female at this firm was talking about a month ago, the one who admitted on air—"

"Yes." She nodded. "Sam Haney, the handsiest handyman in the Twin Cities."

"You *hired* him, knowing he—"

"No. My *mother* hired him." She covered her face with her hands. "Oh, God. This is so complicated. Forget I said anything. I'll figure it out on my own." She shot up from her chair.

"Haley, sit down. Start from the beginning, and give me the short version."

"Are you sure?" She sat back down. "We're still on the clock."

"I'm sure. That's why I asked for the short version." He leaned back in his leather chair. "Start talking."

As concisely as possible, she outlined her mother's dastardly plan and everything that had happened since. "So, that's why he wants to prove to me that I have him all wrong," she said.

"Huh," Brent said, nodding. "Well, it's obvious."

"It is?" She frowned.

"Think about it, Haley. If he didn't have feelings for you, if he didn't care, he wouldn't feel the need to prove anything, and he certainly wouldn't have stopped at kissing." He chuckled. "Poor drooler. Probably doesn't even realize what's happening."

"What's happening?"

"The man who swore he doesn't do relationships is falling into one. With you."

She gasped. "You think?"

"I know. Been there. Wrote the book." He tsked and shook his head. "And what about your mother? How does she feel about the fact that you're dating the one-night stud she set you up with?"

"She doesn't know. I haven't said a word. My personal life is none of Trudy's business."

Brent leaned back and laughed. "Oh, I so want to be there when she finds out."

"You promised you wouldn't laugh," she grumbled.

"Sorry. Can't help it. Ahhh," he sighed, swiping at his eyes. "Haven't laughed this hard in a while. If this were a reality TV show, I'd be your biggest fan."

"Thanks." Haley rose again, glancing at the fancy clock on his wall. "You've been a great help," she clipped out.

"Haley, do you care about this guy, or is it just lust?"

"I care." There was that stomach flip thing again. "But—"

"No buts. Here's the thing. He cares too, and I'm sure it's freaking him out. Be patient. Any guy willing to work this hard to prove himself is a man worth the risk. Give it time."

"Yeah, maybe, but given his past and what I know about him, things could go either way. He could bolt." *Like Michael.* And where would that leave her? With a few more home repair skills and her heart in shambles for the second time in less than a year.

"There's always that possibility. Unfortunately, there are no guarantees for any of us, no matter what the circumstances. Taking emotional risks is not for the faint of heart."

She headed for the door. "That's for sure. Thanks, Brent. You've given me lots to think about. I'd better get going." Was Brent right? Did Sam have feelings for her, other than the obvious lustful kind? She ticked off the evidence, along with the pros and cons of continuing down the path she was on with him.

Bottom line, Sam had issues, but she wanted him anyway. Now, how could she go about getting him past the point where he pushed her out of his arms? "Damn, I'm about to throw myself at the handyman," she mumbled. Hadn't she sworn not to be one of *those* women? Shaking her head at her own idiocy, she gathered her things and headed home.

Chapter Twelve

Sam drove into the parking lot at Haney & Sons and pulled in next to Josey's truck. "I'm going to go inside and make a sandwich before I head to Haley's. See you tomorrow, Jo."

"Yep. See you." His sister hopped out of the van and climbed into her car, taking off in a big hurry.

Was she going out with someone tonight? He still hadn't gotten over the surprise of hearing she dated. How could he not have known? Well, if a husband and family were what she wanted, he hoped she'd find someone really special. He stomped his boots on the step and walked inside, thermal mug in hand. His grandfather stood by the sink, rinsing out a mug. The kitchen smelled like fresh coffee. "Working late, Grandpa Joe?"

"Oh, not too late. I have a few bids to go through, and then I'll head home." He moved to the coffeepot and poured himself a cup. "How's being back on construction working out for you, Sam?"

"It's fine. The job we're working on will be finished on schedule." Sam yawned and poured coffee into his thermal mug. He hadn't been sleeping well lately.

Grandpa Joe leaned a hip against the counter. "Dan says he ran into one of our clients at your hockey game last Wednesday night. Was she there with you?"

He nodded, his heart thumping. "Haley Cooper, and it was a practice scrimmage, not a game."

"I see. Wyatt says she's a real nice gal, a paralegal. He told me you and this client joined him and Josey for dinner after the hockey scrimmage." Grandpa Joe fixed Sam in his sights and took a sip of his coffee. "Is that right?"

When had all this talking about him gone on? He nodded again. "She is nice, Grandpa. Really nice." And sexy, beautiful, smart—he was in too deep and didn't know how to get out—or even if he wanted to get out. Wait. Was Grandpa Joe about to lecture him about some rule against dating clients? Shit, what if Gramps asked if he and Haley were having sex, or he brought up his pre-radio-show activities again? The last thing he wanted was to talk about sex with his grandfather.

What else had Wyatt shared? Sam couldn't remember whether or not he'd mentioned snowmobiling to his brother, but hiding things from his grandfather had *never* worked. *Play it cool, like it's no big deal.* "Haley and I also went snowmobiling on Sunday." His heart hadn't gotten the memo about playing it cool. The thing hammered against his ribs with punishing force.

"Ah, I see." Grandpa Joe's bushy eyebrows lowered. "You're not quite done with her remodel yet, are you?"

"No, not quite, but almost. I'm putting in a tile backsplash in her kitchen tonight, and then all there is left is painting the kitchen and cleanup. I'm taking care of both the Monday after Christmas."

"Is she the reason you wanted to move to construction?" Grandpa Joe's bushy eyebrows lowered even further. "Are you serious about this girl?"

"Serious?" He cleared his throat, embarrassed by the way his voice squeaked. "We've been out twice. No, she's not the reason I switched to construction, and no, it's not serious." He screwed on the top of his thermal mug so tight he might never get it off again. "I'd better get going."

"Well," Grandpa Joe said, straightening away from the counter, "I know I don't have to remind you to be careful. She's a client until after the final walk-through on the job has been completed." He reached over and patted Sam's cheek. "Serious or not, it's good to hear you're dating a nice girl. Your grandmother and I just want you to be happy. You know that, right?"

"Yeah, I know, Gramps." *Happy?* He *had* been happy. His life had been simple, uncomplicated and completely unencumbered—exactly how he'd wanted it to be. And then Haley Cooper happened. Now he was mostly obsessed, missing sleep and finding it difficult to breathe— or eat. Sam averted his gaze and rolled his eyes. *Happy?* Not hardly. "See you tomorrow, Grandpa."

"Yep. Bright and early." Grandpa Joe started down the hall toward his office.

Speaking of eating, he probably should make that sandwich, since he'd be working. Sam scrounged through the fridge and slapped a ham-and-cheese sandwich together before heading to his van. On the drive to Haley's, he thought about what his grandfather had said. It was the subtext that mattered. Grandpa Joe had warned him and given him his blessing all in one short conversation. Cagey old coot.

The drive to Haley's house took about fifteen minutes when there wasn't any traffic, but the closer it got to Christmas, the thicker the traffic, and the longer rush hour lasted. Inching his way to her neighborhood, one of the nicer areas in Saint Paul, he downed his meal. He parked his van behind the dumpster and shut off the engine. One part of him wanted to run to her door, scoop her up and kiss her breathless all the way to her bedroom. The terrified part of him wanted to walk on eggshells around her, keep his distance and lock his heart in a vault.

Why did you stop Thursday night? A blatant invitation if ever he'd heard one, and he'd heard a few. He glanced at her house. "She's a client until after the last walk-through," he repeated the warning part of his grandfather's little talk. That bought him some time to figure things out, keep Haley an arm's length away. "I can do this." He climbed out and unloaded what he needed from the back of his van.

Haley waited for him at her front door, her smile causing its usual internal stir. The impact of all that warmth and adorableness staggered him every time. "Evening, Ms. Cooper."

She held the door open wide for him. "Good evening, Mr. Haney. I cooked my dinner in the new kitchen tonight," she said, her eyes sparkling. "It's wonderful."

Pride swelled his chest and he smiled back. "Good. Are you ready to install the backsplash?"

She took a rubber band from her pocket and lifted her arms to put her hair up in a ponytail. Her breasts lifted in the process, drawing his attention. Where was the old sweatshirt she usually wore when they worked? Tonight she had on a red, long-sleeve T-shirt that accentuated every alluring feminine curve.

She stepped closer, breasts still thrusting, and glanced at him through her lashes. Blood rushed to his groin. *What the hell is she up to?*

"I am ready," she said, her smile a tad too enticing for the question at hand. "I took half the day off, and I've already taped off and covered the counters, removed the outlet covers and measured each area with a mark at the center point like you showed me." She reached out and touched his arm. "I also marked the one-eighth-inch expansion space at the top and bottom."

He chuckled and followed her to the kitchen. "You're hired."

She turned to beam at him over her shoulder. Was she wearing more makeup than usual tonight? *Uh-oh.* His pulse surged, and heat crept up his neck. "The backsplash mortar will have to dry for twenty-four hours before we can do anything else. We'll take care of the grout and the sealer the same day we paint." He scanned the room, careful to keep his eyes off Haley. He and his brother had already prepped the walls, so they were ready to go.

Sam filled a bucket with the mortar and water and crouched down to stir the mixture to the consistency of peanut butter. With Haley hovering next to him, brushing her hip against his shoulder, concentrating turned into a monumental effort. She was wearing perfume tonight, because, yeah, that was a new smell wafting over him. Enticing, but he preferred her natural scent, just her and the shampoo she used with a dash of laundry detergent or dryer sheets. He'd make a mint if he could bottle the way Haley smelled.

Trying his best to ignore the signals she was sending, he pondered the obvious changes in her attitude. Michael had responded to her e-mail. Her confidence had been shaken, and she'd been hurt. Did she look to *him* to be her rebound guy? No thanks. Rebound guy was the last thing he wanted to be to her. Frowning, he blew out a breath and went to work, troweling mortar onto the wall and setting the meshed sheets of tile.

A few hours later, he stood back to admire the job, Haley beside him. The tiles she'd chosen had flashes of turquoise, umber, black and gold, which looked great with the counters, and would go nicely with the paint she'd chosen. "What do you think?" he asked, glancing sideways at her.

"I think it's amazing." Sighing happily, she moved around the room, studying each section of the small colorful tiles. "My kitchen and bathroom are perfect, way better than I imagined." She turned to face him. "You know what? I'm having a New Year's Day open house to show off my new updates. I think you should come. It will be very casual, my family and a few friends. I think everyone would love to meet the man responsible for this," she said, gesturing around the room. "Plus, there will be tons of food."

Adrenaline rushed through his veins. Her family . . . Did he want to come face-to-face with the woman who had wanted to use him to fix her daughter? "Hmm, I don't know, Haley. Your mom——"

"You aren't the man my mother assumed you were, Sam. You've proven that over and over. I want her to see how wrong she was about you, and maybe she'll get how inappropriate it was for her to set us up the way she did."

"You want to rub her nose in it." He snorted.

"Don't you?" she asked.

"Eh." He rubbed the back of his neck. "I get that you want to end her meddling. You said as much, but I don't know that *I* want to be the means to accomplish that particular end."

"I don't want you to be the means to that end either," she said, her tone earnest. "I was thinking more in terms of *we*. We were both set up, Sam. I want Trudy to see how much I like and respect you. What she did was wrong, but look at the good that came from it. We triumphed over her insanity."

But they hadn't risen above or triumphed. Trudy had wanted him to make a pass at Haley. Every time they got together, things between them moved a little closer to the bedroom. "You respect and like me?" He raised his brow, feigning surprise.

"You know I do."

Her shy smile at the admission, a few blotches blooming on her cheeks, and he melted. "All right. I'll come to your open house." Even though he had doubts—serious misgivings, actually—he couldn't refuse her.

"Thank you, Sam. Extend the invitation to Wyatt and Josey. I'd love to have them join us. They're both part of this remodel."

"I will." He'd managed to keep his hands to himself all evening, but sexual tension flared again as Haley helped him take off the plastic sheets covering her counters. She brushed up against him, made sure their hands touched and gave him all the green-light signals. She wanted him as much as he wanted her, and the air grew thick and hot. *Gulp.* She's a client until after the last walk-through. "I'm going to go put this stuff in the trash. I'll be right back for the rest."

He hauled the bucket of leftover mortar and debris to the dumpster. The frigid night air did little to cool his lust. It would be all right to kiss Haley good night, wouldn't it? So long as he didn't take it any further. They'd kissed before. Nothing new there. On the way back to her door, he gave himself permission for one good-night kiss. He drew a long breath before walking inside.

Haley was humming along to the radio, some popular station. Grinning, he followed the sound to the kitchen. At least she could carry a tune, even if he didn't care much for her choice of music. She was busy arranging things on her counter, a toaster, her coffeepot and a few ceramic containers holding cooking utensils. "Hey," he said. "It's going to be a while before we see each other again."

She glanced at him over her shoulder. "I guess so."

"I hope you have a great Christmas, Haley," he said.

"I hope you do too, Sam." Her expression softened, and her eyes filled with warmth.

"Would you like to go snowmobiling on Sunday? We can head to St. Croix Park this time."

"I'd like that. Remember, you said you'd teach me how to drive your snowmobile."

"Like you'd let me forget." He moved closer and put his hands on her waist. "Where's the mistletoe when you need it?" She gave a husky laugh that slid down his spine in an erotic shiver.

"Since when do you need mistletoe?" She laid her hands on his chest.

"Good point. I don't." He drew her close and kissed her. His body responded in record time. On the she-turns-me-on scale of one to ten, Haley easily scored a twenty. What was it about this woman? She rendered him hard, breathless and aching in under ten seconds. He slid his tongue into her mouth. So sweet. Everything about her was sweet, from the way she felt in his arms to her innate goodness. He deepened the kiss, cradling her face and slanting her head for better access. He burned for her.

Haley pressed herself close and tugged at the tee under his flannel shirt. Her hands slid up his bare back, and he backed her up against the counter, thrusting his hips against her. His grandfather's warning echoed in his head. Groaning, he reached around and gripped her wrists, bringing them around to press her palms against his pounding heart. He broke the kiss and struggled to bring himself under control. "Haley . . ."

Her eyes were hazed with passion. He'd put that sexy look on her face, and that humbled him, turned him on even more. She opened her mouth to speak, and he feared she might ask him to stay. He knew full well he wouldn't be able to refuse her. "I'd better get going. I have a long day tomorrow."

The passion in her expression turned to confusion and hurt. "All right."

She tried to step out of his arms, but he pulled her close again. "I'm looking forward to spending Sunday with you." He kissed her once more. She deserved an explanation, but he didn't want to hand her an excuse. Truth was, he had no idea what to say. He wanted her more than he'd ever wanted anyone, and the powerful feelings roiling through him scared him half to death.

He couldn't say with any certainty what role he wanted to play in her life. The only thing he was sure of was that he couldn't hand her a lame excuse, like "Grandpa Joe reminded me you're still a client, which was a veiled reminder to behave myself." He ran his knuckles down her cheek. "We'll grab lunch or a late breakfast on the way."

She nodded, and he let her go. "If it's any consolation," he said, his voice gruff, "I'm just as confused and turned on as you are."

"Is that why you keep stopping what *you* start?" Her chin came up, a spark of irritation lighting her eyes. "You're *confused*?"

"That about sums it up. Would you rather I didn't kiss you? Because, I don't know if that's possible. I'm *trying* to do the right thing here. I'm trying to be a better man."

"I see." She averted her gaze. "Well, I am still a client, and I'm sure you've taken lots of flak about—"

"You have no idea, but it's not about that. It's about who I am, and how I want you to see me."

"Oh, Sam," she said, turning back to face him. "I see *you*."

"Do you?" He searched her eyes, trying to catch a glimpse of some sense of himself reflected back in her steady gaze. "I never was that guy on the radio show, Haley. Things just kind of spiraled out of control." He swallowed hard. "And, yeah, I went with the flow."

"But that's over now," she said. "Right?"

He nodded and cleared his throat. "Well, I really do have to go. I'll see you on Sunday around ten. Will that work?"

Haley went up on tiptoe and gave him a quick kiss on the cheek. "That'll work. I'll be ready."

Sam grabbed the rest of his stuff and left. *I see you.* He'd pay good money to hear what was going on inside her head right now. Damn, but leaving her was becoming increasingly difficult the more time he spent with her. How had that happened, and what did he intend to do about it?

Maybe the way she affected him was strictly testosterone driven. After all, he hadn't been with a woman since *Loaded Question* had aired. If he slept with Haley, would he be free from this hold she had on him? He snorted. "Doubt it." Besides, he couldn't sleep with her for the sole purpose of breaking the spell she'd put him under. She wasn't that kind of woman. His breath hitched. What if he couldn't get Haley out of his system? Then what?

◆ ◆ ◆

Haley popped into Kathy and Felicia's office on the way to hers. "Hey, are you two free on New Year's Day?"

"Sure." Kathy looked up from her keyboard.

"I am," Felicia said. "Why, what's up?"

"I'm having an open house to show off my new kitchen and bathroom." She handed them each an invitation. "From five until whenever for you two, even though the invitation says 'til ten. Bring something to share. I'm providing the beer and wine and some other goodies."

Kathy studied the card. "Can I bring Blake?"

"Absolutely." Haley grinned. "Sam will be there too."

"He will?" Felicia's brow rose. "And Trudy? Did you invite your mother to this shindig?"

"Yes, but . . . I was so wrong about Sam. He's not like everyone thinks. He's sensitive, considerate, sweet . . ." She pointed at both of them. "Promise me you'll be nice to him. I didn't invite him because I want my mom's scheme to backfire. I invited him because he deserves credit for the incredible job he did on my house, and I want people to get to know him the way I do."

"Oh, my Gawd, you've fallen for the handyman," Felicia chortled.

"Shhh." Haley checked the hallway, then moved further inside the office. "Maybe a little," she admitted. "We've been out twice now, and we're going snowmobiling this coming Sunday. But I don't know what to think." She shrugged. "He won't . . . I mean, we . . ." Her face grew hot. "I want him, but every time things heat up between us, he pulls back."

"Hmm." Felicia frowned. "So he gets handy with every woman *except* you?"

"No. It's not like that. He says he's done with being the hands-on handyman. He told me he stops things between us because he's trying to be a better man."

"And you believe him?" Kathy asked, her expression inscrutable.

"I do." Defensiveness on Sam's behalf roared to life. "I've gotten to know him really well these past two months. I've spent time with him and some of his family. I've seen how he is in his personal life. He got caught up in something that was too tempting to turn down, that's all."

"OK, Haley." Kathy shrugged. "If you believe him, then I'm willing to give the man a chance. But if he hurts you, I will hunt him down and kick his ass."

Haley grinned. "He has a great ass."

Felicia giggled, and Haley flashed her a grin. "Do you two want to go out for lunch today?" Haley asked.

"Only if you're willing to give up a few more details about your handyman." Felicia waggled her eyebrows at her.

"I can do that. Plus, I want to tell you about my e-mail to Michael, and his response."

"What?" Kathy's brow shot up. "You e-mailed that skinny twerp? Why didn't you tell us?"

"I haven't had the chance. We'll talk about it over lunch. I'd better go get some work done." Haley backed out of their office. "Later."

Should she tell her mom she'd invited Sam to her open house? No. It wasn't like she'd invited him to Sunday dinner to meet the family. This was an open house—casual, with people coming and going. She was doing the right thing. So, why did she feel as if she needed to justify her actions—to herself?

Trudy picked up her phone and dialed her sister's number. Smiling, she eyed Haley's open house invitation while she waited.

"Is that you, Trudy?"

"It is." She rolled her eyes. "Who else would be using my phone to call you?"

"Never gets old." Nanci chuckled. "What's up?"

"Did you get the invitation for Haley's open house?"

"I did, and I'm looking forward to seeing her new kitchen."

"Me too. Speaking of her remodeling job, I've decided to give up on Sam the Handyman. I have a new plan, and I've already set it in motion."

"Oh? Why is that? Did Haley say something?"

"No, but . . ." Haley liked the handyman a little too much, which concerned her. "It was a mistake to throw them together. I'm afraid Haley has no idea what kind of man he is, and I want to distract her."

"How? Wait. Let me guess. You've pretended to be Haley and set up a profile for her on Match or some other dating site."

"No. Even better."

"Ha! OK, let's hear it. What have you done?"

"I talked to a few friends, asked around to see if anyone knew of a nice young man who might be available and looking to date."

"Hmm."

Trudy forged on, before her sister could snuff out the beginnings of her newest tactic. "Turns out the Meyers have become friends with their new neighbors. The Andersons recently moved into their neighborhood, and they have a son who just finished graduate school. He's accepted a job in Minneapolis and has moved home with his parents while he looks for a place of his own and gets situated with the new job."

"OK, and exactly how does that help Haley?"

"Since he's new to the area, he's eager to meet people his age." Trudy braced herself for a squashing comment. "Frank and I met with the Andersons at the Meyers', and I offered to introduce their son David to Haley. He's a very nice-looking young man."

"He was open to meeting her?"

"Absolutely." She drew a breath. "What do you think?"

"I think it's great. You should've maybe done something like this to begin with."

"I agree, but I have to admit I'm glad Frank and I helped Haley put her house back together. No harm; no foul. Right?"

"We'll see."

She should've known Nanci would throw a fly into the soup. "What do you mean by that?"

"I don't mean anything by it, other than *we'll see*. I have to get going. Today is the day I'm doing the grocery shopping for our Christmas dinner. I'll see you Christmas day."

"All right. Do you want me to come a little early to help?"

"Come as early as you like. We're eating at six."

"In that case, Frank and I will be there around four." Trudy ended the call. Nanci was right. She should've tried to fix Haley up with a nice young man from the start. What had she been thinking, setting her daughter up with Sam the handyman? She shook her head, relieved that nothing had come of her stupid plan.

Chapter Thirteen

Sam checked his new haircut in the mirror again before wiping the traces of shaving cream from his face and slapping on some aftershave. His nerves were strung taut about Haley's open house, but at least Wyatt and Josey would be there. Including Haley, that made three friendly faces he could count on tonight.

Dressed and ready to go, he walked to the kitchen and grabbed the large plastic bowl full of bagel chips. He put on his coat and headed out the door, questions still pinging around in his mind like exploding kernels of popcorn, like: Would Haley invite him to stay after everyone left? How many of Haley's friends knew about his episode on the *Loaded Question* radio show? He sure wasn't looking forward to coming face-to-face with Trudy Cooper. Why had he agreed to attend Haley's open house again? Because she'd asked him to, and he couldn't refuse her.

She wasn't a client anymore. His already overworked nerves fired up even more, but for an entirely different reason. Blood rushed to his groin, and he forced his thoughts away from anything having to do with Haley naked, her soft warm skin against his, or the way he wanted to taste every inch of her.

Even driving way under the speed limit all the way there, Sam still managed to arrive on time. Every light in Haley's house was on, but there weren't too many cars parked in front yet. Wyatt and Josey's vehicles weren't anywhere in the vicinity. By the time he got to Haley's front door, his stomach had twisted into an uncomfortable knot. He knocked and someone *other* than Haley opened the door, a nice-looking black woman with a great smile.

"Come on in. I'm Felicia, a friend of Haley's." Her curious gaze slid over him. "Who might you be?"

"I'm Sam." His mouth had taken on the consistency of the dry mortar they'd used to set tiles.

"Here, let me take that." Felicia took the bowl from his hands. "Sam, eh? Are you the man responsible for Haley's amazing kitchen and bathroom updates? She mentioned you might stop by."

"Haley designed the rooms, but," Sam shrugged out of his coat, "yeah, that would be me."

"Well, both rooms look great. You can leave your coat on her bed. Haley's in the kitchen, by the way. I'll put your bowl on the table with the rest of the food."

"My sister is bringing the dip to go with those bagel chips. Should we wait 'til she gets here to put them out?"

"I'll leave the lid on, how about that? Right now it's just you, me and two others besides Haley."

He nodded, already on his way to the bedroom. His stomach still tight, he dropped off his coat and headed for the kitchen. Haley was opening bottles of wine and talking to a couple who were arranging vegetables on a platter. Every time he so much as looked at Haley his breath caught, and this was no exception.

Tonight she looked especially sexy in a black stretchy skirt, tights and leather boots that came to her knees. Her blouse, which showed an enticing hint of cleavage, was some kind of silky dark red material that brought out the rich tones of her hair and gave her skin a warm glow. She turned, and their eyes met.

A welcoming smile lit her face. "Sam," she said, extending her hand to him.

He moved to her side and took it, even though his palms were still sweaty. Seeing her, having her hand in his settled him somehow.

"Kathy and Blake," Haley said. "This is Sam Haney, the man who worked miracles with the mess I made of my house." Her brow rose slightly as she noticed his haircut.

He nodded at the two. "Nice to meet you both."

"Nice to meet you, too. I love what you've done with Haley's house," Kathy said. "It makes such an amazing difference."

"Thanks." So far, no one had looked at him funny. Could it be that Haley's friends knew nothing about him besides the fact he'd remodeled her house? He breathed a little easier. Other than meeting Trudy, tonight might be OK.

"Would you like a beer?" Haley asked.

"Sure. Point me in the right direction, and I'll get one myself."

"It's in the breezeway. I'll come with you. Anyone else need anything?" Haley asked.

Blake held up his half-full bottle. "I'm good."

"Me too," Kathy added. She held a glass of white wine in one hand.

"We'll be right back," Haley said, tugging him toward the back door. "You cut your hair. I like it."

"Thanks. It was long overdue." He followed her out to the porch connecting the house and her garage. "What, no keg?" he teased, looking at the cases of beer lining the perimeter.

"No. I opted for variety. You look great, Sam. I like that sweater."

"Me too." He smoothed his hand over the front of his new sweater. "It's a Christmas present from my grandmother. You're looking mighty fine yourself this evening." He wrapped an arm around her waist, needing to feel her close if only for a moment. He kissed her briefly. "It's cold out here. We should head inside."

"In a minute," she said, sliding her arms around him. "I'm glad you're here. Are Josey and Wyatt going to drop by?"

"Mmm-mm." He nuzzled her temple, savoring her familiar scent. "They should be here soon." Headlight beams passed through the porch, landing on them briefly before swinging away. "Looks like you have more guests arriving." Reluctantly, he let her go. Sam grabbed a bottle of beer, and trailed her back into to the warmth of her kitchen.

"Haley," a woman called from the living room.

"It's my mother." Haley glanced at him. "Ready?"

Sam nodded. *Not really.* His palms grew damp again. He set his beer on the granite counter and reached for her hand. They were a united front—Team Haley against her meddlesome mother. Three people stood just inside the front door: her mother, a tall man in his late twenties—was that her brother?—and an older man who must be her father.

"Oh, there you are," Haley's mother chirped. She unbuttoned her coat and took it off. Her eyes lit on Sam, and her lips pursed before she turned her attention back to her daughter.

Haley's father took the coat from his wife's hands and draped it over his arm. "Let me take your coat too while I'm at it," he said, turning to the younger man. "Where do you want these, sweetheart?" he asked, kissing Haley on the cheek.

"On my bed. Thanks, Dad." Haley's voice carried the hint of strain. "Who's this, Mom?"

So, not her brother. Sam frowned. Why on earth would the Coopers bring a total stranger to Haley's party?

"I hope you don't mind . . . we brought a guest with us to your open house. David is new in town, and we thought this might be a good way for him to meet people his own age." She gestured toward the younger man. "He's recently finished graduate school, and he has a great new job. I'm sure you two will hit it off." She smiled brightly at her daughter. "This is David Anderson. David, this is our lovely daughter, Haley. She's a paralegal with a prestigious law firm in downtown Minneapolis."

"Hey, I hope it's OK I tagged along." David grinned at Haley and held up a plastic bag. "I brought cookies."

"Oh, sure. Come on in," Haley said. "The more the merrier."

Despite the friendly greeting, Haley tensed beside him, and blotches of red bloomed on her cheeks. Was Haley's mother trying to fix her daughter up with this guy, bringing him to the party uninvited? Wow. Haley had told him stories about her mother. In fact, he was *one* of Trudy's stories. But it still stunned him. Driven by an overwhelming wave of possessiveness, Sam put his arm around Haley's shoulders and drew her close to his side. *Go, Team Haley.* "You must be Mrs. Cooper," he said, sending David a back-off look.

Trudy's gaze went from his arm, to his face and then to Haley. "Yes . . ." The door behind them opened, and they moved in a huddle farther into the living room to accommodate the new arrival, another woman who looked to be in her late fifties or early sixties.

"Happy New Year, Haley." She smiled.

"Same to you, Aunt Nanci. Glad you could make it."

"Aren't you going to introduce me to this young man?" Trudy asked, her smile as fake as faux fur.

"Of course." Haley put her arm around Sam's waist. "Mother, Aunt Nanci, I'd like you to meet Sam Haney. My date."

"No he isn't." Trudy's voice dropped, and she paled, and the casserole dish she held started to slip out of her hands.

Sam caught it before it hit the floor and handed it back, earning him a glare.

"You can't *date* my daughter!"

"Who says he can't?" Haley snapped, folding her arms in front of her.

Haley's aunt made a muffled snorting sound, and Sam cringed. His heart pounded so hard his ears rang.

"Haley, I need to talk to you for a moment?" Trudy refused to look at him. "Perhaps in your bedroom?"

"Not now. I have company."

"Yes, but . . . but I really *need* to talk to you. *Now.*"

Haley's dad returned. He smiled and rubbed his palms together. "So, what's going on?"

"It was all Nanci's idea," Mrs. Cooper blurted, clutching her casserole dish so hard her knuckles stood out in sharp relief.

"I have no clue what you're talking about, Trudy," Nanci snapped. "*What* was all my idea again?"

"Yeah, Mom," Haley said in an overly sweet voice. "Tell us."

"Hmm." Her dad's friendly smile turned to a frown as he looked at each of them. "Trudy, is there something I should know?"

"Nope." Mrs. Cooper's eyes saucered. "Not a thing."

Haley's friends had gone so quiet, you could've heard an eyelash drop on a plush rug. This was a mistake. Coming here tonight had been a colossal mistake.

Felicia shot up from the couch and hurried toward the guy Trudy had *hoped* would be Haley's date for the evening. "Hi, I'm Felicia. How about I show you where everything is, and then I'll introduce you to everyone. Let me take care of that, Mrs. Cooper." Felicia took the dish from Trudy's hands and led David and his bag of cookies away. Kathy and Blake trailed after them.

Mr. Cooper turned to Haley. "Did I hear you say this is the young man who did the work on your house? I took a look at the bathroom. Nice job." He extended his hand. "I'm Frank, Haley's father."

Sam reached out and shook Frank's hand with his once-again-sweaty palm. "Sam Haney." Haley had put her arm around him as she'd introduced him to her mother, and she'd referred to him as her date. She *had* presented a united front as promised. Still, he hadn't been prepared for this sick feeling lodged in his gut. These were her parents, a huge part of her life, and Trudy Cooper viewed him like some kind of millipede crawling out from under the floorboards.

Plus, he no longer had any doubts about whether or not her friends knew about his past or how he and Haley had been set up. They did. Their avid interest in the exchange made that perfectly clear. If he left now, he could text Wyatt and Josey before they got here and head them off.

"Sam, why don't you show me Haley's new kitchen," Frank said. "And then perhaps you can point out where I might find a beer."

"Sure." Sam nodded. "I'd be happy to." His heart had turned into a brick in his chest as he walked Haley's dad to the kitchen. Mr. Cooper had picked up on the tension. What was he thinking right now? One thing for sure, Haley's mother would never see him as anything other than the handyman who admitted on the air that women threw themselves at him—and that he hadn't always thrown them off. For the first time in his life, he regretted his past, and regret was a bitter brew to swallow. He had only himself to blame.

What had she been thinking, blurting out Sam was her date like that? She'd put him in such an awkward position. But dammit, she wouldn't have done it if it weren't for the uninvited stranger her mother had brought to her open house. Haley hadn't been able to help herself.

She'd seen the hurt in Sam's eyes before he left with her dad. What must he be going through right now? Once she'd dealt with Mother Mayhem, she'd find Sam and make things right.

Haley leaned close and lowered her voice. "So, let me guess, Mom. You brought David Anderson, hoping to fix me up."

"He's a very nice young man," Trudy said. "He just finished graduate school, and he has a great job. I thought—"

"You brought a total stranger to my party . . . as a blind date . . . for me." Haley pressed her fingers to her temples. "Without asking first, I might add. Do you have any idea how totally inappropriate that is? I can't believe you would do such a thing."

"I can't believe you tried to throw *me* under the truck," her aunt muttered.

Trudy glanced at her sister. "Bus."

"Wheels. You threw me under the wheels," Nanci huffed and stomped off.

"Haley, you don't know about Sam Haney. He——"

"Yes I do, Mom. I know everything. I know about the radio show, and about how you pretended to be me when you set up the appointment. I even know you told Sam I wanted his"——she made quote marks in the air——"*special touch.*" Her eyes stung. "Can you imagine how humiliating it was to have my own mother set me up for . . . for . . . ? Argh, I can't even say it. And what about poor Sam?" She shuddered. "What is it that makes you think it's OK to manipulate people the way you do?"

"Well I . . . I've been so worried about you. You've been down in the dumps for months and months, and I just want you to be happy. I was hoping——"

"My happiness is up to me, and this intrusiveness into my personal life has got to stop right now, or I will be forced to act accordingly."

"What does that mean?" Her mother frowned.

"It means I'll move to another country to put some distance between us. Lots of distance." An empty threat, but she'd at least stop coming to Sunday dinners. "I won't tell you anything about my life ever again. A few years from now you might have grandkids and a son-in-law, but you'll *never know*, because *I* won't say a word."

Trudy gasped. "You wouldn't."

Haley crossed her arms and squared off with her mother. "Try me."

"Tell me you're not *really* dating Sam Haney. You just said that to make your point, right? He's—"

"Mom, I'm not sixteen anymore. It's none of your business who I date, and if you can't be nice to him, I suggest you turn around right now and go home."

"Oh, no. You *are* dating the handyman." Trudy groaned. "This is all my fault."

"Hello, hello," Brent called, coming into the living room. "I brought my famous buffalo chicken dip." He held up a Crock-Pot, and a canvas shopping bag dangled from his wrist. He glanced between them. "Oh, you must be Haley's mom." Brent closed the door with his hip. "I'm Brent. I work with your daughter."

Her mother went into social mode, and any sign that they'd had words, or that Haley threatened banishment from her life disappeared. "Yes, I'm Trudy Cooper. It's very nice to meet you, Brent."

Haley sighed. She had to find Sam and make sure he was OK. He must be fuming. "Come with me, Brent. I'll show you where you can plug in the Crock-Pot. Mom, there's wine on the kitchen counter and beer in the breezeway. Help yourself." She led Brent to the dining room. "You always seem to show up at exactly the right time," she whispered.

"Where's your studly handyman?" he whispered back.

"Good question." She didn't see him or her father anywhere. Had he left? Were Sam and her dad still in the breezeway? Her house wasn't all that big. "Somewhere with my dad." *I hope.* She moved her mom's wild rice hot dish to make room on the table and showed Brent the outlet for his slow cooker. "Promise me you'll be nice to Sam. My mom . . ." She rolled her eyes. "It was awful. She brought a blind date for me."

"Oh, Haley."

The front door opened again, and Wyatt and Josey walked in. Thank goodness. "Gotta go. Make yourself at home." She hurried to the front door. Her mother had settled herself in the living room, and

David sat on the couch with Felicia. *Note to self: Thank Felicia profusely and buy her chocolates.* "Hey, you two. Am I ever glad to see you."

"Why? What's up?" Wyatt asked.

"Nothing, I'm just glad you came." She glanced at her mother. "Sam is somewhere with my dad. Coats go on my bed, and you can put your dip on the dining room table. Sam's bagel chips are already there in the big green plastic bowl." Her front door opened again, and her brother and his date entered. Dammit. All she wanted was to be with Sam.

Josey patted her arm. "We'll figure it out."

Haley nodded. "Thanks."

More of her friends arrived, and her party went into full swing. Haley mingled, kept the wine stocked and the food table tidy. Every time she set out to find Sam, someone came to talk to her before she could get to him. And though she caught glimpses of him, talking to Josey and Wyatt or to her friends, he made no attempt to come to her. No matter how she spun things, forcing an encounter between Sam and her mother had put a strain on her and Sam.

By eight thirty, she wanted everyone to go home. She headed to the table to get something to eat, and her father emerged from her bedroom with coats in hand.

"Honey, your mother, aunt and I are heading out so you young people can party without us old folks in your way."

"I don't suppose you're taking David Anderson with you," she muttered.

"No." He shook his head. "And for the record, I had no idea your mother hadn't asked you first if he could join us. He drove here himself, but I don't think you have to worry about him." He nodded toward the living room.

Haley glanced in that direction. David and Brent were sitting close to each other on her couch, close enough that their knees touched, and they were talking in that way people did when they didn't want anyone else to join them. Their mutual attraction was obvious. *Ha. Take that, Mom.*

"Thank you so much for helping with my house, Dad. What do you think, by the way?"

"I really like the updates. Sam and his company did excellent work. In fact, it's been years since we've updated anything at our house. I'm thinking of hiring Haney & Sons to do some remodeling." The laugh lines at the corners of his eyes creased.

"Really?" She snorted. "Better talk to Mom about it first."

"No, I don't think I will." He winked. "That's the point."

"Dad . . ."

"I like him, Haley. I have no idea what all that was about earlier, but I do know your mother. Give me some credit."

Her throat tightened, and she hugged him. "Love you."

"Love you too." He patted her on the back. "Good night. We'll see you for Sunday dinner."

"Hey, Haley." Frank Jr. came to stand beside her. "Carrie and I are heading out too. We have another party to hit tonight."

"OK. Thanks for coming." Sighing, she grabbed a bagel chip and dredged it through Josey's spinach dip, admiring the painted ceramic bowl. Sam, Wyatt and Josey would probably be the next to leave, and she hadn't even had a chance to talk to Sam.

"Haley."

Startled at the sound of Sam's voice, she dropped the bagel chip. It landed dip-side down on the table. "Are you leaving too?" She grabbed a napkin. "I'm sorry about Trudy, and I wanted to—"

"There you go, jumping to conclusions again," he said. "I was *going* to ask if you wanted me to stay and help clean up tonight."

"Oh. But . . . but you've been avoiding me most of the evening. I thought you were angry."

"No." He stuffed his hands into his front pockets. "A little uncomfortable with your mother maybe, but it's not like I didn't know what to expect."

No matter what he said, his words couldn't hide the dejected look in his eyes. She shook her head. "I shouldn't have forced you to meet her."

"It's OK. Do you think presenting a united front had the impact you hoped it would?"

He reached for her, and ran his hands down her arms, taking her hands in his. She wanted to purr like a kitten. "I don't know. I told her the intrusiveness into my personal life had to stop, or I'd move to a different country." He chuckled, and she felt it all the way to her toes. She peered up at him. "Yes, Sam. Please stay."

His eyes smoldered into hers, and she could hardly breathe. He bent his head, leaning close, their lips almost touching.

"Hey you two, come join the party," Kathy said. "No more fussing over the food and worrying about empty plates and used napkins, Haley. Time to relax." She handed her a glass of wine.

"You're absolutely right." Bless her dad for whisking her mom and aunt away when he did. Finally she could unwind and enjoy the rest of the evening. Sam twined his fingers with hers, and they joined everyone in the living room.

She and Sam sat on a couple of her dining room chairs, and he slung his arm around her shoulders. Haley sipped her wine while the laughter and conversations flowed around her. She responded when anything was directed her way, but mostly her awareness centered on Sam. His body heat, the way he couldn't seem to stop touching her. Being so close that she was wrapped in his scent . . . he'd put her under a spell—the kind of spell that had her throbbing and needy.

What would her friends think if she stood up right now and ordered them all to take their leftovers and go home, because she wanted to get naked with her handyman? She giggled. Sam hugged her close. She could get used to this, having him beside her . . . having *him*.

"What's so funny?" he whispered in her ear.

A pleasurable shiver tickled its way down to her already-aroused bits. "Do you really want to know?"

"I do."

"I just imagined ordering everyone to leave." She smiled. "Everyone except you."

His blue eyes darkened. "I dare you," he said, his voice hoarse.

"Would you stay if I did, or would you—"

"Absolutely." He ran his hand up and down her arm. "What is this material? I really like the way it feels."

"Silk." When had breathing ceased to be automatic?

"It's already half past nine. According to the invitation, the party is over at ten," he whispered. "We can wait."

"Can we?" She arched a brow.

"Mature adults here. I think so."

By the time everyone left, it was close to eleven, and Haley was about ready to jump out of her skin. All they really needed to deal with were the things that were perishable, and very little remained. She unzipped her boots and took them off, setting them aside. "Finally." She sighed and wiggled her pinched toes. "I'm going to put a few things away, and the rest of this can wait until tomorrow." She padded to the dining room and surveyed the remains.

Sam's arms came around her waist, and he pulled her back against him. "Mmmm." He nibbled her neck. "You always smell so good."

Currents of electrifying heat coursed through her. "On second thought, I don't really need the leftovers." Haley turned in his arms to face him. He kissed her, and all thoughts of cleaning were swept away. His kisses were perfect. Just the right amount of everything, and when his tongue slid into her mouth, her knees almost gave out.

Sam scooped her up, and she wrapped her legs around his waist, her skirt rising to ride her hips. He kept kissing her all the way to her bedroom.

He placed her on the bed and toed off his shoes. "If this isn't what you want, tell me now, Haley." His heated gaze roamed over her from head to toe, the intensity nearly setting her aflame. Sam reached for the wallet in his back pocket, took out a condom and set it on her night-stand. "Do you want this? Do you want me?"

Nodding, she scooted over to give him room. He stretched out beside her, all six feet something of him. She turned to him, and a look of such longing and tenderness filled his eyes that her heart turned over.

"Have I ever told you how beautiful you are?" His hand found its way under her blouse to skim her waist.

"No. You haven't."

"Well, I'm telling you now." His lips grazed her throat and he kissed his way along her jaw to her chin, and finally to her mouth. "And so damn sexy. God, Haley. You have no idea how badly I want you. Ever since that very first day we met, you've been in my thoughts and in my dreams." His breathing grew ragged as he unbuttoned her blouse. He worked it off, and then raised himself to stare down at her.

She shivered under his perusal, and her poor heart felt as if it would burst. He found her beautiful? Sexy. The way he looked at her, the intensity, heat and hunger in his eyes—she believed every word.

She'd planned for this moment, hoped for it and even shopped for the occasion. She wore a brand-new, front-fastening black bra with red over-lace and matching panties. He ran his palm over the material and groaned. His touch elicited a surge of wetness and a throbbing ache. Never had she wanted anyone so badly as she wanted Sam.

His fingers shook slightly as he undid the clasp. "Even though it's a few days late, I gotta tell you, *you* are the best Christmas present ever. Love the wrapping." He kissed the swell of her breasts.

Haley tugged at his sweater. "I like your wrapping too, but this has got to go." He growled low in his throat and pulled off the sweater, revealing a cotton T-shirt beneath. She grinned. Something about the plain white cotton tees he always wore melted her insides. He was an endearing mix of sex god and regular guy, and she found the combination irresistible. "This too," she whispered, tugging at the T-shirt. He raised his arms so she could pull it off. Haley tossed the shirt to the floor, and then she ran her palms over his chest, reveling in the feel of firm muscle under soft hot skin.

He reached for her, and she gasped as his thumbs stroked her sensitive nipples. And when he drew one into his mouth, teasing the hardened bud with his teeth and tongue, all coherency fled. He took his time removing the rest of her clothing, nibbling, kissing and tasting every part of her in the process. His own clothing disappeared as well, though she was barely aware of how or when that happened.

His kisses grew hotter and more demanding, his touches more intimate, and she lost herself in him. Sam's overpowering presence, heat and hardness turned her on in ways she hadn't known were possible. She flicked her tongue over one of his nipples and wrapped her hand around the length of his erection, gratified by the hiss of air escaping from him at her touch.

Haley stroked his broad shoulders, trailing kisses as she explored every inch of his sculpted chest, down to his belly. His muscles twitched under her touch, and he held his breath. She grinned against his skin. How many times had she fantasized about touching him like this? Indulging herself in the feel of him, his strength and heat, the softness of his skin and the tickle of hair on his chest, far exceeded what she could have imagined.

Working her way back up his torso, she nipped and licked, finally taking his earlobe between her teeth, while fondling him from base to tip.

"Haley," he whispered, reaching for the condom. "I want you. Can't wait." He sheathed himself and rolled her beneath him. He took her mouth with a fierce abandon and kneeled between her thighs. He moved his hand down her side, along her hip, finally coming to her most sensitive spot. He drove her wild, stroking her slick heat.

He broke the kiss and held himself up slightly, watching as he rubbed the tip of his penis against her swollen clit. She shuddered and moved beneath him, heightening the delicious sensations pulsing through her. He continued to watch as he brought her close to the edge, and the sound of their breathing filled the room.

"Sam . . . now."

Finally he entered her and stilled. He lowered himself and kissed her again, his tongue ravaging her mouth, and it was the hottest, most erotic thing she'd ever experienced. Being with Sam felt so right it brought tears to her eyes. She closed them, in the throes of an overwhelming intimacy, opening up the rest of her senses to merge with him.

He moved then, setting a steady pace, and she arched into him, trying to get closer, bringing him deeper. Pleasurable tension built, spiraling through her, carrying her along the crest for several glorious moments until she came apart in his arms, pulsing around him. Sam cried out, thrust hard into her and held himself there, his muscles straining as he climaxed.

Supporting his weight with his forearms, he kissed her forehead, cheeks, even the tip of her nose and smoothed her hair from her face. Rolling to his side, he brought her with him and held her close. Slowly their breathing returned to normal. "You're scary amazing, Ms. Cooper."

She laughed against his chest. "You're pretty amazing yourself, Mr. Haney."

"I'll be right back," he said, lifting himself and swinging his legs over the edge of her bed.

Haley slipped beneath the covers and drew them up around her shoulders. Sated and sleepy, she smiled. Sam had worked hard to prove himself to her, and she could no longer deny the truth. He was sweet, considerate, a gentleman and a fantastic lover. She'd fallen in love with the handyman, and she had no doubts that he had feelings for her too.

He returned, turned off the light and climbed into bed with her. She yawned and snuggled close, and he wrapped her in his warmth. For the first time in months, she looked forward to the promise of a bright future, a future with Sam.

Chapter Fourteen

Nothing compared to having Haley snuggled up next to him, all soft, warm and naked. So, why had his mind started to spiral again? Because there was nothing strings-free or casual about what they'd just shared, that's why, and this was a first for him. Yep. He'd just had *superglue sex*—the kind of sex that bound two souls together for a lifetime and led to a mortgage, two-point-five children and a minivan. Maybe even a dog.

He swallowed a few times and rolled onto his back. His arm was trapped under Haley's neck, and her bare bottom pressed against his hip. Sam stared up at the ceiling. What if he did decide to go down the soul-binding path with her? Say they had a family together, and everything was fantastic. And then one day he got another one of those life-shattering phone calls telling him his wife and children were never coming home again. Then what? He wouldn't survive a blow like that. No way would he be able to continue on with his life. He'd be a zombie—breathing, heart beating, but dead all the same.

Or . . . what if he wanted to get serious and she didn't? Or . . . what if, after being together for years, she decided she wanted to quit him?

Loss sucked. Relationships ended. Eventually, everyone died.

Hell, his grandparents were already in their seventies. How much longer would they be around? He had uncles and aunts, cousins, his brother and sister and a few friends. His potential for grief was already huge, and he'd never intended to add to the number.

Just enough light from the street filtered through the blinds that he could make out Haley's slumbering form beside him. Her soft brown hair tickled his arm, and sweat had formed where her cheek rested against him. He was torn between wanting to spoon with her all night and running fast and far away from everything she represented.

Dammit, keeping himself free from further emotional entanglement had been his only defense against the very worst kind of pain—the pain of losing *the one*. The *only*, who had the potential of becoming the very center of his universe—the celestial body his life would orbit around year after year after year. His heart pounded, and his palms were sweaty. Again. Haley turned over, made a soft snuffling sound and snuggled closer, throwing her arm across his waist and a leg over his thigh. Too much. Too intense. Too . . . everything.

Three hundred and sixty degrees of pressure encircled his chest and squeezed until he was sure his heart would explode. This time, a heart attack for sure, because pain closed in around him, leaving him dizzy and breathless. He needed air, needed to get out of here. Sam disentangled himself from Haley and slid out from under the covers. He searched the floor for his clothing, shoes and socks.

"What are you doing?" Haley propped herself up on an elbow and yawned.

"I . . . uh." He stood with his things bundled against his aching chest. "I have to go."

"Go?" Haley glanced at the digital clock on her dresser. "It's two in the morning, Sam. Where do you have to be at two a.m. on a Saturday morning? Come back to bed."

"I can't . . ." He swallowed a few times. "I need to . . ." Blind panic stole his ability to think, much less express what he was feeling. Not that he wanted to anyway. "Have to go."

"Of course you do," Haley bit out. She punched her pillow a few times and laid back down, curling into a ball with her back to him. "Leave then, and don't forget to lock the door on the way out."

There was no mistaking the hurt in her voice and in her posture. A sharp twinge of guilt only added to his panic. He left, tugging on his clothes along the way. He sat on a chair in the living room to put on his shoes and socks and shoved his arms into his coat. Opening the front door brought in a welcome blast of frigid air. Sucking in a huge gulp, he locked the doorknob, shut Haley's door behind him and made a dash for freedom.

The panic didn't recede until he parked his SUV in the lot of his apartment building, and then the full impact of what he'd done slammed into him with Haley-wielding-sledgehammer force. He'd run out on her, leaving her feeling rejected and hurt. He groaned as that realization was followed by another. After trying so hard to convince her he wasn't the love 'em-and-leave 'em lothario she'd assumed him to be, he'd just confirmed every single stereotypical belief about him she'd ever held. He couldn't blame her for thinking the worst.

Something inside him tore, and his eyes burned. No matter how badly he wanted to, the thought of going back sent him reeling again. Sam dragged himself to his apartment, stripped down to his briefs and T-shirt and fell into his cold, empty bed. He stared at nothing, unable to sleep for the painful pounding inside his skull.

Loss sucked all right, whether it happened because of an accident, old age or, in his case, the absolute stupidest thing he'd ever done. He'd destroyed what he'd had with the only woman he would ever love. Sam rubbed his aching chest.

Yes, indeed. Haley was *the one*, his *only*, and he'd run from her. She'd never forgive him, and he saw no way to justify his actions. After everything was said and done, he was a lothario after all.

Showered, dressed and depressed, Haley reached for a large garbage bag from under her kitchen sink. How could she have been so stupid? Tigers didn't change their stripes. She'd believed Sam cared. In fact, one part of her still believed, but the truth was—he'd left. She'd been played. Worse, like every other one of Sam's brief sexual encounters, once the job was finished, she'd thrown herself at him.

A tear slid down her cheek. She sniffed and wiped it away, cringing at the thought of how he'd run out of her bedroom, clutching his things. He couldn't get away fast enough. "Idiot," she muttered. *Have to go*, and *I can't*. A man who says that to a woman he's just slept with does not intend to come back. Hadn't he told her he didn't do relationships? Why had she believed she'd be the one to change his mind?

She had a mess to clean up, and she welcomed anything that would occupy her enough to keep her mind off her foolish mistake. She turned on some music and padded back to her dining room, the garbage bag dangling from her hand. A knock on her door stopped her in her tracks, and she held her breath. *Sam*. She'd been wrong about him again. Relief flooded her system.

Dropping the bag, she hurried to her front door and threw it open. She squinted against the brightness of the morning sun. "Mom? What are you doing here?" Her stomach dropped, and disappointment nearly choked her. Fool. Had she really thought the handsiest handyman in the Twin Cities would return to the scene of yet another sexual conquest?

"I thought you might need some help cleaning up." Trudy stepped inside, her gaze darting around Haley's bungalow.

"He's not here."

Her mother set her purse and coat on the couch. "Who's not here?"

Haley walked back to the dining room. "Never mind. My personal life is off-limits." Haley picked up the garbage bag. "Or it's emigration time for me. I'm thinking Toronto, Canada. I hear it's a great city."

"Hmm."

"Mom, why are you really here?" Haley waved a hand around her house. "I appreciate the offer, but I know you. Whatever it is you have to say, let's get it over with."

"All right." Trudy fetched one of the dining room chairs from the living room and set it by the table. "I'm sorry. I know how wrong it was to . . . to try and get Sam to make a pass at you. But Haley, I knew you would never take him up on the offer."

"Right. Who *does* that, Mom?" Her eyes burned, and she blinked back the tears threatening to give her away. She *had* taken him up on the offer. Even worse, she'd been the one to initiate things.

"I'll admit it wasn't one of my brightest ideas, but I thought if you knew a hot guy found you attractive, you'd get over Michael and get out there and date again." Trudy went for another dining room chair. "I promise I will never meddle in your social life again. All I've ever wanted was for you and Frank to be happy."

"And grandchildren." Haley tsked. "Don't forget the grandchildren."

"Yes, and grandchildren." Her mother grinned. "It would be nice, but whether or not I ever have grandkids is entirely up to you and Junior. I realize that. Your happiness comes first."

Dammit, her eyes filled again. "I want a family, Mom, but fixing me up with . . . with anyone, is not the way it's going to happen. I accept your apology, and I'm going to hold you to your promise."

"That's settled then. Let's clean up this mess."

"OK. I appreciate the help, by the way."

Her mother held the garbage bag open, and Haley tossed things inside. Sam's plastic bowl still sat on her table. He'd left it behind in his haste to escape any possibility of attachment. Josey's painted ceramic dish holding the dried remains of her spinach dip had been left behind as well. A few tears escaped and traced down her cheeks.

"What's the matter, sweetheart?" Trudy straightened.

"Nothing," she said, forcing a smile. "I'm just glad we settled things between us. It's been stressful." Haley lifted Sam's bowl and dumped the leftover bagel chips into the trash bag. She stacked a bunch of other dishes inside his bowl and brought them to her kitchen, setting them in the sink to deal with later. Her phone rang, and again her hopes soared. She hurried to the living room and snatched it from the coffee table. "Hello?"

"Hey, it's me," Kathy said. "I was wondering if you wanted to see a movie tonight, a girls' night out, you, me and Felicia."

This pathetic hope, followed by staggering disappointment, had to stop. Sam wasn't going to call. He didn't do relationships. He only did drive-bys. She'd made him work a little bit harder for it, that's all. Haley steeled herself and pushed away the hurt. "I'd love to. Do you want to meet at the theater, or go together?"

"Felicia and I will come by for you at five. We'll have dinner some-where near the theater first."

"Sounds great. I'll see you then." Haley ended the call and turned to find herself the object of her mother's speculative stare. She shook her head. "Off-limits."

"I know." Her mother's lips pursed. "I didn't say a thing."

Haley stifled the urge to snort. "I appreciate how very difficult not saying anything must be for you."

She would get through this. She would. In a few days—make that weeks—she'd stop thinking about Sam. When that happened, she'd join one of those online dating sites. *Be proactive.* That would be her new motto. Never had she doubted what she wanted, and just because it hadn't happened yet didn't mean it never would. Maybe Kathy's boy-friend knew another single fireman he could introduce her to. Her heart wrenched. She'd ask in a few weeks, not now—not while Sam's rejection still stung.

◆ ◆ ◆

"And then he grabbed his stuff and practically ran out of my house. No explanation, no 'I'll call you later.' Nothing," Haley said, looking from Felicia to Kathy. "All he said was, 'I can't,' and 'Have to go.' If it didn't bite as much as it does, I'd think the whole thing was pretty funny. And no. I haven't heard from him since."

"Oh, my God, what a dip-wad." Kathy gripped the edge of the restaurant table, her eyes narrowing. "I told you if he hurt you, I'd find him and kick his ass."

Haley checked out the diners in their vicinity to see if any of them were eavesdropping. They weren't. "It's my fault. I did what all of his female clients do. I threw myself at him. I practically begged him to stay."

"Your first one-night stand," Felicia murmured.

"My *only* one-night stand." Haley stirred the watered-down remains of her drink with her straw. "You know, it's weird, but my mother's ridiculous scheme kind of worked."

Kathy's brow creased. "How so?"

"She wanted to jump-start my social life." One side of her mouth quirked up. "It sort of did. I've decided to join an online dating site. I'm serious about meeting someone, so if either of you know anyone you think I'd get along with, fix me up."

"So . . ." Felicia played with the stem of her wineglass. "Was Sam any good in bed?"

"Felicia," Kathy cried. "I can't believe you asked her that. Can't you see he broke her heart?"

"What?" Felicia drew back, her eyes wide. "Can't I live vicariously here?"

"He was amazing," Haley said with a sigh. "And my heart's not broken. I'll get over it. It's not like I got left at the altar again. Sam and I didn't even know each other all that long. We only went out a few times."

Yes, but they'd worked together on her house for hours and hours, sharing things about themselves that they hadn't shared with anyone else. As far as she knew, anyway. Maybe he told all the women he met about the way he'd lost his parents. Like her, they'd feel sorry for him . . . and offer comfort sex. *Gah. I'm so gullible.*

Kathy leaned in. "It doesn't take any time at all to fall in love, Haley. We're here for you."

She stared at the glass in front of her. "I appreciate it."

"We've got to get going if we don't want to be late for the movie." Felicia picked up the folder holding their tab. "Should we just have the server split this three ways?"

"Sure," Haley said, reaching for her purse.

By the time her friends dropped her off at home, she felt more optimistic and less ready to cry at the slightest memory of Sam. That lasted only until she went into her newly remodeled bathroom to wash her face and brush her teeth. She and Sam had shared their first kiss here. Every single tile reminded her of the patient way he'd taught her. She missed his charming smile, the way he smelled, moved and talked. Forcing her thoughts away from him, she firmed her resolve. She would get over him. Eventually.

Sam pushed his uneaten bowl of cereal away. He had no appetite, and even if he did, he doubted he'd be able to swallow. His insides felt weird, like all of his internal organs had tensed up in fight-or-flight mode. He rubbed his scratchy eyes. He hadn't slept either. Thank God it was Sunday and he didn't have to work.

He brought his bowl to the sink and dumped the contents into the disposal. The sun pouring through the door to his tiny balcony drew him, and he walked over to look outside. Not a cloud in the sky, and the snow sparkled and beckoned. This would be a perfect day to go snowmobiling. His heart wrenched. Snowmobiling with Haley had been a blast. He'd gotten such a kick out of the way she'd squeal and tighten her arms around him when he accelerated.

Groaning, he picked up his phone and speed-dialed his brother. Wyatt answered on the third ring. "Hey, you want to take the snowmobiles out?" Sam asked. "It's a perfect day."

"Not today. I'm in the middle of a project." Wyatt sounded distracted, the way he always did when he was deep into one of his comic book ideas.

"How about catching a movie tonight?"

"Mmm, how about you come to my apartment later? We can rent a movie on cable and order pizza delivery."

"Yeah, OK," Sam said. "What time?"

"Give me until five."

"Five it is. See you later." Sam let his brother get back to his project. That left him with an entire day with nothing to do, no one to do it with and way too much on his mind. What was Haley up to today? Probably calling all her friends to tell them what an A-hole he turned out to be. He was no better than her ex, bolting without a word of explanation. He should go back to her, at least tell her . . . Tension banded his chest, and he went breathless. He couldn't. Rubbing the painful spot over his heart, he searched for something to turn his mind away from the panic.

Laundry. He'd do his laundry and clean his apartment, and maybe watch football until it was time to go to Wyatt's place. Before Haley, he'd never felt lonely. And now? Loneliness bounced around inside the empty chambers of his heart. Hell, he'd only known her for a couple of months. He'd get over this. He'd get over *her* and carry on. He headed for his bathroom to shower, dreading the hours, days, weeks and months it would take before he stopped missing Ms. Cooper.

As he knew they would, the hours dragged by. Sam watched the clock and channel surfed. Nothing held his attention. Finally, it was time to go to his brother's place. He grabbed the six-pack sitting in his fridge and headed out. How pathetic? He was downright desperate for company.

He parked his SUV in front of the old apartment building Wyatt lived in on the west side of Saint Paul. Located a few blocks from the Mississippi River, the turn-of-the-century brick building had once been luxury apartments. Nothing had been done in the way of maintenance or improvements for decades though, which was why the rent was so reasonable. Still, it was a nice area with plenty to do within walking distance, and Wyatt's apartment had lots of what he called *character.*

He strode to the security door and hit his brother's buzzer. The heavy glass door clicked, and Sam took the short flight of stairs to the first floor. Wyatt waited for him with his door open.

"Hey," Sam said, hoisting the six-pack. "I brought beer."

The sound of a child's laughter behind him seemed to catch Wyatt's attention. Sam turned in time to see a cute blonde with a little boy in tow coming up the back stairs. The woman smiled briefly and continued on her way up the next flight. Wyatt smiled back and watched her, while Sam watched him. "New neighbor?" he asked.

"Not really." Wyatt drew back into his apartment. "She and her son have lived here for about eight months now. She lives in the apartment right above mine, which is great. Unlike the last tenants, she and her son are quiet."

"What's her name? Have you talked to her?" Sam followed Wyatt into his kitchen and handed him the six-pack.

Wyatt's face reddened. "According to her mailbox, her last name is Malone, and no, I haven't spoken to her other than a greeting now and then when we run into each other in the hallway."

Sam nodded. Normally, he'd give his brother a rough time about that, but after what he'd done, giving anyone a hard time about women didn't feel right. "Have you checked out what's available on pay-per-view?"

"Not yet." Wyatt handed Sam a beer and took one for himself before putting the rest into the fridge.

"So, what have you been working on all day? Can I see?"

"Sure." Mentioning his work brought a smile to his brother's face.

Sam followed him to the smaller of his two bedrooms, which Wyatt had set up as a studio. He'd placed a drawing table and stool by the east-facing window, and a large sheet of paper with colorful panels lay across the surface. Sam moved close to take a look. His brother had a unique style, bold and angular, and his hero wielded lightning bolts from his hands to fight the dastardly otherworld creatures of evil. Wyatt's graphic tales often included a damsel in distress, and his latest damsel looked a lot like the blonde they'd encountered in the hallway.

"Wow, you're so freaking talented." Sam grinned at his brother. "Have you heard back from your latest submission?"

"No, not yet, but it's no big deal if I get rejected." He shrugged. "It's not like I don't have a job. I just really enjoy creating the stories and the graphics. In the meantime, I'll keep coming up with new ideas." He took a swig of his beer. "How's Haley? She too tired after her party to go snowmobiling with you today?"

Sam nodded and turned away, his face heating. A lump clogged his throat. No way did he want to tell Wyatt what had happened, especially after he'd told his brother he had no intention of hurting Haley. In fact, he wouldn't tell anyone. Eventually, like the *Loaded Question* radio show, Haley would fade from everyone's memory. Everyone's but his.

Guilt pinched at his heart. He owed Haley an explanation. He couldn't bear the thought that he was no better than her ex, leaving her hanging the way he had. He'd call her soon and ask her if they could talk. Even thinking about facing her stole his breath.

"What kind of pizza do we want?" Wyatt asked, leading the way out of his studio.

"Anything's fine with me. I'm not picky." What difference did it make? His stomach had tightened to the size of a walnut, and he couldn't eat anything anyway. "Order whatever you want."

He moved to Wyatt's living room and took a seat on the couch to search for a movie involving lots of explosions and car chases. Something action heavy and plot light—anything that didn't require trying to keep up or think. "Hey, have you seen the latest Marvel Avengers movie?" he called, scrolling through the options.

"Nope." Wyatt walked into the room, holding a menu and his cell phone. "Sounds great."

Wyatt ordered their pizza, and Sam selected the movie. A wave of gratitude engulfed him. Wyatt had no idea that his insides were in a semipermanent twisted state, yet just being with him helped. Familiar and safe, that's what he needed. Once he apologized to Haley, he'd return to his routine, hang out with family, and eventually he'd feel like himself again. He slouched down on the couch and leaned his head back. He could hope, anyway.

Chapter Fifteen

Haley sat at her computer, scrolling through the pictures Kathy had taken of her, trying to choose a few for her online dating profile. It had been eight days since Sam had fled the scene, and today her insides felt less wobbly. She wasn't quite ready to activate her account yet, but at least she could complete the profile. All that remained were the pictures to upload and completing her method of payment. *Gah.* Would dating other men purge Sam from her system?

Her phone chimed, notifying her she had a text message. Probably Kathy, checking to see how her profile was coming along. She picked it up and looked at the screen. *Sam.* Her heart tripped.

Hey, could I drop by sometime this coming week. If you're willing, I'd like to talk.

She dropped her phone, shot up from the chair and strode to the kitchen. Willing? Did she want to talk to him? Haley paced and wrapped her arms around herself. What did they have to talk about? He probably thought he owed her an explanation, which he did, but was she ready to hear what he had to say?

Wait. She could pretend she hadn't read the message for a while, at least until her pulse returned to normal. His stupid plastic bowl still sat in a corner of her kitchen counter with Josey's ceramic dish nestled inside. She'd meant to get hold of Josey, tell her she'd leave both in her breezeway so one of them could pick them up whenever—meaning at a time when she wasn't home.

Hadn't she learned anything this year? She didn't want to wait for months before finding closure. Despite the fact that he'd flat out told her he didn't do relationships, she'd fallen for him, and he'd given every indication that he cared back. What had happened that night? He'd looked so freaked out, standing there with his things clutched to his naked chest.

If she did agree to talk, it didn't mean she had to admit she'd fallen for him, and honestly, she did want to . . . what? Scold him for being the promiscuous commitment-phobe he'd always been? Lesson learned: No matter how many times you kiss a frog, it's still going to be an amphibian—*not* a prince. Who Sam chose to be and what he chose to do were not her business anymore. She'd talk to him, but on her terms.

Her heart in her throat, she forced herself back to her office and picked up her phone. She wouldn't let him know how much he'd hurt her. Staring at the screen with her insides scrambling for cover, she texted back.

If you want/need to talk, sure. How's this coming Thursday around six? You and your sister left your bowls here. You can pick them up then.

If she stared at her screen any harder, the glass might shatter. She inhaled through her nose and slowly exhaled through her mouth, trying to steady her nerves. Finally, he texted back.

That will work. See you Thursday, six p.m.

Haley dropped into her chair. Her hands were shaking, and her legs wouldn't hold her up any longer. This was Sunday. She had until Thursday to pull herself together. Four days. Did hair stylists keep openings for emergencies the way dentists did? She'd go shopping today. All the winter stuff was on clearance. Hopefully she could find a nice sweater or blouse and a new and perfect pair of jeans or leggings. She wanted to look her absolute best, which also meant a stop at Sephora for new makeup.

Don't show the cracks; don't let him see the dents he put in your heart. She hit Kathy's speed dial number and pressed her phone to her ear.

"Hey, Haley. What're you up to?" Kathy answered in a cheerful voice.

"You'll never guess who just texted me."

"Channing Tatum."

"I wish." Haley huffed. "Sam Haney. He wants to talk."

"Oh no. Tell me you turned him down."

"Why would I turn him down?" Haley frowned.

"You *don't* want to see him, Haley. Not after—"

"You're right. I don't want to see him; I want him to see *me*." Not entirely true; she ached to see him again, but she'd keep that to herself. "I'm going shopping today. I want to look great when he comes over." The night he'd come for his drill, he'd said she looked positively edible. He hadn't been able to take his eyes off her then, and she wanted that reaction one more time. "This is about me, Kathy. I want him to see I'm not falling apart. I want him to know his abrupt exit from my life has had no lasting effect."

"Hmm, which means it *did* have a lasting effect. You succumbed to his charm, and he broke your heart."

"I'll admit I did fall a little bit in love with Sam, but this is my chance for closure, and then I can let it go. I'm not going to fester for a year, wondering why things ended with Sam. I did that with Michael, and it's a waste of time. Do you want to come shopping with me?"

"Oh, gosh. I'd love to, but this is one of Blake's off-duty days, and we have plans. I'm meeting his parents for the first time. What about Felicia?"

"She's in Iowa visiting her grandparents. It's their fiftieth wedding anniversary this weekend, remember? She's not coming home until Tuesday."

"Right. I forgot."

"It's OK. This is going to be a power shopping trip anyway. I'm probably better off going by myself."

"You sure?"

"Yeah. Have fun with Blake and his parents." Haley was truly happy things were going so well for Kathy and Blake, but that didn't prevent a flash of envy from flaring to life. Her turn would come. She'd make it happen. "We'll talk tomorrow."

"All right. Go fire up that credit card, and buy something smoking hot. Nothing is as sweet as making a man who dumped you drool."

"That's exactly what I'm going for." Haley ended the call and saved her dating profile before putting her computer to sleep. Lots to do today, and it was already close to eleven. She hurried to her bathroom for a quick shower, plans for her shopping trip occupying her thoughts.

Four hours later, she pulled into to her garage, her trunk filled with bags of the sweet deals she'd found. The hard part would be choosing what to wear, the black skinny jeans or the burgundy denim. She also had two new sweaters and a tailored white blouse for work, plus a black-and-white Sephora bag holding mascara, a new shade of blush and her favorite eyeliner.

She could manage pretending to be happy and unaffected by Sam's rejection while graciously listening to what he had to say. Taking the high ground, being willing to forgive and forget, would certainly be easier if she could make him drool.

Haley unloaded her purchases and hit the button closing her garage door. One more item remained on her list, and even if it meant taking a few vacation hours, she intended to get in for a brand-new haircut and style, something short to frame her face. Nothing says *fresh start* like a new hairstyle. She walked into her house with a lighter step. *Drool, handyman, drool.*

Once she'd cut off all the tags on her purchases and started a load of laundry, she completed her online dating profile and chose the six-month option. Her finger hovered above the Enter key for several seconds. Nervousness and self-doubt swirled through her. What if nobody responded? Worse, what if only creepy guys flirted with her? She swallowed and hit the Return key. Ready or not, she was going to do this. She needed to get her life moving forward again.

A flutter rippled through her stomach. Sam would be at her house in twenty minutes. What did he want to say to her? At least Kathy and Felicia's positive reactions to her haircut today had buoyed her confidence. Haley washed her face and applied fresh makeup, taking extra special care with her eyes.

Deciding what to wear had taken up at least half her time getting ready. The cream-colored tunic-style sweater she'd chosen had threads of copper, black and pewter woven through the yarn, and the black skinny jeans were casual enough that it didn't appear as if she'd gone to all that much trouble to look good . . . but she had, and she did. If only her nerves would calm down, she might be able to have a rational conversation with Sam.

She stepped back and studied herself in the mirror, turning her head this way and that to make sure every hair of her short bob with the angled sweep of layered bangs, was in place. The new cut set off her eyes and cheekbones, and she really liked how easy it was to style.

A knock on her door sent her pulse racing. She wiped her hands on a towel and forced herself to walk, not dash, to her living room.

Plastering a smile on her face, she opened the door. Seeing Sam in his all-too-familiar Carhartt work jacket and signature faded flannel shirt beneath, she almost burst into tears. She'd been wrong. She couldn't do this. Her plastered smile faltered.

His gaze roamed over her from head to toe and then back again. "You cut your hair."

Her hand came up to touch her bangs, and she nodded.

"It's nice, but I liked the way it was before." Sam's Adam's apple bobbed, and his blue eyes darkened. "I liked the way you'd flip it over your shoulder, and how you'd sometimes put it up in a ponytail."

Her brow rose. "You came here to talk to me about my hair?"

"Uh, no. Sorry." Sam wiped his boots on the rubber mat in front of the door. "Can I come in?"

"Sure." She stood back, still gripping the edge of the door for support. "Can I get you something? Water, coffee?" *A new outlook on involvement?* Her heart wrenched. Sam had been perfect all the way up to the moment he'd made his mad, naked dash out of her bedroom.

"No. I'm fine, thanks." He slipped out of his coat and draped it over the back of the couch.

"Have a seat," she said, moving to the overstuffed chair in the corner. If she sat any closer to him, the meltdown she was struggling to conquer would defeat her. "So, you wanted to talk. Go ahead."

"I . . ." He cleared his throat. "I want to apologize for the way I left . . . things."

"By things, are you referring to the way you ran out of my house at two in the morning after having sex with me, or *things* in general?" The hurt and anger finally overrode her nerves, lending her an odd sort of calm.

"Ahh . . . both." His Adam's apple bobbed again, and his face turned red. "I . . ." He blew out an audible breath. "Look, ever since my parents died, I've had panic attacks. My chest hurts, and I can't breathe. It's like having a heart attack, only it's not. When it happens, I get claustrophobic. I can't think. I just have to get out. That night, after we made love—"

"Had *sex*, you mean." She lifted her chin.

He stared at her intently for a second before averting his gaze. "I had a panic attack, and I ran. I'm sorry, Haley."

She'd seen the panic in his eyes that night. Come to think of it, he hadn't really been *all there* when he'd left. He hadn't even been coherent. She frowned. "What were you thinking about before the panic attack?"

"Us."

Us? In his mind there had been an *us?* Wait, did he come here to talk her into giving him another chance? Damn this annoying spark of hope. She squelched the sucker. Devastating disappointment was not something she cared to set herself up for again. Still . . . it had to take a lot of courage to face her and admit to a panic attack. "What about us?"

"You know, what if we went down this path or that path, stuff like that."

"Relationship stuff."

He nodded, his expression bleak.

He'd lost his parents, and she'd wondered if his aversion to getting close had been a defense mechanism. The sudden flash of insight penetrated the hurt and anger. "Oh, Sam. This is about those unresolved issues we talked about, isn't it? Look, I understand how a childhood trauma like losing your parents can lead to irrational fears, but don't let it control your life. Don't cut yourself off from having feelings for—"

"I never said I didn't have feelings for you, Haley," he said, his voice hoarse. "My heart functions just like everybody else's." His eyes met hers, and he leaned forward, placing his elbows on his thighs. He scrubbed his face with his hands for a second. "Yeah, I'm sure it has something to do with losing my parents. The problem is, I feel too much, and the thought of facing more loss isn't something I want to put myself through. *That's* why I don't do relationships." He lifted his head, his gaze intense again.

All her desire to come away from this the victor fell away, and she looked, really looked at Sam. His face was leaner, pale, and he had dark circles under his eyes. He did care about her, but he wasn't here to ask for a second chance. Her heart broke all over again. "So, let me get this straight. You would rather throw *us* away, because somehow, suffering *now* is preferable to suffering *later*. Is that it?"

He shrugged his broad shoulders, and a wave of frustration tinged with empathy swept through her. "What makes you think you'd be the one to lose me, Sam? Maybe I'd be the one to lose you."

He made a muffled snorting noise and shook his head.

"Can I ask you a question?"

"Absolutely." He sat back up and took a deep breath, as if bracing himself. "That's why I'm here, so we can talk this through. I don't want there to be any hard feelings between us. It's just that . . ."

"You don't do relationships."

He nodded again. God, her heart and her head hurt, not just for herself, but for him. To be so trapped by fear and panic must be awful for him. She couldn't imagine cutting herself off from the possibility of love and a family of her own. Haley ran her damp palms along her jeans. "So, say we had chosen to be together and you did lose me. What would that be like for you?"

He shot her a puzzled look. "What do you mean?"

"Well, like . . . would you have trouble sleeping?" The dark circles looked like bruises beneath his eyes.

"I suppose."

Yep. He was definitely thinner, his face more angular and way less boyish. "And you might lose your appetite, have trouble eating?"

"What's your point, Haley?"

"It seems to me . . ." She paused, searching for the words that might penetrate his irrational thought processes. "It's obvious you've lost weight, and looking at you now, I can see you haven't been sleeping well. Am I right?"

"I guess. So?"

"So . . ." She threw up her hands. "What's the difference, Sam? You're putting us both through this misery, and it's needless. We could be together." Her eyes filled, and she forced herself to calm down. Now was not the time to cry. "But we're not, because you've decided—without giving me a say, by the way—that it's better to be in pain now rather than later." She shook her head.

"That makes no sense. Sooner, later . . . again, what's the difference? Hurt happens, but so do love and happiness. Don't you see? You're *not* . . ." Her voice hitched. "You haven't prevented anything. All you've done is cut yourself off from a huge part of what life has to offer. Just think of the memories we could've made together."

She was grasping at straws here, but she couldn't seem to stop. "Memories sustain us when loss happens. They're like . . . well, they're like flotation devices that keep us afloat through the tough times."

Was anything getting through to him? She couldn't tell. He sat like a statue in her living room, like one big tragic work of male performance art. "I saw you with the kids you coach and with your cousins. You'd make a great dad, and I have no doubt you'd enjoy the role. You have so much to offer. You're sweet, considerate, compassionate, affectionate—"

"Great in bed," he added, still averting his gaze.

She rolled her eyes. "The point is, things don't have to be like this. *I'm* sad. I have feelings too, and *you've* hurt them."

"I'm sorry, Haley. I never set out to cause you any grief. For what it's worth, you're the closest I've ever come to serious involvement, but I just can't do the relationship thing." He scrubbed his face with both hands again. "I choke up, panic, and I'd rather . . . It's better for all involved if I don't have to experience that on a daily basis."

"Have you thought about, you know, maybe talking to a professional about this?"

"No. It wouldn't do any good, and it won't change my mind. My grandparents put me, Josey and Wyatt through therapy after our parents

died. If it didn't help then, it's not going to make a difference now." He
stood up. "I'd better get going. It wasn't you, Haley. You're amazing, and
never doubt it—I have very strong feelings for you. This is *my* issue."

"Yes." Anger and defeat exhausted her last hope. "It *is* your issue.
Obviously, I can't talk you into or out of anything, so I'll stop trying.
It's your life, your decision." She wanted to scream, cry and argue with
him until he realized what an idiot he was being, but it wouldn't do any
good. He was stuck, and it wasn't up to her to unstick him.

"I wish you all the best. No hard feelings." She followed him to the
door, catching a whiff of his unique scent as he put on his jacket. "Say
hello to Josey and Wyatt for me."

"I will. Thanks for being—"

"Understanding?" She searched for some spark in his eyes, any
shred of evidence that he'd heard what she'd said. But they held only a
flat kind of resignation. The shutters were drawn tight. "I'm not *understanding*. I just know when I'm wasting my breath."

He nodded, kissed her forehead and left. The tears didn't start until
after she shut and locked her door. That's when it hit her. This was the
last time she'd ever see her handyman, and she still loved him every bit
as much today as she had two weeks ago. "Big stubborn idiot."

Sniffling, tears running down her cheeks, she headed for her fridge.
A bottle of chardonnay left over from the open house called to her, and
she wasn't about to ignore the summons. Having Sam in her house
tonight, listening to him explain why they couldn't be together was like
losing him all over again. A glass of wine, maybe two, mindless TV and
bed—that was her plan for the rest of this disastrous evening.

Thank God tomorrow was Friday, and she only had to get through
one more day at work before she had the weekend to mourn in the
privacy of her own home. Maybe she'd meet an emotionally available
someone online to chat with—anything to take her mind off Sam
Haney, the most stubborn, wrong-thinking, commitment-phobic
handyman in the Twin Cities.

She reached into her new cabinet for a wineglass. Sam's stupid plastic bowl tucked into the corner beneath caught her eye. *Dammit.* One more link when all she wanted was for this to be over so the healing could begin.

Sighing, she poured herself a glass of wine, filling it to the rim. Tomorrow she'd call Haney & Sons and leave a message for Josey. Until then, she didn't want to look at the bowl. Wasn't it bad enough she'd live with reminders of Sam in her house every day?

Haley grabbed Sam and Josey's bowls and stomped to the breezeway. She placed them on the stacked plastic chairs she stored there over the winter. Done. Josey would pick them up, and that would be the end of the Sam Haney chapter of her life.

Still a weepy mess, she returned for her glass of wine and grabbed a few paper towels as well. A comfy spot on her couch, a nice cozy throw over her lap, and she settled in for her own personal pity party. She picked up the remote control and searched for something on TV. One night of feeling sorry for herself was all she'd allow, and then she'd start a new chapter, hopefully one that didn't lead to more heartache.

Sam pulled his van into his spot at Haney & Sons and cut the engine. He sat for a minute and stared through the windshield. Seeing Haley last night had done him in. His arms and legs still had the consistency of overcooked spaghetti noodles. His weakened state might have something to do with a lack of sleep and a lack of protein, but both of those problems were Haley related. So, yeah, his plug had been pulled, and he'd been drained of every last ounce of energy.

If he kept this up, he'd be a boneless blob soon. Wyatt could turn him into one of his cartoon characters. Blob Man. What would his evil superpower be? Breaking hearts? *I have feelings too, and you've hurt them.* Haley's words refused to leave him in peace. They'd kept him up all night, left fresh score marks on his heart and a load of guilt squatting in his gut.

He'd better eat something, or he wouldn't be able to work. Maybe someone brought pastries this morning. He climbed out and headed for the kitchen and his assignments for the day. Now that the custom house had been completed, he'd been put back on the handyman roster. So far he'd been lucky, and his clients had been elderly couples with simple maintenance jobs they wanted done.

Was Grandpa Joe giving him those kinds of assignments on purpose? Gramps still liked to do things the old-fashioned way, handing out jobs in person. It would be so much easier if they switched to tablets. An e-mail with an address first thing in the morning, and he wouldn't have to see anybody. After all, that's how they coordinated their contracted workers, but then the contract workers already owned tablets. Convincing Grandpa Joe to buy technology for Haney & Sons would take a miracle.

"Hi, S-Sam." Jerry smiled as he hung his coat on the coat tree in the corner.

"Hey, Jerry. How's it hanging?" Nope, not even a stale doughnut on the table. He'd have to do a drive-through on his way to his first job, grab a breakfast sandwich and eat it on the way.

"It's h-hanging. Want to see a movie with me t-tonight, Sam?"

"Absolutely, let's hang out. I'd like that."

"I miss h-hockey."

"Me too. Hopefully, we'll do better in the tournament next year. In the meantime, we have hockey camp to look forward to." He took a seat at the table. "I'll come get you at your house around five thirty. Choose a movie sometime today."

"Brrr, I hate winter." Josey stomped through the door, shivering and rubbing her arms. "Good morning, Jerry, Sam. Where is everybody?"

"D-dad and Grandpa are checking phone messages," Jerry told her. "Wyatt is in the bathroom."

"Thanks for the Wyatt update," Josey said with a snort. "You OK, Sam? You don't look so good." She tugged off her mittens and came at him with a hand outstretched, like she intended to feel his forehead.

He leaned out of her reach. "Yeah, I'm fine, just fighting something, I guess." Heat crept up his neck. He was fighting something all right, but it had nothing to do with germs. "A cold maybe, and it's wearing me out."

Hurt happens, but so do love and happiness. He shook his head, attempting to dislodge Haley's voice from his mind. That last bit should be in one of those positive affirmation books, or better yet, made into a bumper sticker. Add a stick figure family at the end, tweak to read *Shit happens, but so do love and happiness*, and it would be perfect.

Grandpa Joe walked into the kitchen, a clipboard and a few yellow message sheets in his hand. Wyatt strolled in behind him. "Here are today's jobs," Gramps said, putting the clipboard on the table. "And a few leads for estimates." He handed out the messages to each of them. Josey read one of hers, raised her head and scowled at Sam.

"What?" Had she gotten a lead from one of his pre-radio-show clients, and it included a coded phrase or something?

"Nothing." She moved to the clipboard and paged through the sheets until she found hers. She tugged it out from under the clip and left.

Sam studied his. Simple. Leaky faucets, clogged drains, install a new ceiling fan, nothing too challenging. Scanning his jobs, he mentally arranged them in order to minimize mileage and bring him the closest to his apartment at the end of the day. He'd change, and head to his uncle Dan's house for Jerry.

Regretting the lack of doughnuts, he headed out the door in search of the nearest Mickey D's before giving his first client a call. He was driving to his first job when his phone rang with Josey's ringtone. He hit the Speaker button on his phone. "What do you need, Jo?"

"Hello to you too. I don't need anything. I called to see if we could meet at The Bulldog after work."

"Not tonight. I promised I'd take Jerry to see a movie."

"How about lunch at Keys then? We could meet around one."

"I could do that. Which one? Lexington or Raymond Avenue?"

"Lexington. Text me if we need to change the time. See you."

She ended the call before he could respond. Even for Josey that had been abrupt. Something must be bugging her. He pulled up to the curb in front of his job. He'd be installing a ceiling fan in the family room of a two-story home. A daycare sign in the yard caught his eye, and the tension he hadn't known he carried, eased. The homeowner would be occupied. Grandpa Joe was obviously filtering the jobs he assigned to him.

"Thank you, Gramps." He wasn't in the mood to fend off advances. Would he ever be in the mood again? Maybe not now, but dammit, he'd been happy before *Loaded Question* aired. At least, he'd thought he'd been. Could he be happy again if he went back to the strings-free, recreational safe-sex lifestyle? Worth thinking about, anyway.

He worked his way through the morning, finishing his third job in plenty of time to reach Keys Café. By the time he pulled into the lot of the strip mall, Josey's and Wyatt's vans were already there. Josey hadn't mentioned Wyatt, but no big deal. Sam parked and climbed out of his van, already mentally going through the menu to see if anything sparked his appetite.

The scent of baked goods and burgers frying on the grill enveloped him. He caught sight of Wyatt and Jo sitting in a booth toward the rear of the café, and made his way toward them. Josey slid out of the seat, gesturing for him to sit on the inside. OK, that was different, but maybe she had somewhere to go soon. "Hey, how's the day going for you two?" he asked, sliding into the booth and picking up a menu.

Josey sat back down. "Fine, Sam. How about you?"

Both of them were eyeing him intently. "What?"

"This is an intervention," Wyatt informed him. "We're concerned about you. You've lost weight, you have dark circles under your eyes, and we haven't seen you smile since Haley's open house."

"You look like shit," Josey added with a nod.

"Come on." Sam rolled his eyes. "I'm not doing drugs or abusing alcohol, if that's what's worrying you two mother hens."

"Not that kind of intervention," Josey said, sliding one of Grandpa Joe's yellow messages toward him. "What happened?"

Frowning, Sam snatched up the scrap of paper and scanned it. Haley's name, the date the call came in and the time were all filled out in Grandpa Joe's familiar scrawl.

Haley Cooper called and said you and Sam left your bowls at her house. They're in the breezeway. She wants you to pick them up ASAP.

"Oh." All the air left his lungs. He could insist it was none of their business, but they'd peck at him until he caved. No wonder Josey had sat on the outside. She'd blocked his escape. Their server appeared then, giving Sam time to avoid the topic. "I'll have the grilled cheese, tomato and bacon sandwich with chips and a cup of tomato soup," he said, stacking his menu on top of Wyatt's and Jo's. "And a Coke."

While his keepers ordered, he contemplated how much he had to share to satisfy them. The minimum. The two turned back to him the second the server walked away. Best to get this over with. "Things ended with Haley before they went too far," Sam told them.

"How far is *too far* in your world, Sam?" Wyatt asked. "You stayed at Haley's the night of her open house. Was it to explain your aversion to emotional intimacy and end things there, or did you wait until *after* you'd slept with her?"

Sam's jaw clenched. "That's none of your business."

"I've got to say this, because I'm your brother and I love you. The way you treat women really bothers me. It's wrong. You have some serious issues." Wyatt's jaw muscles ticked away. "You said you weren't going to cross the line with Haley. You *said* you wouldn't hurt her."

"Hey, in case you haven't noticed, I'm the one with the circles under my eyes and no appetite," he snapped. "Haley looks great. Got her hair cut short and everything. *She* didn't appear to be suffering last Thursday night when I went to see her."

"She dumped you?" Jo reached out and patted his arm. "Oh, God. We had it all wrong. I'm sorry, Sam. We could see how into her you were, and we hoped—"

"No." He squirmed, unable to look either of them in the eye. "I had a panic attack the night of her party, well, early the morning after, actually. I had to get out of there, and I left in a big fat hurry without telling her what was going on. I went back to apologize and to explain. We left it there with no hard feelings." His chest tightened. "I never meant to hurt her, and yeah, she got to me, but . . ." He shook his head. "I can't do the relationship thing." His brother and sister shared a long look.

"Sam, do you remember how it was with Mom and Dad, how they were with each other?" Josey asked.

He nodded.

"Me too," Wyatt said, his tone wistful. "Even when they disagreed about something, it was crystal clear they loved each other."

"Exactly." Josey sighed. "I remember our house being filled with happiness. They made each other laugh, and they were always hugging and kissing—each other and us. I want that again, which is why I keep looking for Mr. Right. How can you not want what we had as kids?"

"Haley was great, Sam. We liked her a lot," Wyatt added. "With her, you could've had what our parents had. It was obvious you two were falling for each other. Don't you want a family for yourself? I know I do."

Sam's eyes burned, and he kept his gaze fixed on the table.

"Do you think if Mom or Dad were here right now, either one of them would say they regretted the love they'd shared, even though it meant one of them would suffer losing the other first?" Jo asked. "What do you think they'd say about the way you keep that heart of yours locked away? It's like you're betraying what they taught us through their example."

"I'm not betraying anything. You don't know what it's like for me," he rasped out. "The panic attacks . . ."

Wyatt tugged at his sweatshirt's hoodie on his head. "Right. No possibility of understanding here," he said with a grunt.

"Look, I appreciate what you two are trying to do here, but it's over. Haley would never take me back now anyway."

"You don't know that." Josey shot him an exasperated look. "Do you love her?"

"I'm afraid so." And it wasn't the kind of love that would fade with time either. His was the kind of love that robbed him of sleep, stole his breath and gave him no peace.

"Then *do* something about your panic attacks and go beg her for a second chance." Wyatt scowled at him. "What you're going through right now, the loss of appetite and sleeplessness, listen to your body, because it's telling you turning away from Haley was the wrong thing to do. There are antianxiety meds for the panic attacks. Get a prescription already, talk to a shrink and get a life."

"I will if you will." Sam scowled back.

"If that's what it'll take, then make the appointment. We'll go see a shrink together."

"Thank God I'm well adjusted." Josey cracked a smile.

Wyatt laughed, and Sam couldn't help but grin. "You know what Haley calls memories? She says they're *flotation devices*, there to help keep us afloat through the tough times."

"Smart woman," Wyatt said. "Not to mention she's really pretty, and then there's the way she handles a sledgehammer."

Sam chuckled. "There is that." And so much more. "I'll think about it, and as lame as this *intervention* has been, I do appreciate your concern."

"Plus our support. Don't forget we're here to help." Wyatt smirked. "If you want, we can all go to Haley's house together. Jo and I will stand right behind you while you beg her to take you back."

"Humph." Their food came, and Sam forced himself to eat, while memories from his childhood bobbed around in his head. Happy memories of his mother and father and how secure he'd felt back then. He tried to imagine himself as a father, a husband. Haley had told him he'd make a great dad. *We could be together. You haven't prevented anything, Sam, all you've done is cut yourself off . . .*

What would his parents have to say about that? It was true; he had cut himself off. He'd made that choice long before he met Haley, and it had served him well. He'd been satisfied with his life, and now he was a wreck. What a mess.

He didn't know what to do, but he had a feeling he'd be up all night thinking again. If by chance he did manage to sleep, he was certain his dreams would be filled with Haley dressed in a superhero outfit, her sledgehammer at the ready and her face flushed with passion. God, he missed her.

Chapter Sixteen

Haley sat on her living room couch, Kathy beside her. Missing Sam was a constant dull ache, but it didn't do her any good to isolate herself. At the very least, the flirts and likes she got online gave her a distraction. "Thanks for volunteering to go through these profiles with me. I need your objectivity," Haley said, turning her laptop toward Kathy. "So what do you think of this guy? Rad7 and I have been chatting all week. He seems nice. He asked me to meet him for coffee, but I haven't replied yet."

Once she'd told her friends she'd joined an online dating site, the advice and support had poured in. Brent had even suggested he show up on her first meets and pretend he didn't know her, just to keep an eye on her to make sure she was safe. Haley smiled, gratitude for the people in her life warming her heart.

"Hmm." Kathy took her computer and scrolled through Rad7's profile and their chat history. "He does seem nice, and he's cute." She kept reading. "He left the meeting place up to you. That's a good sign."

"I thought so too." If only her heart weren't still set on a certain carpenter with commitment issues. "Coffee with Rad7 it is, then." She tried to muster some enthusiasm for Rad7 and took the laptop back.

She replied to his latest message, suggesting they meet at the Caribou Coffee on Grand and Oxford in Saint Paul. He wasn't online now, so she moved on to bachelor number two. "Here's the other guy I've been chatting with."

"BlueHeeler?" Kathy laughed. "You want to date another hound dog?"

Haley's stomach twisted at the reference to Sam. "This guy owns a Blue Heeler. If you check our chat history, you'll see where we talk about his dog. Besides, Sam is a horndog, not a hound dog."

"Well, BlueHeeler is definitely good looking."

The instant message pinged and the box popped up on the screen. Rad7 typed, "Hello, Comet. Caribou works for me. How's Sunday afternoon around three?"

Haley glanced at Kathy.

"Go for it, Haley."

"Perfect. See you there," Haley typed back.

"Great! I'll wait for you outside by the door. I'd like to stay and chat, but I'm heading out with friends. I'm looking forward to meeting you tomorrow. Later, Comet."

"Me too. Later," she typed and he went offline.

"How'd you come up with Comet?"

She shrugged. "Halley's Comet. It's not easy to come up with a fake name." She went back to her recent flirts. Even though she'd specified an age range and nonsmokers only, she still got hits from men in their forties and fifties and guys who described themselves as social smokers. She skimmed the new profiles sent to her as matches. *Delete, delete, delete.*

"Have you heard anything more from Sam?"

She shook her head. "I don't expect to. Josey hasn't picked up the bowls either, which is strange. Maybe she didn't get the message. I suppose I could drop them off at their office."

"Do you want me to take them to Haney & Sons? That way there's no chance you'll run into Sam."

"That's sweet, but no. I'm fine." Not really, but she'd fake it till *fine* became her reality. Meeting new men would help. That was the plan, anyway. At least she hadn't allowed herself to sink back into the isolation-from-men cave she'd been in after Michael left her for adventure. *Haley, you are the adventure.* How could Sam say that to her, and then just walk away? He'd certainly come across as sincere.

Sam had known exactly what to say to make her feel better. He'd been so sweet about bolstering her self-confidence, praising her efforts at home repair, telling her she was a goddess with a sledgehammer. Her heart gave a painful thud, and the back of her throat burned.

Being with Sam had been good for her, and no matter how much his rejection hurt, she didn't have a single regret. Well, other than the fact that they weren't together. Stupid stubborn man.

Haley parked her car a block away from the Caribou Coffee on Grand Ave. She checked her phone for time. Two minutes to three. Her nerves revved up. She got out of her car and surveyed the coffee shop. An older man stood by the curb smoking a cigarette, but there was no sign of Rad7.

Great. She hated being the first to arrive. It made her look a little too eager. Blowing out a breath, she crossed the street and walked toward Caribou, the rich scent of coffee filling the air. Maybe Rad7 wouldn't show. They hadn't exchanged phone numbers, so there'd be no way to let her know. Fine. If she got stood up, she'd buy herself a latte and a cookie and call it a day.

"Comet?" the older guy asked.

"Yes?" Confused, she glanced at him.

"It's me." He smiled, his teeth stained with nicotine. "Rad7."

She gaped. "No."

"Yeah."

"How old is your profile picture?" Too stunned to be polite, she gawked. His hair was graying and he had a paunch.

"It's a few years old."

More like fifteen or twenty. Incredible. What a jerk. "You smoke. I *did* put nonsmokers only in my preferences, and I also included an age range, twenty-five to thirty. You're well out of my range. Did you even read what I wrote in my profile?"

"Sure, but hey, everybody fudges the truth on those sites."

"I didn't. Does this work for you? Misrepresenting yourself, I mean." No way was she having coffee or anything else with him. If he lied about his age and whether or not he smoked, he'd lie about other things. Haley peeked at the ring finger on his left hand. Sure enough, that finger had the telltale indentation from a wedding ring recently removed. She wanted to give him a finger herself. "Never mind. I don't even want to know."

"Suit yourself," he said with a shrug. He reached for a cigarette from the pack in his pocket and lit up. "So, do you want coffee or what?"

"No thanks." She turned on her heel and marched back to her car, careful to make sure he didn't follow. *Yuck.* The minute she was safely in her car with the doors locked, she called Kathy.

"Hey," Kathy answered right away. "Why are you calling me? Aren't you on your date?"

"He lied about his age by twenty years." She huffed out a laugh. "Oh, my God, Kathy, he was so creepy, and I'm pretty sure he's married too." She started her car.

"I should have warned you about this, Haley. A lot of guys view online dating sites as a hookup place for sex."

"So I've heard, but it still took me by surprise."

"I'm sure. Don't give up after one creep though."

"Is there a specific number of creeps I have to go through before I *should* give up?"

Kathy chuckled. "No, that's entirely up to you, but at least move on to bachelor number two and three. I know couples who've met online and are happily married now."

Haley wanted to put her head down on her steering wheel and weep. She missed Sam, dammit, and forcing herself to get out there to date because he'd dumped her made her angry at him and herself. Meeting new men to get over the one she'd fallen for didn't make sense after all. She swiped at the tears on her cheeks. "Are you just saying that, or is it true?"

"It's true. I swear. My cousin and her husband met on the same site you're on, and if you want, I'll introduce you to them."

"Not necessary. I believe you." She pulled a tissue from her jacket pocket and wiped her nose.

"Go home and make yourself a cup of tea. Then check your site. I'll bet you have a ton of new flirts, and one of them is bound to be a really great guy."

Doubtful. "Sounds like a plan. Thanks for being there for me."

"Always."

"Say hi to Blake. I'm glad things are working out for the two of you. At least one of us is happily involved. It gives me hope."

"It'll happen for you, Haley. I know it will."

Her vision misted over again. "Hope so." Haley scanned the avenue for any sign of Creepy Guy, relieved when she didn't see him. She and Kathy said their good-byes, and she pulled her car away from the curb. On to bachelors number two and three. She headed for home—where she'd be surrounded by reminders of Sam in every room. At least she had dinner at her folks to look forward to later, so she wouldn't be alone.

As she drove, the temptation to call Sam overwhelmed her. Maybe if she did, this time she'd come up with the right words to get through his irrational fears. He cared for her. He'd said as much, and she didn't doubt him. She wouldn't call him, though.

If he didn't want to work through things with her, nothing she said or did would make a difference. The best she could do was to focus on forgetting him. "Bring it, bachelor number two. Here's hoping your picture isn't twenty years old, and your profile isn't a lame attempt at fiction."

Sam pulled his van into the condo parking lot, the late afternoon sun nearly blinding him through the windshield. He flipped the visor down and found a spot to park. Gathering his clipboard, catalogs and tool belt, he thought of Haley. The St. Paul Winter Carnival had begun. Weeks ago he'd asked her to go with him to check out the ice sculptures. Did she remember? Did she ever think of him? She was on his mind twenty-four-seven.

After Wyatt and Josey's intervention, he'd tried to work through his fears. He'd even made an appointment with his doctor to ask about antianxiety medication, but then he'd changed his mind and canceled the next day. Which only made him feel worse about everything. What if he did need Wyatt to hold his hand and take him to the doctor? *Loser.*

He turned his mind to the job before him, a new bathroom faucet to install and a kitchen remodel estimate for—he lifted the clipboard to read—Janice Lynch. Pushing his way into the vestibule, he hoped she was a little old lady in her eighties. He searched the list of names and condo numbers next to the intercom buttons, found the right one and pressed.

"Yes?" a feminine voice answered—not sounding at all old or frail.

"Sam Haney with Haney & Sons," he said into the speaker.

"I'm on the third floor. Take a right as you leave the elevator. Come on up," she said.

The heavy glass door buzzed. He entered the building and walked to the elevators straight ahead. He steeled himself on the way up. The construction season couldn't start fast enough as far as he was concerned. At least he always knew what to expect with new construction. The elevator stopped on the third floor. He made his way down the hall, found the right door and knocked. The door swung open, and a pretty redhead smiled at him. No ring on her finger. She wore yoga pants and a casual fleece top that showed a bit of strap from the camisole beneath, along with a glimpse of bare shoulder.

"Hi, I'm Janice. Come on in." She stepped back.

"I'm Sam," he said, handing her a card. Her fingers brushed his. *Hmm.* Could be his imagination, or an accident, but . . . was she being less than businesslike? "Bathroom faucet first?"

"Sure." She grabbed the box containing the new fixture from her kitchen counter and handed it to him. "The bathroom is the first door on the left down that hall. I'll be in the dining room working if you need anything."

"OK. Thanks." He'd imagined the finger brushing. Things were going to be fine. She was all business, not flirty. Box in hand, Sam set out for the bathroom and settled into the job. He'd been happy before he met Haley. Hadn't he? At least he hadn't been aware of how empty his life had been of any meaningful relationships outside of family.

It didn't take him more than thirty minutes to change out the old faucet for the newer, more stylish fixture. He cleaned up, put the old fixture in the now-empty box, and brought it back to the dining room, setting it down on a placemat.

"Do you want to check out the new faucet while I start measuring the kitchen? I understand you want to keep the room the same, only with new cabinets, countertops and appliances, is that correct?"

She had a bunch of papers and a laptop set up on the table. "That's right. New cabinets, counters, sink and appliances. Oh, and flooring. I forgot to mention the floor when I called."

"No problem." Sam took out his tape measure, and Ms. Lynch left to check out his work in the bathroom. He measured, made notes and drew a diagram.

Ms. Lynch returned and leaned against the wall to watch him. "The faucet works great, and I appreciate the way you cleaned up."

"Part of the job." He measured the space for her stove. "Do you want to keep the sizes of your appliances the same as they are now? They're pretty standard, and you shouldn't have any trouble finding replacements that will fit."

"Yes. I don't want to spend a ton, but it's overdue for a change, and since the appliances are beginning to show their age, I figure I might as well do everything at once. Then I won't have to worry about my kitchen for another twelve or fifteen years."

"Hmm." He flashed her a grin. "That's optimistic. For the appliances, anyway. Things don't last like they used to."

"I suppose." She moved back to the table.

Sam continued to measure and make notes, conscious of the fact that her gaze kept landing on him. Once he was done, he joined her in the dining room. "Do you mind if I sit here to write up the estimate?" he asked, handing her the catalogs he'd brought.

"Not at all. Have a seat," she said with a smile.

"We can save you money on materials if you order through us. Appliances, cabinets, everything Lowes, Menards and Home Depot carries, we can get for you at a nice discount. Everything you'll need can be found in these catalogs." He tapped the catalogs she'd placed on the table.

"You know, you come highly recommended," she purred.

"Oh?" *Gulp.* His heart kicked up a notch. He kept his attention on his cell phone calculator, crunching numbers. Was that a cat under the table? Damn. Not a cat. Ms. Lynch's foot continued to slide up his leg, past his knee to his inner thigh. Sam shot up from the table. "Look, I don't know who recommended me to you, but—"

"Yvonne sings your praises."

"—I don't do this kind of thing anymore. Are you serious about the remodel quote, or—"

"Probably not. Why don't you do *this kind of thing* anymore?" she asked, her face a pout.

"Because . . ." *I've fallen in love, that's why.* None of her business. He raked his fingers through his hair. *Guess this answers the question about returning to my old ways.* "I'm not interested, but thanks." He wasn't that guy anymore, and he never would be again. Being with Haley had ruined him.

He wrote out a quick bill, padding it for the wasted time spent doing the estimate, and handed it to her. "I'll leave the kitchen estimate with you in case you change your mind. Will that be check or credit card today?"

"Credit card," she said, her tone flat.

Sam rushed through the transaction and got out of there as fast as he could. Was his sex life over forever? Had falling for Haley doomed him to a life of self-gratification only? Come to think of it, wasn't that exactly what he'd been having all along, only with partners? He made a beeline for Haney & Sons, full of questions only one person could answer. He parked, climbed out and strode into the kitchen. His uncles were putting on their coats. "Heading out?" Sam asked.

"Yep," Uncle Dan said. "What about you? Aren't you finished for the day?"

"Yeah, but I want to talk to Gramps before I head home. Is he here?"

Uncle Jack nodded toward the hallway. "In his office."

"Thanks. See you tomorrow." He hurried down the hall. Grandpa Joe sat at his desk, which was a mess as usual. Still, as chaotic as the work space appeared to be, his grandfather always knew exactly where everything was. "Hey, Gramps. Do you have a minute?"

"For you? Always." Grandpa Joe leaned back in his chair and smiled. "What's on your mind?"

Too keyed up to sit, Sam wandered around the office, looking at stuff on the shelves, parts catalogs, bowling trophies, the things he'd grown up seeing every day. "How come we don't have a bowling team anymore?"

"You came to talk to me about joining a bowling league?"

"No." Sam cast him a glance. "Do you remember when that whole radio thing happened?"

Gramps grunted. "I wish I could forget."

Guilt pinched at his heart. Or was it shame? "You said something that day." Sam took one of the bowling trophies from the shelf and wiped the dust off with his fingers. "You said once you met Grandma Maggie, the thought of being with any other woman made your . . . uh . . ." He cleared his throat.

"Junk shrivel up?" Grandpa said. "I remember."

"You said you had eyes only for Grandma, and that we Haney men are like that once we meet the one." He set the trophy back on the shelf. "Is there any truth to that, or were you just trying to make a point?"

Gramps gestured toward the chairs in front of his desk. "Sit down, son. You can talk to me about anything. You know that, right?"

"I know, but talking about this just . . . it isn't *easy.*" Sam slid into one of the chairs and slumped down.

"Things weren't any different back in my day than they are now. Women propositioned me on the job more frequently than you'd imagine, and no—I didn't always turn them down. I even dated a few. But once I met my sweet Maggie, that was it." He shook his head. "Mind you, we men are visual, and I still appreciated the occasional *view,* but the thought of touching anyone but your grandmother turned my stomach and yes, shriveled the family jewels." Grandpa Joe's eyebrows rose. "Does that answer your question?"

"Yeah." Sam chewed on that for a bit. "Gramps, if Grandma Maggie passes before you, how the hell will you survive? How do you even deal with the possibility?"

"Your grandmother and I have had a lot of wonderful years together, and God willing, we'll have many more. I love her more today than I did yesterday, and the thought of losing her *would* terrify me if I didn't believe we'd somehow find a way to be together again. Either through reincarnation, or in heaven or whatever it is awaiting us on the other side."

"Really? You believe that?"

"Really. Not only that, but she will always live on through all of you. Our children, grandchildren and great-grandchildren carry a part of us forward, and that's a huge comfort. I have all of you, and if I should lose her, having family makes living worthwhile."

Sam nodded. "Flotation devices."

"Come again?" Grandpa Joe grinned.

"Uh, just thinking about what someone told me once. So, you're saying that having family around helps keep us afloat through the hard times."

"Ah. Good analogy, and it's true. Grieving for lost loved ones is painful but unavoidable, and every family goes through tough times. You have to take the good with the bad. There are no easy streets through life, Sam. Every road has its own unique set of potholes." Gramps leveled a serious look his way. "Does this have something to do with Haley Cooper?"

"Yeah." Sam's eyes stung. "I blew it."

"Well, if she's the one, I suggest you un-blow it. You're a Haney. You have skills. We Haney men can fix anything."

Sam huffed out a breath, his eyes a little moist. "Don't let Josey hear you say that, Gramps. It's sexist."

"Ah, well." He waved a hand in the air. "You know what I mean."

"I do." He rose from the chair. "Thanks, I . . ." He cleared his throat. "You and Grandma Maggie mean the world to me."

"We love you too, Sam." He got up from the desk and stretched. "All this talk has me wanting to put my arms around my sweet wife. Every day I have with your grandmother is a gift, and I consider myself a very lucky man. Let's get out of here. We can lock up and walk out together."

Sam waited while his grandfather bundled himself up in his coat, scarf and gloves. The two of them walked outside together, and he waited while Gramps set the alarm system and locked the door. Grandpa Joe gripped the back of Sam's neck as they walked.

"Sam, I know how tough it was on you kids when you lost your mom and dad, and you've always taken things the hardest out of the three of you. Don't let losing them prevent you from reaching for your own happiness. That would break your mom's and dad's hearts. It would break mine and your grandmother's hearts too."

"Oh, great. Lay *more* guilt on my shoulders." A mirthless laugh escaped.

"Ah, I've always wondered and worried." Grandpa Joe stilled, and his brow furrowed. "You think what happened to your mom and dad is somehow your fault?"

He shrugged. "If it hadn't been my birthday, if they hadn't been flying home for my party—"

"Bullshit. We could've put your party off for a week, or they could've decided on a different weekend for their anniversary trip. If this. If that." Gramps shook his head. "So many variables, and you had nothing to do with a single one of them. You were a kid. You didn't get to make the decisions. You didn't have any control, and what happened was *not* your fault."

"OK, Gramps." His throat tightened, and the familiar sense of helplessness gripped him. He'd been unable to prevent his parents' deaths, and then he'd made a conscious decision to shut himself off from emotional attachment. Had his decision been all about control—at least the illusion of control? "Good night. I'll see you tomorrow."

"Good night, Sam. Think about what I said."

"I will." Sam climbed into his van, his mind a whirl of connecting dots as he drove home to his bare white walls and lonely apartment. Even where he lived had been about distancing himself. His apartment was not a home; it was a place to stay, nothing more. He hadn't made a personal investment. No decoration on his walls, no photos of family or much of anything having to do with his life or personality. He'd kept the place pretty much the way he'd found it—impersonal.

And then Haley Cooper had looked down her pert nose at him, and any illusions of control he'd ever had shattered. He'd fallen for her before he'd even realized what was happening. He had worked so hard to convince himself that proving she'd been wrong about him had been about the insult to his skill. How could he have been so blind? She was his *only*.

If he didn't fix things, he had nothing but an empty future to look forward to, with no memories, no family of his own to sustain him. Not to mention he'd be sentenced to a sex life involving only himself and his right hand. After having experienced superglue sex with Haley, that alone was enough to knock his ass off the fence he'd been sitting on for far too long.

He had to come up with a plan. Somehow he had to find a way to convince Haley to give him another chance. He only hoped he wasn't too late.

Chapter Seventeen

Haley placed her lunch order at Panera's counter and took the pager from the cashier's hand. Getting out there to date had only made the pain of missing Sam worse, and her heart grew heavier with each passing day. "So, I met bachelor number two after work yesterday." She stepped aside to wait while Kathy and Felicia placed their orders.

"Yeah? Where'd you go?" Felicia asked, handing over her credit card to the woman behind the counter.

"I met him at Nina's Coffee Café." Once Kathy had ordered her lunch, the three of them moved to the beverage stand, and Haley filled a large mug with coffee.

"Was this BlueHeeler?" Kathy asked.

"Yep." She scanned the restaurant. "There's a table. Let's grab it before someone else beats us to it."

"BlueHeeler, huh?" Felicia giggled. "I'll bet his tail wagged when he met you."

"Ha, ha." Haley slid into a chair. "Actually, he was really weird. He just kind of sat there and stared at me. He hardly said anything, and it made me really nervous. And when I'm nervous, I babble."

"Maybe he's shy." Kathy settled on the seat across from her.

"Could be, but there was no chemistry. I'm not going to see him again." She sipped her coffee. "At least his profile picture matched his current age. That's an improvement over Rad7."

"So, who's next?" Felicia asked.

"I'm meeting bachelor number three after work today. He goes by Waiting4U, and he works as a financial advisor." She wasn't really up for number three. Maybe she'd pull a no-show.

"Waiting4U. Huh, his online handle sounds kind of corny but sweet." Kathy grinned. "Where to this time?"

"J&S Bean Factory on Randolph. It's close to home." She could swing by, take a look and then keep going if she wanted. Haley huffed out a breath. "By the time I meet someone decent, I'll have visited all of the coffeehouses in St. Paul. In less than two weeks, I've been to Caribou, Nina's and now the Bean Factory." Her pager started to buzz. "I'll be right back."

She went to pick up her soup-and-sandwich combo from the counter. Waiting4U might be a great guy. She hoped so, but she wasn't counting on it. Still, three men in two weeks' time, and nothing to show for it? Her stomach dropped. If bachelor number three didn't work out, she'd take a break. The fact that she compared them all to Sam didn't help. Well, nothing could've helped Rad7. One more date like that, and she really would be ready for a man ban.

Haley parked her car across the street and half a block down from the coffeehouse. Waiting4U stood on the corner. He'd seen her and waved as she'd driven by. OK, he was nice looking, and she liked the way he dressed. She'd smiled and waved back. Thank goodness he matched his profile picture. She climbed out of her car, crossed the street and made her way down the sidewalk. "Hi," she said. "I'm Haley."

"Nice to meet you, Haley. I'm Jason." He gestured toward the coffeehouse. "Shall we?"

"Sure." She moved to the door, expecting him to open it for her. He didn't. Sam would have, but then he was a throwback. *Let it go.* Most men didn't open doors for women anymore. She walked into the small café. The smell of coffee and the savory scent of food permeated the coffee shop, and her stomach grumbled.

Jason pulled his wallet from his pocket and ordered a coffee for himself before stepping back to give her room. "I hope you don't mind going Dutch." He flashed her a smarmy grin. "I mean, since it's just a meet and greet. Not really a date at this point, right?"

"Oh." No door opening, and cheap. *Hmmm.* "No, that's fine." Did that mean he'd taken one look at her and decided she didn't do it for him? Haley ordered a chai tea—in a to-go cup just in case—and by the time she got her beverage, Jason had already seated himself at a table. Another point gone. He hadn't waited for her. She'd give him twenty minutes to redeem himself, and if he didn't, she'd leave.

She set her tea on the table and started to take off her coat. "So, you're a financial advisor. What's that like?"

"It's great," he said, launching into all the high-profile clients he had, their portfolios and his own financial goals. "I own a nice house in Edina, and a rental property in south Minneapolis. This summer I'm going to look into buying a vacation home somewhere on a lake up north."

He hadn't even waited until she'd sat down before giving her a list of his assets. Was she being nitpicky? "Sounds great," she muttered as she took her seat, and he was off again.

"Yep, it is, plus I have a Chaparral Signature 31, which is a great boat, by the way. I keep it at the King's Cove Marina on the St. Croix

River. I also have two four-wheeler all-terrain vehicles if you're into that sort of thing, and a membership at the Interlachen Country Club. I golf a lot."

Did he think telling her what he owned made a difference? Not once did he ask a single question about her. "Besides boating, golf and ATVs, what else do you like to do for fun?" she asked, hoping to steer him away from his materialistic monologue.

"I like to travel, especially to tropical places. In fact, next week I'm going on a vacation to Jamaica. I'll be staying at the Sandals Negri Spa and Resort. It's all-inclusive, top of the line."

She nodded, and sipped her tea. Disappointed, she fought the urge to roll her eyes, and only half listened as bachelor number three went on and on about the ritzy places he'd been, and where he wanted to go in the future. Her boycott on men looked better and better by the minute. She could always start the remodel on her downstairs bathroom.

Her heart ached as images of *Instructor Sam* flashed through her mind. Thanks to him, she now knew how to get the job done herself. Had she kept all the catalogs Sam had given her? She'd go with a lighter decor this time, a cream-colored vanity, shiny subway tiles on the walls, and a nice one-piece shower insert. Or, maybe it would be fun to do it up in a fifties motif to match the post WWII era her bungalow had been built. She'd do an online search for retro stuff once she got home.

"So, what do you think?"

"Huh?" Her attention returned to Jason. "About what?"

"My Mercedes is five years old now, and I'm shopping for a new car. Should I buy a BMW or a Lexus? Which do you prefer?"

"Oh." Haley stood up and reached for her coat. "I'm sorry, Jason. This just isn't working for me. It was nice meeting you though. Best of luck in your date search." She grabbed her chai and headed for the door. Once she got home she'd go downstairs with her tape measure—which she could use properly now, also thanks to her relationship-phobe handyman—and start planning her new home improvement project. To hell with online dating. If she was meant to meet someone, she would. And if not? Her eyes stung a bit at the alternative.

She could join a few clubs, find volunteer opportunities. Perhaps it made better sense to meet a man in a more organic way, so the two of them would be drawn together by mutual interests. Or not. Again the urge to call Sam overwhelmed her. Did he miss her even a little bit? She waited for a break in traffic so she could cross the street.

"Hey, wait up, Haley." Jason joined her. "I'm sorry."

"For what?"

"When I'm nervous, I get . . . Well, you're much prettier in person than you are in your profile pictures. I guess I was trying too hard to impress you, and it came off as shallow."

She got that, and she may have been a smidge judgmental. "It's OK."

"Let me walk you to your car. I'd love to take you out for dinner. If you're free tonight, that is."

"All right." He did have a nice smile. "You have until we reach my car to convince me you're worth another shot, and by worth, I don't mean *things you own*," she teased.

Sam drove down Randolph, heading downtown to meet Wyatt and Josey at The Bulldog. After talking to Gramps two days ago, he'd racked his brain for a way to redeem himself with Haley. He needed to run things by his siblings. Stopping at a red light, Sam tapped his fingers to the rock music blaring from his radio.

The scent of coffee infiltrated his van, and he looked for the source. J&S Bean Factory on the next block up and to his right. A woman walked out and stopped by the curb as if waiting for someone. There was something so familiar about her that he stared harder. She turned then, and his lungs seized. *Haley.*

A man joined her. They talked, and Haley smiled. The two of them crossed the street together and disappeared from his view. Sam's heart pounded. She was on a date. He'd been losing sleep, losing weight, hemming and hawing over what to do, and meanwhile, some other man had swooped in to steal her away.

He had to do something fast, or he'd lose her for good. The light changed, and he hit the gas, praying she hadn't seen him. He wasn't ready to plead his case to her yet. A new kind of panic welled. He loved her, and she'd said she had feelings for him too. He'd been insane to push her away, and now he might miss his chance to win her back.

Sam parked his van and hurried into The Bulldog. He caught sight of Wyatt and Josey and wended his way through the packed bar and grill. "I need help," he said, sliding into his seat.

"Been telling you that for years, bro," Wyatt said, saluting him with his bottle of beer.

"Seriously." Sam signaled the server, holding up Josey's Michelob and pointing to it. "I need help coming up with a plan to get Haley back in my life. I saw her with another guy about ten minutes ago."

"Glad to hear you've finally come to your senses," Josey said. "Roses. Show up at her house with a dozen long-stem red roses, and beg for mercy."

"No." Wyatt's expression turned pensive. "The begging part is good, but roses are temporary. If I were a woman, I wouldn't want flowers. They don't last."

"Neither do chocolates, unless you count the extra poundage they cause," Jo said with a smirk.

"Nope, chocolates won't do either," Wyatt said, straightening in his chair. "Given the way Sam left her, he needs to stay away from anything that implies *temporary*. Flowers or candy might even come across as an empty gesture. Sam needs to come up with something meaningful and Haley-specific, something that says *I paid attention and I know you.* You want to make a statement, Sam, like, *I'm here to stay.*"

"Wyatt is right," Jo admitted. "What you need is a grand gesture, something that screams you want a future with her."

"She enjoys snowmobiling, and she did say she ought to get one for herself. I've considered buying one for her. Would that work?" Sam's hopes soared. Although, if Haley had her own snowmobile, he'd miss the fun of having her arms around him.

"Too much and not sentimental at all." Jo pursed her lips. "Besides snowmobiling, what did the two of you enjoy doing together the most?"

"I enjoyed everything we did together, which wasn't much. We . . . we'd just gotten started." Sam rubbed the stubble on his chin, remembering the way he and Haley had worked side by side on her house. "We enjoyed remodeling her house together," he offered. "She's great with tear-outs and installing tile. I'd buy her a new sledgehammer, but she already has one."

Wyatt straightened. "Oh, man. I have the greatest idea."

"Me too." The perfect gift came to Sam in a flash. He explained what he had in mind, and certainty welled in his chest.

"Perfect." Wyatt grinned and high-fived him.

"What do you think, Jo?" Sam asked. "You're a girl. Would something like that work for you?"

"First of all, I'm a woman, not a girl." She scowled at him.

Their server came to the table with his beer, and the three of them ordered food. Now that he'd come to grips with his need to have Haley in his life, Sam actually had an appetite. "Sorry. A *woman*. Would it work? Will it be a grand enough gesture?"

"It might work if you're not too late, and *if* she isn't over you yet." Her pitying expression put a damper on his spirits. Josey shrugged. "I hope it's not too late, Sam, but you said you saw her out with another man, and it may have been a date. What if she really likes the guy?"

"It's only been a couple of weeks since I stopped by to talk to her. She can't be that serious about him yet."

"No? Well, here's a question for you." Wyatt flashed him a pointed look. "How long did it take you to fall for Haley?"

"Ten minutes." He buried his face in his hands and groaned. "Oh, God, I'm screwed."

"Not necessarily. Tomorrow is Saturday. As soon as Home Depot opens, go get what you need." Wyatt did a search on his phone. "The Target on University Avenue stays open until midnight. After we eat, go buy her a sentimental card to go with the gift. Women love that kind of thing."

"We do," Josey added.

"I will." Sam took a fortifying swig of his beer. He had one more thing in mind to get her, but at this time of year, he wasn't sure if he could find what he wanted. His cousin might be able to help. He pulled his phone from its holster. "I'll be right back. I need to call Andrea."

"What for?"

"To ask a favor." He headed to the street where it was quiet enough to hear her. Goose bumps formed on his arms and his hands froze, but he toughed it out, made the call and got the answer he needed. He'd stop at her house on the way to Target. Smiling, he walked back to their table. "All set."

"What was all that about?" Jo asked, her forehead puckered.

"It's no big deal, an added prop is all."

"If this doesn't work, you're going to feel like shit," Wyatt said. "Call if you need company."

"I will."

"And if it does work out"—Wyatt smirked—"and you end up marrying her, you do realize there's only one letter difference between her first name and our last name, right?"

Sam frowned. "Yeah, so?"

"She'll become Haley Haney. Isn't her middle name Helen? Her initials will be H.H.H. She'll be one H short of four. I'm going to have to tease her."

"Good thing her name isn't Laney." Josey snorted. "Then she'd be Laney Haney. In fact, if you two ever have a daughter—"

"You're both idiots." Their food came, and Sam wolfed his down. He laid fifteen dollars on the table and put on his coat. "If that's not enough, I'll pay you back later."

Josey picked up the bills and handed them back. "Don't worry about it. Dinner's on us tonight. Go."

"Thanks. Wish me luck." He started for the door.

"Good luck. Text us," Wyatt called after him.

Sam held up his hand, letting his brother know he'd heard. He headed to his cousin's house first. He had a plan. Haney men had skills, and there wasn't anything he couldn't fix.

Haley's phone pealed. She dropped her toast on the plate and chewed fast while reaching for her cell. Swallowing, she checked the ID and brought it up to her ear. "Hey, Felicia. How're you this fabulous sunny morning?"

"Well aren't you perky as hell? That must mean yesterday's date with Waiting4U turned out OK."

"Not really. It started out horribly, but he talked me into having dinner with him, which I did." She moved to her living room couch and curled up in the pool of sunshine beaming in from her east-facing window. "He's a very ambitious and materialistic man. Nice, but not at all my type. I ended up paying for my own dinner and telling him I wasn't interested in seeing him again."

"I don't get it. If Waiting 4U was a bust, then why do you sound so cheerful?"

"Because I've decided to take a break from online dating."

"But you just started. At least give it a few months."

"Nope. I'm going to remodel my downstairs bathroom instead."

"By yourself?"

"Yes, by myself. I'll hire an electrician and a plumber when I need to, but there's no reason I can't do most of the work on my own."

"Oh?"

"You don't sound convinced." Haley recalled the disastrous state of her kitchen and bathroom pre-Haney & Sons. She couldn't blame her. "Sam taught me a lot, and I'm confident I can pull it off."

"I'm sure you can remodel your bathroom, Haley. I'm just disappointed I won't get to live vicariously through you now that you've decided to take a break from online dating."

"You could always sign up on an online site yourself, you know."

"Mmm. Do you need any help with your new project? I'm pretty good at painting. I'd appreciate it if you'd teach me a few new skills. There are things I'd like to do with my townhouse, but with my student loans and car payment, I can't really afford to hire anybody to do the work."

"I'd love to teach you what I've learned. If you want to pitch in, get your hands dirty and callused, that'd be great." Excitement for her new project surged. "I'm going to need help with carrying things out to a dumpster, like the old vanity, the toilet, buckets of construction debris and stuff like that. Do you think your brother would be willing to lend a hand? I'd pay him, of course."

"He's always looking for a way to earn some cash. His college classes keep him too busy to take on more than temporary jobs, and something like this would be perfect."

A knock on her door startled Haley, and she glanced out the front window toward the street. Sam's SUV was parked in front of her mailbox—in the same spot where he'd always parked when they were working on her house. Her heart leaped up her throat. "Oh my God, you'll never guess who's at my front door."

"Kathy told me about this game. Wait. Isaiah Mustafa?"

Her mouth dry, Haley walked to the door. "Who's Isaiah Mustafa?"

"The hot brother who made Old Spice famous a few years ago."

"Oh, I remember him. Gotta go. I'll call you back later."

Felicia sighed. "You'd better."

Haley ended the call. Her hand shaking and her heart thumping, she opened the door. "Sam. What are you doing here?"

"I brought you a present." He lifted a gift bag in the air for her to see. His gaze roamed over her. "Along with fresh cinnamon bagels and cream cheese." He lifted the other hand to reveal a Panera bag.

She was still in her pajamas, flannel pants and a snug long-sleeve T-shirt. No bra. Great. "Wait here." She slammed the door in his face and hurried to her room to dress. She had no idea why he'd shown up at her door, but she didn't need him ogling her braless, traitorous breasts. Her nipples had pebbled at the sight of him, or maybe it was from the cold coming in through the door. Must be the cold.

She tossed her phone on her dresser and rummaged through the drawers. Haley dressed in record time, jeans, a sweater—with a padded bra beneath that would *not* show off the state of her nipples. Running a brush through her hair, she struggled to calm her nerves.

She marched back to her front door, and once again threw it open. "If you're here for your bowls, they're *still* in the breezeway." It hurt to look at him, so she didn't.

"I'm not here for the bowls. If you don't want to invite me in, I'll understand completely, and I'll leave these for you." He tried to hand her the two bags.

She didn't take them. "Come in." She moved aside, and he stepped over the threshold, close enough that she caught a whiff of his aftershave. That hurt too. "Coffee?"

"I'd love a cup, thanks."

"Have a seat." Haley hurried off to the kitchen, buying herself a few more seconds to pull herself together. She poured herself a fresh cup, and another for Sam. Taking a deep breath, she returned to the living room and set the mugs on the table next to the Panera bag.

Sam had placed the gift bag on the floor by the couch. Curiosity burned through her, but she was distracted by the very sight of him. He wore the nice blue sweater his grandmother had given him for Christmas, and a pair of jeans that looked as if he'd ironed them. They had a crease in front. As surreptitiously as possible, she drank him in.

She reached for her coffee, going for casual nonchalance. Ha. Her insides quaked and stirred like some kind of off-kilter washing machine in a mad spin cycle. "So, what brings you here today, and bearing gifts no less? A consolation prize?"

"No." Sam raked his fingers through his hair, his Adam's apple bobbing.

Good. At least she knew he was nervous too. "What is this for then?" She set her coffee down and leaned over the gift bag, trying like hell to catch a glimpse of what might lie beneath the tissue paper.

"Haley, I can't—"

"I know you *can't*, Sam." She shot up from the couch and paced. "We've already been through this, haven't we? Did you show up today just to—"

"Are you *always* going to jump to conclusions every time I open my mouth? Is this what it's going to be like for the rest of our lives? You interrupting me?"

Stunned, she stopped her pacing and wrapped her arms around herself. She stared out her front window, unsure she'd heard him correctly and unwilling to ask him to repeat himself.

"I was *going* to say that I can't sleep. I've lost weight, and you're on my mind pretty much around the clock. And with you so close right now, I can hardly breathe. I was wrong, Haley."

"About what?" she asked, afraid she'd break down into a weepy, snotty mess if she looked at him.

"Pretty much everything. I've kept myself cut off from becoming seriously involved with anyone because more than anything, I fear losing the people I love. I believed that losing my *one and only*—that would be you, by the way—would be the very worst kind of loss, and it would destroy me."

She nodded, conscious of the way he watched her. *Wait.* Did he just say . . . Her stupid hopes shot up again. She put a lid on them, unwilling to allow herself to go *there*. Besides, she wasn't about to jump right back into his arms.

"I asked Grandpa Joe how he dealt with loss, how he coped with the possibility that Grandma Maggie might go before him. Do you want to hear what he had to say?"

Her eyes filled. Still giving him her back, she nodded again.

"Then come sit with me, Haley. Please come sit with me."

She shook her head, and a tear slid down her cheek. She so didn't want to blubber in front of him, and she was definitely on the verge.

"OK. I respect that." Sam sighed heavily. "Grandpa Joe believes he and Grandma Maggie will somehow be together again once they both leave this world, and even without her, having family around will help make his life worth living. He says if Grandma Maggie goes first, a part of her will live on in us, so it's not like he'll ever lose her completely."

The rustle of paper behind her piqued her curiosity.

"Here," Sam said, coming up beside her. "I brought you these, because I wanted you to know I heard what you said. I paid attention. You got through to me."

He handed her a pair of water wings, the kind little kids wore while swimming. She turned them over in her hands, staring at them. "You brought me water wings?"

"I brought you *flotation devices*. Remember? You said memories are like flotation devices, and they keep us afloat through the tough times. When Grandpa Joe talked about how his children, grandchildren and great-grandchildren will sustain him if he loses Grandma, I figured families are also flotation devices. I get it now. I want to make memories with you, Haley. Please give me a second chance, because I fell in love with you the day we met, and I'm not going to fall out of love with you. Ever."

A sob broke free, and she covered her mouth. Sam drew her into his arms and held her just right. The water wings fell to the floor, and she wrapped her arms around his waist. She wanted to stay right there for the rest of the day. "I fell in love with you, too. I've missed you so much."

"Please," he whispered into her ear. "Come sit on the couch and see what I brought you."

"All right," she said, wiping her eyes. "We need to discuss a few things, negotiate terms."

"I'm all ears, Ms. Paralegal." He led her to the couch and settled her there. "I have a feeling I'm going to need sustenance for this conversation. You sit. I'm going to go get plates, a knife for the cream cheese and napkins."

"Bring me a few sheets of paper towel, too," she said, tossing him a watery smile. She sagged into the couch cushions, drained, hungry and optimistic.

Sam returned and set two places at the coffee table. He reached into the Panera bag and brought out two bagels, placing one on her plate and one on his. "I'm starving," he said, handing her a wad of paper towels.

She wiped her nose and sopped up her tears. As hungry as she was, she couldn't eat, but she let him fix a bagel for her anyway. "Panera's cinnamon bagels are my favorite," she said, her voice quavering.

"Mine too. See? We're perfect for each other." He grinned. "Do you want to open your present or negotiate first?"

She sniffed and hiccupped. "Negotiate."

"I figured, what with you being a paralegal and all." He straightened and placed his hands on his knees, bracing himself. "OK, shoot. What do you need?"

"How do I know I can trust you when you're working? Women are still going to throw themselves at you." She gestured toward him. "You're hot, Sam, and you have this scruffy-little-boy-who-needs-care thing going on. It's irresistible."

"You find me irresistible?" His grin grew wider. "You think I'm hot? How hot?"

"I do think so, and you are *not* helping your cause right now." Haley crossed her arms in front of her and lifted her chin.

"Aw, Haley. You're pretty irresistible yourself." He laughed. "I love it when you look down your nose at me. You have no idea how much I've missed you."

He reached for her, and she held herself stiff in his arms. "Negotiations first."

"OK." He let her go, his expression solemn. "Haney men don't stray. According to Gramps, fidelity is part of our DNA. When all that stuff happened on the job, I wasn't involved with anyone, and I've never hooked up with a woman who was involved with anyone either. That's not who I am. If I had been in a relationship, none of it would've happened. The women who threw themselves at me, what we did together, it was . . . empty. Physical gratification, and that's all. I lost interest in *empty* the minute I laid eyes on you."

His gaze met and held hers. "When we made love, it blew me away, freaked me out and brought on a panic attack. Do you know why?"

"No, why?" Her heart danced around in her chest, her pitiful hopes soaring.

"Because making love to you was so much more than physical gratification. *Intense* doesn't even begin to describe how I felt that night. I bonded with you at a soul-deep level, and it scared the shit out of me." He took her hands in his. "I won't do anything to threaten that bond, Haley. What I feel for you is a once-in-a-lifetime thing, and I realize now what a fool I was to run from you the way I did. I won't make the same mistake twice."

Her breath hitched, she wanted him so badly right now. "*Have* there been other women since we met?" Haley lifted her chin again, determined to get all of this out of the way. She stared deeply into his eyes, so she'd be able to tell if he told the truth or not.

One of the things she loved about Sam was his basic goodness, his forthright nature. What you saw was what you got with him. He was as salt-of-the-earth as they came, a throwback and a gentleman. She understood how he'd gotten caught up in the whole handsiest handyman thing, but that was over now. Still, she needed him to say the words—for his benefit as well as for hers.

"No, Haley." He continued to meet her gaze, his steady and sure. "I have not been with anyone else since the day we met, and it has nothing to do with flak from my grandfather or the stupid radio show. It has everything to do with you. My heart knew you were the one for me right away, but I fought it, and it took a while for my head to catch on." He ran a knuckle down her cheek, and she leaned into the caress.

"There have been offers, but even the thought of touching another woman makes my skin crawl. Plus, if you want, you can stop by my job sites to check on me at any time."

"Not necessary."

"Well, you still could." He waggled his eyebrows. "We could do some role-playing. Me, handyman; you, sexy client in need of my *special touch*."

She laughed. "We'll talk about that another time."

He blew out a breath. "How long before you trust me?"

"I did trust you until you pushed me away. I want to trust you again, Sam. I really do, but—"

"Let me prove to you I'm worthy of a second chance."

"All right." Her heart melted. "I'm willing to try."

"Good." He leaned back. "What else?"

"I understand about the trauma from your childhood and the panic attacks, but can we come up with a plan to deal with them that doesn't include you running away from me?" Another tear slid down her cheek. "I have a hard time dealing with . . . with—"

"I'm sorry," he whispered. "I'm so sorry I hurt you."

"I know you are." She sighed. "What if when you feel a panic attack coming on, you tell me what's going on? Maybe we can talk things through?"

"I swear to you that's exactly what I'll do." Sam lifted her to his lap.

Haley leaned against him, savoring his scent. He smelled like home. "There's one more issue, and it's huge," she murmured.

"Oh?" He kissed her.

She put her arms around him and kissed him back, so happy more tears flooded her eyes. She could hardly wrap her mind around everything he'd said, everything he was willing to do for her.

Sam broke the kiss and reached for a paper towel to dry her tears. He studied her. "Uh-oh." He sucked in a huge breath. "OK. Lay it on me. What is this huge issue I must face?"

"T-Trudy Cooper," she managed through more hiccups. "What about my mother?"

Sam chuckled and wrapped his arms around her. "She's going to have to get used to me, because I'm not going anywhere."

"I'm not worried about her getting used to you; I'm worried about you getting used to her." She huffed. "You have no idea."

"I kind of do. It's a nonissue." He grunted. He reached for the gift bag and handed it to her. "Open your present."

Haley scooted off his lap and removed the white tissue paper. She gasped. "A tool belt!" She laughed. "I love it. I absolutely love it." She hugged the stiff leather to her chest.

"There's more," Sam said, putting his arm around her. He reached into the bag and pulled out an envelope. "Here," he said, handing it to her.

Haley opened the flap and pulled out the thick folded sheets. Flattening them on her lap, she frowned. "This is from Haney & Sons, an estimate form."

"Yep. Read." He ran his hand up and down her arm.

"One thousand forty hours of handyman/carpenter labor at no charge, no matter what." Her eyes widened. "That's a lot of hours."

"I figured it out. If I put in twenty hours a week, it'll take me a year. I hope that will be long enough for you to see you can place your faith in me."

She smiled, unable to speak for the strong emotions swirling through her.

"Can I start proving myself right away, Ms. Cooper?"

"What did you have in mind?" she asked as he swept her into his arms.

"Let's spend the weekend together. We can go snowmobiling today, and—"

"It's far too cold out for snowmobiling today." She shrugged and sent him a sultry look.

"OK, how about the winter carnival? Do you want to go see the ice sculptures?"

"Again. Too cold." She sighed, and studied her nails. "Maybe tomorrow we can see the ice sculptures. It's supposed to be warmer, in the twenties I heard."

"What then?" Sam gave her a squeeze. "What would you like to do today?"

"I thought maybe we could do some of that soul-deep bonding thing you mentioned earlier." She bit her lip, and heat flooded her cheeks.

"Are you suggesting I take you to bed? Are you propositioning the handyman?"

"I am, and feel free to tell my mother if you want." She rose from her place and held out her hand. "It's a test. If you stick around afterward, you pass."

"I can do that." Taking her hand, he allowed her to lead him toward her bedroom. His cell phone pinged, and he stopped. "Wait." Sam took it from his back pocket and checked his texts. "It's Wyatt. He and Josey made me promise I'd let them know how things go with you today. Do you think you might let me out of bed later this afternoon?"

"Maybe. Why?"

He shot her an amused look. "Do you want to get together with Wyatt and Josey this evening? We can shoot some pool or play darts."

"I'd like that. Plus, I can finally get Josey's bowl back to her."

"See?" he said, texting back. "We're perfect for each other."

"Prove it."

Laughing, Sam tossed his phone on the dining room table and scooped her up. He carried her to her bedroom and laid her out on her bed, where he proceeded to undress her—slowly enough that he drove her crazy.

"I love this spot right here where your neck and shoulder meet. Mmm." He kissed her there before nibbling his way down her torso.

"And this bit of skin right here," he said, swirling his tongue along the curve of her waist. "And this one." He ran his cheek over her belly, causing delicious currents of heat coiling through her.

Haley moaned and pulled him up to her for a kiss. The tenderness in his touch, the reverent look in his eyes, was a balm to her heart. Haley lost herself in his arms, reveling in the way he loved her, the way she loved him.

Running her hands down his shoulders, across his chest, she savored the feel of him under her palms. His sudden exhalations as she explored every inch of him sent her desire to new heights.

"You drive me wild, Haley." Sam cradled her head and kissed her forehead, each cheek and finally her mouth. With every touch, nibble and bone-melting kiss, he loved her fears and doubts away. When their bodies joined, he stared into her eyes, his love for her shining through.

And when they were both breathless and replete, he stayed with her in a tangle of arms, legs and sheets.

"I love having superglue sex with you," he said, turning on his side to wrap her in his arms.

Haley giggled. "Superglue sex? Are you saying I'm sticky?"

"Exactly. I'm involved, bonded—heart, soul and body. I'm sticking to you, which means you're stuck with me. Superglue sex."

"Wow. That's deep, Sam," she said, her tone teasing. "And so hot. I'll never be able to look at glue the same way ever again. Elmer's, Gorilla, Titebond, talk dirty to me, baby." She sighed. "Now I want you again," she teased.

He tickled her ribs, and she giggled and tried to squirm away. Her threw his leg over hers and tightened his hold. "I don't know about you, but I'm ready for a nap."

"Me too." Haley pulled the covers up over their shoulders. "I need to rest so I can kick your ass at darts later."

"Dream on, Ms. Cooper. Dream on."

Once again he wrapped himself around her. Surrounded by his heat, scent and strength, Haley succumbed to drowsiness, the kind that only happened when she was perfectly content and happy. She fell asleep, secure in his arms and certain her handyman would still be with her when she woke.

Epilogue

Six Months Later

Sam wrapped up the cord to Haley's Shop-Vac and surveyed the newly finished downstairs room. After they'd torn out the old bathroom and put in all new fixtures and tile, including a sauna, they'd started on the new family room, putting in an egress window on the west side. A wide-plank, rough-hewn pine floor, insulation, new walls, a closet and built-in bookshelves turned the space into an inviting gathering place for family and friends. He'd also installed a small wet bar, and a gas fireplace.

He and Haley had worked well together, hardly any fights at all during the months they'd remodeled the basement. And the arguments they did have, he'd pretty much started for the fun of having makeup sex. Side by side they'd transformed the dark, cold space into a bright, warm room, a perfect place to hang out. If that didn't mean their relationship worked, he didn't know what did.

"Wyatt is coming over later to help me move my entertainment center, TV and couch out of storage and into our new family room." He turned to Haley. "So? What do you think?"

She crossed the room and slid her arms around his waist. "I love it. How about you?"

"I'm happy with the way it turned out, but . . ." He sighed dramatically for effect.

"But?" Haley's eyes filled with concern as she searched his face.

"Well, I've been thinking." He kissed her forehead and wrapped his arms around her. "Once we turn the upstairs into a master bedroom suite, along with this room, we'll have added significantly to the usable square footage. We could make a nice little profit if we sold this house."

"Sell our home?" She frowned. "But I thought you liked living here with me."

"I *love* living with you, Haley, but this is a small house. I have money saved. I thought we could sell this place, put the profit and my money together and buy a house that will be *ours*. We need a home big enough for a growing family, something we want to stay in for years and years."

"Oh, Sam, I love you so much," she said, her voice hitching. "I'd like that."

"We could build new, or buy a place worth fixing up. I enjoy remodeling with you, so I'm leaning toward an older home with character." He tucked an errant strand of silky brown hair behind her ear, and cradled her face against his shoulder. His heart turned over, and tenderness for her swamped him.

The depth of his love for her grew with each passing day, expanding him and enriching his life in ways he'd never imagined possible. She truly was his greatest adventure, and absolutely nothing in the world would ever compare to having Haley by his side. "I love you," he whispered.

She made a muffled, soggy sound, and the place where her face rested against his shoulder grew damp. "Oh, no. Don't cry, Haley." He drew back to peer at her. "I thought you'd be happy. I got you a present. That should cheer you up."

"I'm not sad, Sam." She let out a shaky laugh. "Tell me you bought me a new miter box. If you did, you're the best boyfriend ever."

"Really?" he said. "That's all it would take?" He pulled the small velvet box from his back pocket. His poor heart pounding away in his chest, he went down on one knee. He opened the box to reveal the engagement ring he'd chosen for her. It was classy and beautiful, like Haley. "What do you say, Haley? This handyman's heart beats for you and you alone, and it always will. Marry me?"

Squealing, she threw her arms around his neck, knocking him off balance. But then, he'd been off balance since the day they'd met, and he discovered he liked the dizzy way she made him feel. He caught himself with a hand on the wall and stood up. Haley continued to cling to him, and that was perfectly fine with him.

"Yes, Sam. Yes," she murmured against his neck.

"Good." He held her tight, his eyes tearing. "What about a winter wedding, a nice honeymoon somewhere warm, and then we can get busy making a few flotation devices together. I was thinking five is a good number."

She laughed. "I'm thinking two is enough."

"Three it is."

Proud and happy beyond belief, Sam kissed her, drawing his bundle of wonderful as close as possible. "Tomorrow, let's gather the troops and make our announcement." He chuckled. "Trudy's going to shit a brick."

"She's coming around. She likes you, and it ticks her off, because she can't help herself."

"Pick a date, and we can start looking for places for the reception. Grandpa Joe and Grandma Maggie will want us to get married in their church. Is that OK with you?"

"I'd like that very much."

"Love you." He wrapped his arms around her, content to spend a few more minutes celebrating. Sam closed his eyes and sent a silent thank-you to his mom and dad. He hoped they were looking down at him now, pleased to see he'd honored their memory by reaching for his own happiness. He'd asked the love of his life to be his forever, and doing so hadn't caused even a smidgeon of panic. "I'm glad I called in that morning to the *Loaded Question* radio show."

"Really?" Haley shot him an incredulous look.

"If I hadn't, Trudy never would've fixed us up. I wouldn't have met you, and I'd still be fooling myself into believing I didn't want anything or anyone tying me down. So, yeah. Really. I'm happy, Haley. Happier than I've ever been. In fact, I might write the radio station and let them know how it all turned out." He chuckled.

"Or maybe not. I do plan to thank your mother though." He would, too, from the bottom of his reformed heart. He imagined the expression on his future mother-in-law's face when she discovered exactly how well her scheme had worked out after all.

Sam twined his fingers with Haley's, every chamber of his heart full to bursting. "Are you disappointed I didn't get you a new miter box? Does this mean I'm not the best boyfriend ever?"

"*Fiancé*," she said. "And you're definitely the best."

Acknowledgments

The saying, "It takes a village to raise a child," is applicable also to producing a book, which to my way of thinking is a "child of the mind." I am deeply grateful to all of the folks at Montlake Romance for giving *What You Do to Me* a home.

I'm also grateful to my agent, Nalini Akolekar, my cheerleader and coach. My village also includes Tamara Hughes and Wyndemere Coffey, critique partners and dear friends. I also have a writing community to thank. Without a village of writers and supportive organizations, writing would be a solitary endeavor indeed.

Finally, I must thank my readers, who make it possible for me to do what I love most.

An Excerpt from
Whatever You Need
(Book 2 in The Haneys)

Editor's Note: This is an early excerpt and may not reflect the finished book.

Wyatt sat at his drawing table and worked on a new panel for his latest comic book. In the first edition, *Elec Tric*, his superhero, had been hit by an otherworldly bolt of lightning one sunny day. Twice. Since then, he's been able to generate his own electricity. Even stranger, an unseen world of demons and super beings became visible to him from that day forward. Tric had been forced to make a choice: join the forces of evil intending to reign supreme over the innocent inhabitants of earth, or . . . join the forces of good who kept the evil in check.

"*Join me, Tric, or I will destroy you,*" *Delilah Diabolical, the demon queen, shouted.*

"*Never!*" *Tric shot a lightning bolt at his archenemy, sending her reeling.*

The first comic book in the series had been all about world building. Now Wyatt got to take his ongoing saga in new directions, adding characters, creating fresh storylines and plot twists. He colored the bolts of lightning shooting from Tric's hands and eyes, and the pesky lower-level demon, sent to distract the superhero, turned into a pile of cinders.

Of course, Tric had chosen to use his powers for good, and in this graphic tale, he would once again come up against Delilah Diabolical—DD for short. Unfortunately for the unsuspecting and unseeing civilian population, DD didn't care who got caught in the crosshairs. It was Tric's job to protect the unsuspecting public.

"Help!" the pretty blonde shouted, as two minor demons attempted to drag her off to the underworld. "Somebody, please help me!"

Wyatt's hero rushed to rescue the mysterious Ms. M again, which gave the superhero pause. Why did fate keep throwing the pretty blue-eyed blonde in harm's way? In *his* way? Was she another distraction sent by the evildoers to keep him from finding out what they were really up to? If not, then what did the demon realm want with Ms. M?

Cue foreshadowing dramatic music. Da-da-duhhh. Wyatt grinned. Sometimes, his stories played like cheesy movies through his mind, and when that happened, he was in the zone. Nothing made him happier than working on his comics while in the zone.

Noise at the back door leading to the parking lot pulled him out of his imaginary world. He rose from his stool and glanced out the window. There *she* was, the pretty blonde who lived in the apartment above his—the blonde who'd been his inspiration for the mysterious Ms. M. Her little boy carried a jug of laundry detergent, while Ms. K. Malone—he'd read her name on the mailbox more than once—lugged two large plastic tubs full of laundry, one stacked on top of the other.

His pretty neighbor did her laundry every Saturday morning. Wyatt knew this because he took the opportunity to observe her as she left, and every Saturday morning he wondered the same thing: How would K. Malone react if he ran downstairs and out the door to help her with her heavy load? Would she turn her thousand-watt smile his way, introduce herself and ask if he'd like to get together with her soon? He wished.

Longing filled him, and he moved back from the window—as if K. Malone might be able to see him from the parking lot. "Curse this wretched shyness," he muttered in his best cartoon character superhero voice. He wanted so badly to talk to her, to introduce himself and maybe ask her out. He'd even tried a few times, but the words stuck in his dry mouth, his face turned to flame, and his lungs refused to do their job. He was a hopeless mess.

Wyatt peered out the window until mother and son drove off to the Laundromat. Letting loose a heavy sigh, he returned to his drawing table, immersing himself in his made-up world of alter egos and heroic deeds.

Forty minutes later, he got up to stretch. The panel he'd been working on was finished, and his stomach rumbled. Lunchtime. He walked to the kitchen to make a sandwich, when he smelled . . . smoke? A second later, the fire alarm shrieked in the kitchen above his.

"Damn." K. Malone's apartment was on fire. Wyatt took his cell phone from his pocket and dialed 911. As he gave the dispatcher all of the pertinent information, he grabbed his fire extinguisher from under the kitchen sink. Snatching his keys on the fly, he dashed out into the hall and down the stairs to the caretaker's apartment.

He pounded on the door and listened for any signs of life from inside. No movement. Not a sound. He tried once more just to be sure. "Floyd," he shouted. Nothing. Wyatt took the stairs three at a time, racing to the top floor. "Fire. Get out!" he pounded on doors and shouted. "Fire," he called, making his way through all the floors. In old buildings like this, fires could spread quickly. Extinguisher still in hand, he followed the last person out the front door.

The blare of sirens reached their quiet street, and by the time he made it to the sidewalk, the engines were close. Two trucks with lights flashing pulled up to the curb next to the hydrant on the corner. Wyatt stepped forward to meet the firefighter who seemed to be directing the crew. "The fire is in the apartment on the southeast corner of the second floor."

"Your place?" a fireman asked, as the rest of the crew scrambled with gear and attached a hose to the hydrant on the corner.

"No, my neighbor's. She's not home, and neither is the caretaker, otherwise I would've tried to put it out." He lifted his extinguisher. "I'll open the security door." Wyatt ran to unlock the deadbolt. He held the door wide as two firefighters rushed in, dragging the hose with them. "It might be electrical," he called out.

"Got it." Two more men followed, canisters strapped to their backs and gear in hand.

"Stay out of the building until we give the all clear," the firefighter in charge yelled.

Wyatt cringed at the sound of Ms. Malone's door being hacked open, but what choice did the firefighters have? Floyd had the master keys, and he was nowhere to be found. As usual. The guy was so lame. He did a piss-poor job of keeping the place up, and Wyatt often smelled pot smoke coming from the basement apartment. He'd turned the caretaker into a really stupid demon character in his comic books—and then he'd killed him off.

Another point against the caretaker, Wyatt had complained to him about the wiring in the building, and asked him to contact the owners. He'd noticed right off the building didn't even come close to meeting code. When his requests failed to produce the much-needed improvements, Wyatt had resorted to sending letters to the city. He'd also researched who owned the complex and sent letters himself to the holding company in California. That got him nowhere either.

If his suspicions were correct, and the fire started because of faulty wiring, something had to be done. What if a fire broke out in the middle of the night when everyone was sleeping? There was no guarantee all the ancient smoke detectors were in working order. His hand went to the scars on his neck and jaw. Burns were excruciatingly painful, and things happened so fast. He didn't wish that kind of misery on anyone.

"Hey," one of his neighbors said, coming to stand beside him. "You're the hero of the day. I'm Mariah Estrada," she said. "Thanks for pounding on my door."

Hero of the day? He let the words trickle through him. "No biggie."

"I've seen you around. You live in the apartment beneath Kenzie's. I guess you heard her alarm go off, huh?"

Wyatt nodded. *Kenzie. Kenzie Malone.* He liked the way the syllables rolled around in his mind. The mysterious Ms. M had a name to go with his fantasies, a name that would lend itself well to a heroine in his comic books. He'd give her superpowers in the next story.

"You gonna introduce yourself? I know you only as 'Hoodie Guy,' because you always have that sweatshirt hood up even when it's hot out. Like today."

Heat crept up his neck. Did the rest of the residents know him as Hoodie Guy too? Great. At least the hoodies he wore in the summer were lightweight with short sleeves, or sleeveless. Still, his neighbors probably thought he had a few screws loose. He couldn't help himself. The hoods were a habit he couldn't break. That's all. Glancing at her, he expected to find derision. Instead, her espresso eyes held only warmth and a teasing sparkle. "Wyatt Haney," he told her.

"I'm a nurse at Fairview Riverside Hospital," Mariah continued.

Not knowing how to respond to that, he nodded again, and other neighbors drifted over, thanking him for alerting them to the fire. He tried to edge away, and even pulled out his phone, pretending he had important texts to read. What he wanted right now was to go into the apartment above his to see where the fire had been and to discover the cause.

He couldn't though, not without Kenzie's permission. His heart thumped. Dammit, he'd find a way to ask her, because if he was right about what caused the fire, Wyatt intended to raise holy hell.

All he had to do was find out which insurance company to contact, and he'd mention the many letters he'd written. He'd even provide copies. Then he'd have his family's company, Haney & Sons Construction and Handyman Service, bid on the job to make the repairs and to rewire the entire building. The outlets weren't even grounded, for cripes sake.

His heart thumped again. Harder this time. If he got the job, he'd be spending time in his pretty neighbor's apartment. If he had any luck at all, she might be there some of the time too, and maybe . . . just maybe . . . he could muster up the courage to ask her out.

Kenzie unlocked the back door to the apartment building and propped it open with one of the tubs of clean, folded laundry. She returned to her car to help Brady out of his booster seat before grabbing the second tub. "Let's get these things put away, and then we can go to the playground at the park."

"What's that smell, Mommy?" Brady asked once they were inside.

She sniffed, and a prickle of concern traipsed down her spine. *No, don't borrow trouble.* There were twelve apartments in the complex, not counting the caretaker's—giving her a one-in-twelve chance the smell came from her apartment. Since she hadn't cooked anything that morning, used her curling iron or burned any candles, the odds were in her favor the smell was *not* coming from her apartment.

"Smells like somebody had a fire earlier. Let's go, buddy." She climbed the back stairs, struggling to prop the tubs against the wall so she could open the door, when it opened without her. Her downstairs neighbor held the door for her and Brady.

"Thanks." She smiled. Though she'd been curious about her hooded-but-good-looking neighbor, smiling and the occasional "hi" were as far as they ever got.

Most of the folks in their building were friendly, but this guy kept to himself. Just as well. Though she couldn't deny the attraction, between school and single parenthood, she had no time for anything else. She was far too busy to pay heed to the loneliness filling the odd moments she found to think about such things.

"There's been a fire," he said, his face turning red. "In your apartment."

Dammit! So much for the odds. Of course the fire had been in her apartment. That's just how her life unfolded. The minute she believed things were going great for a change, *BAM*—an accidental pregnancy with her unemployed boyfriend. A few years later . . . *BAM* again—she's a war widow and a single mother at the ripe old age of twenty-two.

Obviously life saw her as its own personal soccer ball to kick around, because not long after losing her husband, she'd lost her job. The only factory in her small town had closed, and . . . *BAM*. Now there'd been a fire in her apartment. At least the building hadn't burned to the ground. She still had a home. Didn't she?

Why couldn't fate or Mother Nature or whatever go pick on somebody else for a while? She tried to dislodge the lump of self-pity clogging her throat. Everybody went through rough patches, but her patches had turned into acres. What on earth could've started the fire in her place?

Her neighbor took the tubs of laundry from her. She was too stunned to react for a second. "How bad *was* this fire?"

"I don't know. I'm Wyatt Haney, by the way. I called the fire department when I heard the alarm." He nodded toward the stairs. "I was hoping you might let me take a look inside."

"How'd you know I wasn't home to call the fire department myself?"

"Your apartment is right over mine. I heard you leave earlier this morning."

"Oh." Kenzie frowned, and Brady grabbed her hand. "Why do you want to look at the damage?"

Wyatt took a long breath, and his face turned a deeper shade of crimson. Was he painfully shy, have some kind of an anxiety disorder, or was she just really that scary? Maybe she gave off warning pheromones: Stay away, because if you're in my proximity, shit *will* happen.

"I've written more than one letter to the owners about this building not meeting electrical code," he told her. "The wiring is really old, and the outer covering is showing its age, cracking, splitting. If this was an electrical fire, I want to know." He shifted the tubs and propped them on the banister. "I'm an electrician."

"Ah, I see. Sure, you can take a look if you want. I'm Kenzie Malone, by the way," she said, glancing down at her son. "And this is Brady."

Wyatt smiled and held out his fist for Brady to bump. "Hey, little dude."

Brady smiled and bumped Wyatt's fist before moving closer to press himself against her legs. Her five-year-old had always been shy with people he didn't know. "Thanks for calling the fire department and for carrying my laundry."

Wyatt really was a handsome man, especially when he smiled. She liked the striking combination of tawny blond hair and dark brown eyes, not to mention his angular face and straight nose. Plus, he was tall. She was five feet nine herself, and she appreciated a man she could look up to. Though he was on the slender side, Wyatt's shoulders were broad. Very broad, and he was well proportioned, nicely put together, and . . . *Stop. It.*

She started up the stairs, hyperaware of Wyatt's masculine presence behind her. In what shape had she left her apartment? She did a mental inventory: Dishes in the sink, toys strewn all over the living room floor. What kind of mess had the firemen made? *Argh.* Wyatt was willing to carry her tubs of laundry upstairs, and that made letting him take a look worth it, no matter how messy her place might be.

"You don't use the machines in the basement to do laundry?"

His deep masculine voice caused a tummy flutter. "No. The two washing machines here are really old and kind of funky. Besides, if I go to a Laundromat, I can do all my loads at once," she said, turning to look his way, finding his gaze on her backside. "Saves time, and I don't have to run up and down stairs all day."

She'd caught him checking her out. It had been way too long since she'd wanted to *be* checked out. A section of the ceiling outside her apartment had been torn down, and scorch marks spread out like fingers against the exposed wood beneath. White residue covered the blackened areas and the carpet below. The smell of burnt wood assaulted her senses.

Her door had obviously been attacked by an axe, but someone had reinstalled her deadbolt above the wrecked part. The caretaker? Doubtful.

She stuck her key in the lock. "My legs aren't long enough for this," she muttered to herself.

"I beg your pardon?"

Kenzie shrugged and cast him a rueful look. "Don't you ever feel like you're running through life, trying to stay a few steps ahead of trouble?" She arched an eyebrow. "No? Well, I do, and my legs just aren't long enough to run that fast."

"Ah. I get it." One side of his mouth turned up as he set the tubs of laundry on the floor. "I reinstalled the deadbolt for you. You'll need a new door, but at least you can still use the lock until the insurance company settles and you get a new one."

"*You* called the firemen *and* moved the lock for me? Where was Floyd while all this happened?" Their caretaker was pretty much useless, and this only proved the point.

"No clue."

"You ought to send an invoice to the landlord." Kenzie steeled herself for what she might find, and walked inside, Brady's hand in hers. Wyatt followed.

"Yuck. Stinks in here," Brady said, pinching his nose.

"Yeah, it does." Kenzie opened the windows in the living room wider, before joining Wyatt to survey the damage. The ceiling in the dining area was now a gaping hole, and her table and chairs were covered in debris and more of that white residue. "I've had nothing but trouble with that light fixture. Bulbs make this weird *zzzzt* noise and blow out like every few days. Another one went out this morning. I told Floyd about it, but of course nothing was done."

"Mmm. The circuit was left open." Wyatt pointed to the light switch she'd left in the on position after the bulb had burned out. "Exposed electrical wires arcing started the fire," Wyatt muttered, walking around the table with his eyes on the blackened ceiling.

"So, if I'd flipped the switch to off, the fire wouldn't have happened?"

"Not today, but eventually."

"At least it's not dripping wet in here. What a mess that would've made, what with the plaster and soot. Would've ruined the wonderful oak floor."

Wyatt took his phone out of his back pocket. "Water and foam are dangerous in an electrical fire. They're conduits."

"Oh." She ran a finger through the residue on her table and rubbed it between her thumb and pointer. The stuff felt like talcum powder between her fingers, only smoother. "So, what *do* firemen use to put out fires like this?"

"Dry chemicals, like PKP, or they use carbon dioxide." He glanced sideways at her. "My guess is, it's going to take several weeks, maybe months before things get settled with the insurance company." He took a picture of the ceiling. "Do you have a place to stay in the meantime?"

"No." Kenzie's chest tightened. She had enough to deal with as it was. Having to look for a new apartment, packing and moving would definitely be more than she could handle right now. She'd already been through that nightmare once during her two-year program. The rent at her last place had gone up so high, she'd been forced to move. She leaned against the built-in oak buffet. "Why can't I stay here?"

Wyatt shrugged. "I guess you could, if you don't mind the smell and the destruction. The fire marshal is the one who will make that call, though. No family nearby?"

Why did that question cause him to blush again? Was he phishing for personal details about her life? He went back to his picture taking, studying the screen on his phone before taking another.

"Nope. They're all in Iowa. I came to the Twin Cities to go to school." She could've gone to school in Iowa and saved herself some money by living with her folks. But the truth was, she'd been eager to get away from her family, especially her clingy in-laws, and she'd always wanted to live in a big city. Besides, after all the *BAMs* she'd suffered in the past few years, she wanted a fresh start somewhere new.

"I have less than six months to go before I graduate as a dental hygienist. My life will be more manageable if I stay here despite the smell and the hole in the ceiling." Now that she got a good look, this mess didn't really qualify as a *BAM*, more like a *bam*. The landlord's insurance would take care of the damage, and she could live with a torn-up ceiling for a while. She'd be done with her program in December, and then she could get a really good job. Dental hygienists were in demand, and she'd done very well in her program, which would earn her great references from her instructors.

Once she earned a decent living, she'd look for a nicer, more up-to-date place to live. Maybe a townhouse complex in the suburbs, one with a pool and a playground for Brady. Somewhere in a good school district, because her baby would be starting kindergarten next fall.

She studied the chunks of ceiling all over her floor, but then her gaze snagged on Wyatt and traveled up his tall form as he took pictures from every angle. All serious like this, he looked way too studly, entirely masculine. He studied the ceiling, a determined set to his angled jaw.

Sexy. Definitely sexy. How nice would it be to wrap herself around his lean form, and . . . *Down, hormones. Sit. Stay.*

He tucked his phone back into his pocket. "All right if I see where you still have power and where you don't? Since you're going to stay, we might have to rig a few things."

We? He didn't know her at all, and she didn't know him. Should she be worried about him in her home? What motivated him to help a perfect stranger? Well, not perfect by a long shot, but she *was* a stranger. He seemed nice, and he *had* put her deadbolt back on her door, which showed genuine concern. During the months she'd lived here, no police officers had ever come looking for him. Her gut told her he was safe. Surely the fact that he kept to himself had more to do with shyness than felonious tendencies.

"Be my guest." She followed him as he checked the fridge and flipped switches.

"Kitchen power's out. Do you have any extension cords?"

"I think so. Two maybe." Wyatt continued to check the rest of her place. Thank heavens she'd changed the sheets and made the beds this morning. She didn't want him to know what a total slob she was when it came to that stuff, but making their beds every day had never made sense. Why bother when you were just going to unmake them again that night? The only time she made the beds was when she changed the sheets or when she was expecting company.

Someone knocked on her door, and she left Wyatt to the task of turning lights on and off. Maybe their caretaker finally decided to make an appearance.

Brady got to the door before she did. "Who's there?" he called, as she'd taught him.

"It's Mariah, and I brought pizza."

Kenzie opened the door and let her in. "You are the best neighbor ever." She and Mariah were both single moms, and they'd become good friends from the first day she and Brady had moved in. "Thanks for bringing pizza. I don't have any power in my kitchen. I guess I missed all the excitement this afternoon, huh?"

"You're welcome, and yes. You missed the thrilling evacuation of our building and the sight of hunky firemen running around." Mariah set the pizza on the living room coffee table. "I also brought beer. I figured you might want one after coming home to find a mess," she said, lifting the six pack.

"Where's Rosie?" Brady asked. "Can she play with me?"

"Rosie is with her daddy on the weekends." Mariah tousled Brady's mop of blond hair. "Remember? She'll be home tomorrow afternoon though, and the two of you can play then."

Brady nodded, and went back to his superhero action figures, his favorite toys.

"The electrical is on everywhere except the kitchen and the bath-room." Wyatt strolled into the living room. "Where do you keep the extension cords?"

"Oh. Look who's here, our hooded hero." Mariah grinned. "Join us for pizza and beer?"

"Uh . . ." He glanced at the door leading to the hallway, looking as if he might bolt.

"Please stay, Wyatt. I'll get the extension cords." Kenzie headed for the walk-in closet by the front door. The huge storage space was one of the reasons she'd chosen this apartment, that and the elegant wood-work and the great neighborhood. They were only two blocks from terrific biking and walking trails, and a block from a nice park with a playground for kids. She rummaged through a cardboard box of stuff and pulled out her two extension cords.

"Pizza and a beer sound great," Wyatt said from the closet door. He glanced at the cords in her hands. "These aren't going to work. Too short, but you can use them for your toaster and coffeemaker. I have something you can use until you can get a cord of your own. I'll be right back."

"Thanks." He was out the door before she even finished speaking.

"Can I have pop with my pizza, Mommy?" Brady had his Superman and Spiderman dolls clutched to his chest.

"You can have milk."

He shrugged, his expression one of abject disappointment. "Chocolate milk." She compromised, and Brady graced her with a cherubic smile.

"It took a fire to bring Hoodie Guy out of his shell." Mariah grabbed a roll of paper towels from the kitchen counter. "After he called 911, he herded us all out of the building. He had a fire extinguisher in his hands, and *he* was the last one out."

"Oh?" Kenzie found paper plates and set them on the counter. She grabbed milk and chocolate syrup from the fridge. "I wouldn't say he's out of his shell. The poor guy turns scarlet if you even look at him." She shook her head. "Poor guy. I'm grateful he was home to call the fire department, *and* he also moved my deadbolt." She mixed Brady's chocolate milk and put the ingredients back in the dark fridge.

"I know. I helped by handing him tools and offering an extra set of hands while he worked. I tried to chat him up, even though he hardly spoke three or four words. Not much of a talker, but he's hot, that's for sure."

Kenzie chuckled. "He's definitely hot." Hot or not, she'd never felt drawn to shy silent types. Besides, she didn't have any desire or time for a man in her life right now, so what difference did his hotness make?

Her gaze touched upon the shadow box on the wall, the one holding the folded flag from her husband's casket, along with his formal military picture, name and rank. Regret and sadness gripped her, and all the happy plans she and Bradley had made for their future together came back in a rush. She still missed him, still railed at the unfairness of it all. They'd barely gotten started on their lives together when everything came crashing to an end. The day the two men in uniform showed up at her door had been the toughest day of her life. *BAM.*

"I'm hot, too," Brady piped in. "Can we turn on the window air?"

Kenzie shared a grin with Mariah, mentally thanking her little boy for once again turning her thoughts away from her sorrow. "Not now. Only when it's eighty-five or above."

The window air conditioner blew fuses if any other electrical appliances were on, even the vacuum cleaner. Wyatt was right. This place was an electrical disaster. Even she knew there should be circuit breakers instead of fuse boxes. She'd spent a fortune keeping herself in fuses and lightbulbs. Thanks to her downstairs neighbor, only the dining area had suffered damage today. Things could be a whole lot worse.

"It's obvious Wyatt is painfully shy, and it's clear he's self-conscious about the burn scars on his neck." Had he been in the military too, like her husband? Maybe he'd been close to an exploding IED, and that's how he got the scars. She and Mariah carried everything to the living room and set it on the coffee table.

"You should flirt with Wyatt," Mariah said, taking a seat. "If I wasn't already seeing someone, I'd be after him myself."

Kenzie set a place for Brady and lifted him onto the couch. "We don't know that Wyatt's not already involved, and I'm not interested. Being a single parent and trying to get through school are enough."

"It's been two years since you lost your husband, Kenzie. Going out on a date now and then would do you a world of good. I'll even . . ."

Wyatt walked into her apartment before Mariah could finish. He had a long coil of bright orange industrial-size extension cord looped over his shoulder. Mariah had stopped midsentence. Even Brady had stilled. All eyes turned to the hot guy in the hoodie. Had he heard any part of their conversation?

"What?" he muttered, his face once again turning crimson.

"Pizza and beer, that's what. We've been waiting for you. My fridge can wait a few minutes. Let's eat this pizza while it's still hot." Kenzie scooted over to make room for him.

Maybe if she made an effort to be his friend, she could help him get over his shyness a little bit. *Stop.* She didn't know anything about him, and he wasn't her pet project. Who did she think she was, anyway?

Mariah nudged her with her elbow and whispered, "I'd even babysit for free."

"Like you'd ever charge me," she whispered back, shaking her head slightly. "Not going to happen," she mouthed. Nope. She had her hands full, and no matter how hot Wyatt might be, she was not interested in dating or fixing him. Didn't mean she couldn't be friendly though, and she owed him. Kenzie smiled and patted the spot beside her on her ratty old, smoke-scented couch. "Join us."

About the Author

Award-winning author Barbara Longley moved frequently throughout her childhood, but she quickly learned to entertain herself with stories. As an adult, she's lived in a commune in the Appalachians, taught on a Native American reservation, and traveled extensively from coast to coast. After her children were born, she decided to make the state of Minnesota her permanent home. Barbara holds a master's degree in special education and taught for many years. Today she devotes herself to writing contemporary, mythical, and paranormal stories. Her titles include *Heart of the Druid Laird*, the Love from the Heartland series (*Far from Perfect, The Difference a Day Makes, A Change of Heart*, and *The Twisted Road to You*), and the Novels of Loch Moigh (*True to the Highlander, The Highlander's Bargain, The Highlander's Folly*, and *The Highlander's Vow*).